In solidarity!

Githa Hariharan

PRAISE FOR GITHA HARIHARAN

On *The Thousand Faces of Night*

'(The novel) shows, with exceptional fictional skill, the subtle and everyday way in which women are bludgeoned to play male-scripted subordinate roles...'—*India Today*

'Githa Hariharan displays a control of the medium, a sophistication that would be the envy of any contemporary writer. Her diction is pointed and the textures communicated exquisite. In terms of technique, her writing is masterful...she cannot write of an experience but will animate it with sharp and vivid life. There is not a single flat sentence in the book.'—*Economic Times*

'...remarkable for the clarity and subtlety with which it articulates a young woman's search for selfhood...fresh and poetic...entirely free from clichés...'—*Deccan Herald*

'A novel that every Indian woman must read...and every Indian man.'—*Society*

'Commandingly articulate...'—*Bookseller*

'Hariharan's language is poetic and teasing, but always measured, drawing us in and never providing answers...(an) exquisitely woven tale...an important and truly international book...'—*Mail on Sunday*

On *The Art of Dying*

'Compassionate yet ruthless in their honesty, these beautifully written stories about death and its place in life mark Githa Hariharan as an outstanding new writer.'—J.M. Coetzee

'There is luminous resonance in the images of Githa Hariharan, an author clearly engaged in creating metaphors for different states of being.'—*Economic Times*

'Her sentences are controlled, all extra words shaved away. The distilled brevity is delightful, the unsaid hovers everywhere.'—*Business Standard*

'...an insatiable urge to turn a situation inside out and pin it down...Her stories drag you in right under the skin and make you squirm...'—*Illustrated Weekly of India*

'...her writing pulsates to the soft sound of an unusual life force...hitches the most unthinkable of ideas into a graceful arc of images...sunny and well-lit prose which conceals nothing, reveals everything.'—*The Times of India*

On *The Ghosts of Vasu Master*

'This is a book written with a rare lyrical grace, and one that consistently reveals new depths.'—*Business Standard*

'A marvelously written book with wit as corrosive as dry ice...'—*India Today*

'...Hariharan's achievement lies in teasing new meanings out of old ways of life and old modes of storytelling in an immaculately ordered narrative...'—*Telegraph*

'...a silken web of fables and parables...'—*Indian Express*

On *In Times of Siege*

'Hariharan writes with anguish, pain and anger about what is happening to our country. I put *In Times of Siege* on top of my list of books that must be read.'—Khushwant Singh

'*In Times of Siege,* is not only quite as contemporary as today's newspaper, but tomorrow's as well.'—Alok Rai, *Outlook*

'A chilling novel for the times...She writes with an unflinching eye for painful details, often cloaked in a dry, almost black, humour, and all of it drenched in a simmering violence...'—*Indian Express*

'A must-read novel...Lucid, sparse prose with images Ezra Pound would love...Delhi comes alive in a most realistic, yet fluid and plural way, rather like history itself.'—*Newstime*

'An absorbing book...reads almost like a well-crafted thriller.'—*Deccan Herald*

'A heady mix of myth, modern mores, politics and lust...Heartbreakingly funny, moving and as relevant as today's headlines.'—*Washington Post*

'Hariharan amplifies the themes of courage, dissent and responsibility in her protagonist's private life...The result is an engaging portrait of the mild-mannered professor, who, even as the crises engulf him, marvels that his scholarly discipline "has become a live, fiery thing".'—*New Yorker*

'Intelligent...[Hariharan's] deceptively simple prose belies the artistry of her phrasings and she writes with an infectious concern for her characters.'—*San Francisco Chronicle*

'[A] witty, insightful novel.'—*The Seattle Times*

Thoughtful and perceptive...succeeds in illuminating the siege-like mentality that exists when extremists set the agenda for intellectual culture.'—*Publishers Weekly*

'A tale told with wit and grace...enriched by elegant narration and a light touch.'—*Kirkus Reviews*

'A disturbing fictional portrait...[a] persuasive work that tells of the perils of sectarianism and silence in the face of oppression.'—*Far Eastern Economic Review*

'A modern fable...beautifully told in a spare style that is as modern as its subject.'—*Baltimore Sun*

On *When Dreams Travel*

'A dizzying, dazzling performance.'—J.M. Coetzee

'I loved every page of *When Dreams Travel*, and Borges (whom Hariharan quotes most knowingly) would no doubt have loved it too.'—Alberto Manguel

'...a beautifully written and evocative novel...one of the threads that Hariharan skilfully weaves into her narrative is the mutability of tales, their tendency to shift as they pass from one person to another...'—*Times Literary Supplement*

'...a sly retake on Orientalism from within the Orient...rich, supple, sensuous and cerebral...'—*Independent*

'This is a wonderful book...a beautifully lyrical, subtle novel that is just sheer pleasure to read.'—*Herald* (Glasgow)

'...her control is sure...vibrantly reworks *The Thousand and One Nights*, weaving into the great myth the "traveled dreams" of other myths and stories—Muslim and Hindu—from across Asia.'—*Guardian*

'...a story that is told with such surefooted style and panache that it lights up forgotten corners of the reader's mind.'—*Outlook*

'She can do magic...reading her is an effortless pleasure.'—*India Today*

'Hariharan's prose glitters like a gem-encrusted sword...an amazing feat of the imagination.'—*Hindu*

On *Fugitive Histories*

'*Fugitive Histories* is Hariharan's most compellingly simple book.'—*Tehelka*

'Spartan, elegant and nuanced prose...at times luminous and sharply perceptive, *Fugitive Histories* is perhaps Hariharan's most mature work to date.'—*Outlook*

'Her prose [has] an exquisite awareness...the daily lives of individuals and those of history appear to blur and seep through time and memory till they...become all of a piece.'—*India Today*

'There are many compelling stories wrapped in the pages of *Fugitive Histories*...The revisiting of life in Gujarat after 2002, and Yasmin's story, in particular, draws you to Githa Hariharan's powerful new novel like little else.'—*Financial Express*

'...effortless straddling of different geographies...Delightfully nuanced...'—*New Indian Express*

'A powerful read...a quiet, powerful churning in which the whole heavy weight of history comes to rest on you, asking of you an engagement.'—*First City*

'...a compassionate, controlled, compelling narrative.'—*Mint*

'Sparkling clear prose...lays bare disturbing truth...a distressing but redemptive book.'—*Elle*

'...Hariharan's writing is spare, punctuated with passages of brilliant clarity and compassion.'—*Verve*

On *Almost Home*

'In essays that bespeak a thoroughly cosmopolitan sensibility, Githa Hariharan not only takes us on illuminating tours through cities rich in history, but gives a voice to urban people from all over the world...'—J.M. Coetzee

'Hariharan is a complete cultural encyclopaedia...Each essay will add depth to your understanding of the complicated, nuanced relationship between daily life and history, no matter what city or country you call home.'—*Chicago Review of Books*

'A fascinating book...a well-conceived, layered narrative, a work of excellent prose.'—*Frontline*

'A travelogue with a difference, this...it tells us very human stories that make us smile, laugh out loud and sometimes get jolted. Hard. At other times it evokes poetry that makes the heart sing.'—*Outlook*

'...The book is part memoir, part travelogue and part literary and cultural criticism and it's through its irreverential blurring of these lines that the book delights...'—*Biblio*

'This is the best travel book I have ever read...'—*NewPages.com*

'Complex and fascinating.'—*World Literature Today*

'A treat for globetrotters who like to get under the skin of complex places.'—*Bedford and Bowery*

'A beautifully crafted memoir...'—*GoNOMAD*

'Spunky...It is both Hariharan's singular, home-grown cosmopolitanism and her mellow perspective as a distinguished Indian novelist that inform the book's story...'—*Open Magazine*

'...presents a new kind of travel writing that is intellectually adventurous but never detached, couched in personal experience but deeply engaged in the world.'—*Fantastic Fiction*

'Hariharan...employs abundant creative imagination as she conjures the centuries past that have shaped the present in which she finds herself...'—*Kirkus Reviews*

'...an illuminating and unexpected view of a familiar place, a comparison that can in turn spark a cascading line of thoughts on the way that cities and empires relate.'—*Literary Hub*

I Have Become the Tide

GITHA HARIHARAN

SIMON &
SCHUSTER

London · New York · Sydney · Toronto · New Delhi

A CBS COMPANY

First published in India by Simon & Schuster India, 2019
A CBS company

1 3 5 7 9 10 8 6 4 2

Simon & Schuster India
818, Indraprakash Building,
21, Barakhamba Road,
New Delhi 110001

www.simonandschuster.co.in

Hardback ISBN: 978-93-86797-38-4
eBook ISBN: 978-93-86797-39-1

For sale in the Indian Subcontinent only.

Typeset in India by SÜRYA, New Delhi

Printed and bound in India by Replika Press Pvt. Ltd.

Simon & Schuster India is committed to sourcing paper that is made from wood grown in sustainable forests and support the Forest Stewardship Council, the leading international forest certification organisation.
Our books displaying the FSC logo are printed on FSC certified paper.

This is a work of fiction. Apart from named public figures, the characters are fictitious, and so are their stories. The specific events in the novel are also fictitious. But much of the novel may bear resemblance to reality, both past and present. The cruelty of discrimination, bigotry and violence is only too real; and so is the bravery of those who dissent.

For Prabir

I'm the sea; I soar, I surge.
I move out to build your tombs.
The winds, storms, sky, earth.
Now all are mine.
In every inch of the rising struggle
I stand erect.

From 'I Have Become the Tide' by J.V. Pawar,
translated by Jayant Karve and Eleanor Zelliot

Contents

Words like walls

1

Chikka's running hard, a drum held close to his chest. The midday sun beats his body, but he can't stop. He has to get away.

He's almost at the pond at the edge of the settlement—no one could call their awful cluster of hovels a village. Chikka stops to catch his breath. His stomach is so empty it aches; his heart pounds. There's no one at the pond, only the filthy heap of a sleeping dog. For once he can be alone here.

Chikka sinks to the ground then falls flat on his stomach at the edge of the water. The mud feels hot and hard. It's almost like the mother he has seen only in his dreams. Their skin is the same colour. This is what unfamiliar mothers must be like; this is what the familiar mud under his feet is like. It can take a thousand bodies and their multitudinous miseries on its back.

Chikka wants to lie forever in the embrace of this hard-hearted mother. Or he wants to lie here on the mud as long as he is alone, while the villagers finish burying his father and eating a meal in memory of the departed. But the drum Chikka still clutches pokes mercilessly into his chest. He rolls over, looks at the sky hanging far above him. The sky tells him that even he, a cattle skinner's son, can gaze at its wondrous expanse, look into the distance, and see places that the roof of all humanity has seen. Chikka narrows his eyes and looks. But the sky is only playing a trick. It's empty. Really, all he has is the patch of dirty mud under his back, what he has had all his eighteen-year-old life.

Chikka pulls himself to his feet. He stares at the pond without a name, the untouchable pond he, and others like him, cannot do without. The pond means water for people and animals to drink; water for people and animals to bathe; water to wash clothes and bums in; water to play in; water to throw dead and living refuse into; water to be filled in pots and taken home. It's an untouchable pond they touch all the time, a pond that touches their lives like a lover devoted to them, doing his duty day and night. There's nothing Chikka doesn't know about this still pond. It has no surprises for him. It's muddy always; the blue of the sky struggles to swim to the surface in a few brave patches. Otherwise the pond is every colour but blue. Mostly it is a shiny green, spreading like oil. In some places the green algae has come to a boil; it's bubbling, cooking poison with a hundred sparkling eyes. The flat stones here and there force brown clumps of algae into a twisted trail, a sluggish snake-shaped body of scum.

Above the pond, above Chikka, is the over-bright sun, shining as if there is something to celebrate. Or obliterate. Its blaze lights the pond now, transforms it into a glittering mirror that lies shamelessly. Chikka peers at the water again. He can no longer see the filth he knows is there. Instead he sees layers of gleaming pictures blurring into each other. The slurry at the top swirls and blooms into delicate flowers. Frothy white lines float here and there, as if the stagnant pond has learnt to hint at waves. As if the water has learnt to flow at last.

There's a buzz in his ear. He doesn't know whether it is a fly or whether he is just lightheaded. He slaps his ear. The fly sings a quick line in farewell, crash lands in the water. Chikka sighs. The sun, the sky, the water, even a common fly—everything has got together to have a laugh at his expense. They have nothing better to do for a few minutes.

Then he hears voices. The mourners must be done with their meal; they must be getting back to work. Not one of them can afford more than an hour of grief. Chikka scrambles to his feet, takes off before he can be seen. He does not stop till he is at the very edge of the untouchable settlement, an edge marked with thick wall-like bushes beyond a sharp dip in the land. This dip is a wide trench, like a dry moat to keep away the villagers—the people from the real village across. Really the moat is to keep Chikka and his like away from the real village. They can negotiate the pit when their duties call them to the village: when they go there to take away baskets of what they call night soil but is really shit; when they climb upper caste trees that need their coconuts plucked; or when they drag away cows and goats that have fallen dead on upper caste streets and upper caste farms.

Chikka slips into the pit at one end and scrambles up at the other. It's effortless; he's had years of practice. Once he is past the bushes though, he stops. He has no work in the village ahead. He has not eaten since the day before. *What is he doing here?* He falls to his knees.

Chikka is on his knees, alone in no-man's-land, the untouchable colony behind him, the upper caste village before him. He has not let go of the drum all this time.

He bends over it now, sees his father. Not the light bag of bones he helped carry and lower into the narrow hole in the ground, not the body he threw handfuls of mud on. It's his father Chikka sees, alive, lying in their hut. It's his father he hears.

Chikka can hear his father groan. It will go on and on, this groaning, till the rattling snore begins. When the snoring stops, the groaning will begin again. In between the groans, his father will call Chikka in the querulous tone reserved for a useless son. 'I'm hungry,' his father will say for the tenth time that day. 'Chikka, you good-for-nothing, bring me something to eat.'

Chikka sees himself pouring thin gruel into an open toothless mouth, gruel or a watery soup of a few grains of rice, usually flavoured with leaves, and sometimes, on good days, with bones. On the best days, the rare days, Chikka chews small pieces of meat then places the gristly pulp on his father's tongue. The mouth never closes. The tongue and throat have forgotten what they are supposed to do with food. His father chokes. When he gets his breath back, he shouts hoarsely, 'Don't feed me this pulp, you sonofabitch. Get me my lota, get me my drum. I want to drink. I want to beat my drum till I die.'

Most days Chikka gives up at this point. He pours the rank-smelling liquid into the dented lota and helps his father sit up. He gives him the drum. The liquor burns its way down the old throat, brings it to life for a moment. The old man can no longer beat his drum, but he rests it on his stomach, his hands stroking it restlessly. He tries to sing. When all he can do is croak, he is enraged. He throws the drum then the lota across the hut. That calms him down for a while, or exhausts him so much that he is quiet. Sometimes Chikka tiptoes his way to the sleeping body—is it already a body or is it still his father? But his father is awake; the querulous voice is back. 'Didn't I say I want my drum? I want to beat it. It will help me go. Drum and drink. Let me drink, you bastard.'

'Drum and drink, you bastard.' His father's last words to him.

Chikka gapes at the drum now, waiting for it to deny those words. Or accuse him of what he did. The skinning tools his father and he used on cows, goats, whatever cattle died of disease or old age: Chikka threw them into the grave this morning. The village elders were shocked, but not into silence. They let him know their shock in many words, all of them yelling at the same time. That's when Chikka ran away from the funeral. A few of the mourners chased him but quickly gave up. They had to finish the business at the grave, send off the old man with some dignity and a meal for the living. If Chikka was shirking his duty, they would have to see to the end-of-life meal themselves, then carry on with their day.

Chikka had run away from his father's funeral. He had run to the hut. Once inside, he looked around wildly. How empty! A whole life, and this is what remained to prove his father had lived: a couple of bent vessels; a few rags; a drum; a reeking lota; and the smell of vomit, shit, death. Chikka kicked the lota exactly as his father used to on the days he was filled with shame, saying tearfully, 'I will never touch a drop again.' The promise never lasted more than a glum night or two. Soon his father would be shouting in rage, 'Drink. Beat the drum. How else do we keep living?' He had longed for his father to be quiet then. But now that the old man was silent, Chikka felt furious with the hut, its empty place where his father used to be, its miserable lota, and the drum finally gone mute. Here in this silent shambles lay Chikka's life that was, and Chikka's life that was to be. He grabbed the drum and ran out of the hut.

The drum in his hands now: looking at it means looking at himself over the last few months, seeing himself grudging the old man his slow death, seeing himself searching for work that would feed the two of them and buy his father's drink. He strokes the drum as he has seen his father do so many times, as if it is a pet, or a small child's head.

At work, inserting the knife into the dead animal, drawing lines carefully so that the hide could be pulled off neatly, Chikka would sometimes hear his father sing minus the drum. If he was singing, it meant the carcass they were skinning was a good one. They would soon share some edible meat, not meat that made them vomit or run all day to the pond to wash away their watery shit. His father's good-meat songs had nothing to do with their real lives. In these songs, his father always got the girl, the willing naked girl, along with everything he rarely got to eat. Chikka has not heard his father sing any happy songs for years, but he wills himself to remember one:

That girl—
    fish for eyes, mangoes for breasts,
    buttocks like golden pumpkins.
She'll come to me,
Oh yes she will!

But the drum is looking at Chikka steadily, daring him to remember an everyday song instead.

He hears his father again. It's night; the old man is drunk; the stick in his hand is going at the drum as if he wants to beat it to death.

Where is that land
where water flows free?

Tell me. *Tell me.*

Always, most nights, dead drunk, his father would seize the drum and the stick and begin singing his only two questions. He sang or growled or slurred the same words, the same lines, over and over. In the last year, he added a word, the word *my*, so he sang,

Where is that land
where water flows free?

Tell me. *Tell me.*

Where is *my* land
where water flows free?

Just that and the drum beating. Did he think that if he sang it again and again, every night, the stick beating the drum to say it as hungrily and angrily as possible, that someone would hear him? That someone would answer his questions?

Sometimes Chikka couldn't bear it. 'What's the rest of the song, old man?' he would yell over the grating voice and the fierce drumbeats. His father always ignored this question. Only once, on a night when he swayed more than usual, his words leaning against each other for support, the stick on the drum skipping a beat or two, his father paused, then said, 'The drum will tell you, you cunt.' Then he worked himself up to one last furious moment of singing and drumming before he collapsed into a stupor. Chikka only knew his father was still alive because every now and then a snore blew a horn out of his open mouth.

Chikka mutters to himself now: *Where is my land where water flows free?* The question is a pesky fly buzzing around inside his head, jumbling up everything. Where? Where? What land? What flowing water? There are only the tears that flow down his cheeks. He hangs his head, whispers, 'Where, father?'

'Son,' he hears a gentle voice.

Chikka's head flies up. The voice is coming from behind a bush. Then the voice emerges. It's a stranger, a man who smiles at him then asks, 'Did I frighten you?'

Another man emerges from behind the bush.

Chikka stares at them, forgetting to wipe his tears. The man who spoke has a baby-smooth face and a perfect round head, clean-shaven. He is simply dressed, just a dhoti and an upper covering cloth, but both look too clean to be anything but upper caste. The other man: he is a laughable contrast to the first. He's hairy. He looks like a tough furry animal with great big swirls of hair on his bare chest, his arms and what can be seen of his stomach and legs. He has just one grey cloth tied around his waist, folded up so it covers only part of his thighs. The hair on his head and his moustache and beard are equally unruly, declaring cheerfully, *Nothing upper caste about this one.* He too is smiling at Chikka. The gap between his two front teeth makes the smile appear wider.

The smooth one walks toward Chikka. Chikka drops the drum, jumps back then looks down at the drum. That too can pollute. He bends over as if ready for a beating. Is the man picking up a stick? Does he carry a whip in the cloth bag hanging on his shoulder? What is this man doing here, outside the village, as if he wants to get polluted? And what is he doing with the other one, clearly lower caste, and what do they want with him?

'Look at me, son.'

Chikka can't. He crawls forward, grabs his drum. At least he won't lose his wretched father entirely.

He hears the gentle voice again: 'Look at me. Get up, my son.'

My god, the man is coming closer. Soon they will break all caste rules. Chikka can hear and feel the man's breath on him. Chikka looks up bravely, but he is trembling.

The men are still smiling; there's no sneer or threat in their smiles, Chikka can see that now. But his heart still pounds. There's a shrill whistle in his ears; or the whistle is coming out of his ears, emptying the air, emptying everything in his limbs, his stomach, his head.

When Chikka wakes up again, it's to the feel of water. There are cool drops falling on his face. When he opens his eyes, he is in the shade of a wide-branched peepal tree, every leaf tip pointing like a slim finger. The hairy man is sprinkling water on him. Seeing Chikka awake, the man helps him sit, feeds him water from a curled leaf-cup as if he is a baby. The man sits on the ground, holding Chikka. He smells of sweat, but Chikka has a mad desire to sleep in those arms that are as solid as tree trunks.

'What is your name, son?' It's the smooth one again. He's still standing.

'Chikka, master.'

'I am not your master, I am your brother.'

Maybe he is a mad man, thinks Chikka. Oh god, a high-caste mad man and his kind beast of a keeper. Who are they, what are they doing here?

As if he has heard him, the smooth man says, 'I am your brother, Chikka.'

'Yes, my master.'

The man laughs. 'I am no master, I told you. I am just your brother. Your elder brother.'

The other one, still on the ground cradling Chikka, says, 'He's my Elder Brother too. And I am Puttanna. The little elder brother,' he adds, his body shaking with laughter. 'No point having only one sort of elder brother.'

Chikka is speechless. And he is hungry, and still thirsty. He is not sure if he can get up, scramble across the ridge and run back to the old pond.

'No, don't move,' says his new Elder Brother with authority.

The other one, Puttanna, unwraps a bundle, pulls out a piece of dry fish and an onion. 'Eat first,' he says. 'There's time?' he asks Elder Brother. The other man nods.

No one speaks till Chikka has eaten the fish. Now that he is eating, he can hardly eat fast enough. He drinks more of the water Puttanna fetches him. Elder Brother is also sitting with them now; he's eating fruit. He offers a piece to Puttanna, then Chikka. Chikka stares at the ripe red piece of fruit in the hand held out to him. Slowly, Chikka stretches his hand forward. Skin brushes skin as he takes it, mumbling, 'Elder Brother.'

Once they are done with eating, the two men look at Chikka. Though they are so different, the way they look at Chikka is the same. It's a look that melts Chikka, makes him feel a new kind of hunger.

'So tell me, Younger Brother Chikka,' says Elder Brother, 'what you are doing here alone. Where are your people?'

To his shock, Chikka hears himself speak. 'I have no one. I had my father but he is—he is gone. They buried him this morning.' Chikka says *they*; he cannot bring himself to say *I*.

The men listen in a way no one has ever listened to Chikka before. Chikka tries to hold back the flow of words from his mouth. But it's impossible. His stomach is full. He can no longer see and hear and smell hut and father and pond. One loving stranger has fed him. Another stranger is calmly listening to him as if he understands every word Chikka says.

The words flow out of Chikka's mouth like gushing water; they are as audible as his father's stick beating the drum. Chikka says things he has told no one before. His horrible secret thoughts, his impatience, his yearning for he doesn't know what. There's a voice inside him whining in fear, *What are you doing, what are you saying?* But Chikka brings out the worst of it. He might as well get it over with, say aloud what may instantly change this new Elder Brother.

'My father skinned dead cows. I helped him. That's who we are. That's who I was.' Chikka notices he has said *was*, as if that life of his died along with his father.

Chikka falls silent.

Puttanna wipes his eyes. Elder Brother takes Chikka's hands in his, rubs them gently as if warming them. Chikka feels a trembling begin somewhere around his neck and shoulders. It spreads downward till he, all of him, is shivering. Elder Brother strokes Chikka's hands till the shivering stops.

When Elder Brother speaks, it is not about what Chikka has said. He says instead, 'Would you like to come with us? We are going home.'

Chikka is too surprised to ask where this home is.

As before, the man reads his mind. 'It's across the river. We're going past the village and ahead to the river, then we will take a boat across to the other side. From there we will walk home.'

Chikka turns to Puttanna.

'Elder Brother and I have been travelling,' Puttanna explains. 'We meet people, give them courage with our message.'

'Message?'

'Yes, that we are all brothers. And sisters,' Puttanna laughs.

'We are going to the river,' Elder Brother repeats. 'If you have nothing left here, there is the rest of the world. There's always a river you can cross. Come with us.'

The river! So near, yet so far from Chikka's place. To get onto a boat, cross the river, go away, live another life! But can he really walk through the village, or the parts of it out of bounds to him, and reach the riverbank? Elder Brother and Puttanna seem to think it is entirely possible.

It's a walk Chikka's legs do on their own as if the rest of him is not there. Every time he sees someone in the distance, then growing bigger as they get closer, Chikka hangs his head. Elder Brother is, of course, walking with his head held high; but so is Puttanna. Neither has a sacred thread across the chest, nor caste marks on the forehead, and both walk through the village as if they own it. The terror in Chikka waits to hear someone say: 'What is he doing here, doesn't he skin cows and goats, doesn't he cook and eat them, isn't he *untouchable*?'

But Puttanna is clever. He has chosen a longer, winding route to the river so the walk through the village is brief.

They do come across people, both in and beyond the village; it's impossible not to. Chikka does get a couple of stares; so does Puttanna. But then the villagers' eyes shift to Elder Brother, his bland, confident face, his brisk no-nonsense stride. Chikka shuffles behind the other two, making himself as small and invisible as possible. To his amazement, it works. No one says a thing to him.

Then they are there. There it is, the river he has heard of but never seen. But even before he can take in his luck, or admire the water that flows like a rich spread, a feast, Chikka sees the boat coming toward them. It's made of dark mango wood, this boat shaped like a neat little almond. Puttanna waves, shouts a friendly greeting to the ferryman as he brings the bobbing boat right to the bank. 'Ey Peddi. Good to see that dirty face of yours!'

Elder Brother steps into the boat. Puttanna follows him. Then Elder Brother gestures invitingly at Chikka. 'Come,' says Puttanna. Even Peddi the ferryman seems to expect Chikka to get in. It seems like the most natural thing in the world to do, no questions asked.

Chikka steps in gingerly, the drum his only baggage.

2

It's amazing how much hate can be packed into a single line. The one-line message is inaccurate and ignorant, but it's the hatred that strikes Krishna. Hate is what holds those thirteen English words together before they end with an open, ominous dash. Professor P.S. Krishna re-reads the note he has just found: *Bastard Hindu hater, making up lies about a saint, you should do suicide before—*

There's no sender's name, no postage stamp either. There's no specific charge, no particular reason given for why Krishna should 'do suicide'. It's definitely addressed to him. *Mr. P.S. Krishna* says the red scrawl on the envelope that was sealed with several strips of sellotape. Though it's obviously been hand delivered, slipped into his mailbox in the university department, the title Professor, often shortened to Prof, has been dropped, and he has been demoted to a Mister. Krishna crushes the piece of paper, aims it at his wastepaper basket. That's where he sends the worst, the most hopeless work from his students. The others he is willing to read and comment on any number of times.

This is the second critical response Krishna has got to a lecture he gave at a recent 'cultural meet' at the Town Hall. His lecture was on the mystic Kannadeva, going beyond the usual sobriquets of 'saint poet' or 'saint reformer'. A week later, there was a one-inch comment by some Guru (Sri Sri Sri) Santosh in the inner pages of one of the local newspapers. Shiva, Krishna's research assistant for more than fifteen years, brought the paper to him, looking apologetic. 'Sorry, Prof. It's not nice coverage. But I don't like to keep anything from you.' Krishna thanked Shiva and read:

> In our tradition, we have examples of how wise men have lived before us. We are also blessed with their words of guidance handed down to us over thousands of years. These days it has become the fashion to question all this or claim to have made some discovery which turns our historic legacy into something ugly.
>
> Professor of Literature P.S. Krishna has also fallen into this trap. In a lecture in Town Hall last week, he was supposed to describe the uplifting songs and sayings of Saint Kannadeva. Instead the professor mocked the Saint's verses and songs, saying many of them sound like they were composed by someone else. Even more shocking, the professor insulted the Saint by saying he may have committed suicide by drowning in a river. Anyone knowledgeable in such matters knows Sri Kannadeva attained Samadhi in two stages, once in the hoary temple by the Devika River, then in the river itself.
>
> It is sad that this professor, who has taught for more than forty years, is still connected to the university though he has already retired, and will be allowed to continue misleading students and hurting the sentiments of devout Hindus.

The cultural meet at the Town Hall: Krishna had wanted to speak of something new, not his usual readings of what he calls the people's epic poetry. The earnest young man who introduced Krishna had said, in a very long introduction, something to the effect of 'We are honoured to have with us Professor P.S. Krishna who has taught many of us. He has continued to be our teacher, guide and friend even after we have passed out of college. He is well known for his pioneering work on local versions of epic poetry. Professor sir, we are sure that today too you will increase our knowledge and answer many of our questions.'

Krishna had felt guilty somehow, as he always did after a well-meant but fulsome introduction. And that day he felt particularly guilty because he did not plan, especially, to either 'increase knowledge' or 'answer questions'. He had thought he would ask some questions for a change, because his own knowledge needed increasing on the subject.

Krishna had begun with a disclaimer. 'As our young friend here has pointed out, most of my work has been on retellings of epic poems in several languages and dialects south of the Vindhyas. I like to think of these retellings as the people voicing their own versions of grand epic poetry, in words and stories that made and make sense to them. But enough of that. Today I am not going to talk about epics at all. Though devotional literature is not really my area of study, I want to share a few thoughts on the poet and mystic Kannadeva. I came across some of his work, thanks to a student of mine, and I was fascinated. Why?'

Krishna's lecture had bypassed the two words 'saint' and 'reformer', used most frequently to describe Kannadeva. He spoke of him as a poet, and suggested there were some intriguing inconsistencies in his poems. As usual, there had been no cleverness or jargon in Krishna's lecture. He had a few questions, and he asked them simply.

'First, a matter that may seem like a detail to some of you,' he began. 'Many of Kannadeva's poems end with the line "O river of a thousand faces". It appears often enough for it to be a signature line. But why did Kannadeva change his signature line now and then? A few poems use the line "O river that moves to stillness". Yet other poems do not use either line.'

Krishna had cited an example or two. (He didn't sing, but he had a fine reciting voice, sensitive to every nuance in word, pause and punctuation.) 'Consider this,' Krishna said, then recited:

This potter hums with spinning wheel,
that cobbler drones a note for each nail.
The weaver's song twines thread
    with thread.
I too sing when cloth slaps stone.

But you, you don't raise your voice.

My lord, my friend:
You're the song,
the song that sings itself,
O river of a thousand faces.

'Then compare it with this:

    He dives into himself,
    practises his alchemy.

Bodies melt into words,
Word turns spirit.
    Friends, foes,
    all buried
    one by one,
    ash in his earth.

There's only one man left.

Is he the one?
Who's left to tell him?

'Not only is the river missing in the second poem, it's also somewhat different in style. And if I read out a few more examples, you may hear more differences … Some address God directly; others find God in the land, or the river, or even a tree or a bird in flight. Still others seem to be speaking only to men and women, not God. You may argue that all this only shows the development of the poet from a young seeking mind to a full-fledged mystic. But both callow and mature writings show these noticeable differences, not just of signature line, but also tone, even concern.'

Krishna had paused to indicate that he was coming to his main point. 'It is almost,' he continued, 'as if Kannadeva was several people. Sometimes he was one person or the other. Sometimes he was all of them at once. There was more than one person speaking here. The multiple voices cannot simply be explained away as interpolations, the sort that could occur as songs and poems were handed down orally, or in written form, moving from palm leaves to writing on paper to print.'

Krishna had also referred to the limited biographical material on Kannadeva. 'There are very few studies devoted entirely to Kannadeva. He is usually mentioned as part of the larger "singer saint" family. Mostly he tends to be given just one paragraph with a verse quotation—sometimes just two lines—in essays and books on the "saint poets" of India.'

'Given how little we know about him,' Krishna added, 'there is also a question about his life. Or the end of his life. Did he commit suicide by drowning himself in an unnamed river? And why?'

Krishna had made sure to emphasise that all the questions he had raised were preliminary. They were speculative, though he was confident about his theory that Kannadeva's poems gave voice to more than one person.

Who was Kannadeva, really? This question now floats back to the surface, insists that Krishna look at it afresh. The question pushes the anonymous letter writer and the self-proclaimed Guru (Sri Sri Sri) Santosh out of his mind. Krishna drums the table with two fingers to help him think. There are the fragments of "biographies" he should go back to, such as they are. He has read them before, but then he may see some new hint, some fresh lead he can follow.

But for now, Shiva is here, papers in hand. Kannadeva's life will have to wait for the consuming staple of university life, Admin. There's much less of it now that Krishna is no longer head of the department, but still a lot of "official papers" find their way to him as if they can't get rid of the habit. Shiva is, as usual, trying to make himself smaller, holding himself so all six feet of him, and the necessary weight required to fill up that frame, can be reduced to respectful humility.

'If you have a few minutes, Prof sir,' Shiva says, his usual way of beginning their meeting every day. He sits like a coiled knot on the chair before Krishna, places a mess of papers on the table, dropping a few in the process. Shiva gets flustered. He picks up the papers and goes through them one by one, his right forefinger making a swift trip to his tongue each time a page has to be turned. The touch of saliva tames the paper, helps him get to the next sheet.

Krishna watches him, trying not to sigh or say anything.

Any sign of impatience will only make Shiva slower. As it is, this is going to take a while. Krishna can see, on the top of the pile, a proforma from the library, clearly designed to make life so miserable for any professor that he may decide he does not need to order books today.

'This one from the library, Prof,' Shiva says. 'It's a little complicated.' *Complicated* is the word that rules Shiva's life; it makes him nervous but he also loves it, considering how often he uses it. Shiva looks worried but also a little pleased. He loves this quiet hour with the kind-hearted professor, with just the two of them unravelling something complicated.

It's only in the evening, when Krishna is home and sitting on his favourite cane chair in the sit-out, his coffee by him, enjoying an hour alone before everyone else comes back, that the question comes back to him like a reminder. Who was Kannadeva? Krishna swallows the rest of his coffee, looks at his watch. He has a little time.

He makes his way to the study. That's what it is called, and that is where study actually happens, though it is such a mess of papers and books. The new desktop computer his son Ram has bought him sits like a conqueror amid the spoils.

Krishna picks up a fat plastic file, throws it aside. He pulls out a transparent plastic folder which has flowers on it and the words 'My Plastic Folder' in case the owner is on the way to dementia. The papers in the folder spill on the floor. My god, he's getting as bad as Shiva. He picks up a couple of sheets, sees Shiva's signature line *Research for Prof Krishna, Subject Kannadeva life, date 24/3/2010*, and the initials *S.M.* for Shiva Menon. Krishna does not recall reading this. Or maybe he read it and forgot about it, given sweet Shiva's research abilities. But what's the harm in a quick second read? Krishna sits down in the rocking chair by the window.

Kannadeva (circa 1150-1180)

The life of Saint Kannadeva is another example of the heights a mere mortal can aspire to. Kannadeva dedicated his energy equally to self-realization and peace and friendship among all in society.

His birth and pedigree

Kannadeva was born in the cradle of nature, among verdant fields not far from the river. His parents, Chikkiah and Mahadevi, were simple pious folk, tending to their fields and the needs of their neighbours and community. They knew that their son was destined for greatness, so they nurtured him in his early years for a higher purpose.

His initiation into bhakti

Kannadeva was only a day old when he broke into a bright smile at the sound of the big bell being rung in the temple near his parents' home. He learnt to walk at three months, as if he couldn't wait to go to that temple with the big bell, and ring it himself. Even while he was a boy of tender years, he could not bear to see or hear about the rich not sharing their blessings with the poor, and equally, he could not bear to see cruelty to cows …

Kannadeva began, at a tender age, to recite long slokas and mantras. He also began to compose his own songs about the simple sights and natural wonders around him, viz. the river, the boats, trees and flowers, and the daily lives of simple folk like fishermen and farmers. His parents often took him to the town nearby, what in those days was a glorious city, capital of a rich kingdom. Here Kannadeva's young mind was nurtured by the prayers and pujas in the hoary temples. But nature has her own plans to teach her chosen ones. Kannadeva went, again at a tender age, to a school near another river, a quiet but beautiful one. The river was the perfect place for solitary contemplation, leaving all vanities of life behind. Among monks and scholars who meditated on the Absolute all day long, Kannadeva mastered the abstract principles of self-realization. He did not marry. His entire life was devoted to the service of the divine, and to teaching the common people how they could cope with the sufferings of this world and prepare the way for the next. He emphasized constant spiritual development for all, from the most powerful of kings to the humblest of slaves. Often called the Messenger of Peace, Kannadeva attained Samadhi in the temple by his beloved river.

Krishna looks at the second research contribution from Shiva, just in case it is any better than the first. This second Life of Kannadeva is entitled 'On whose wisdom no human hand can improve', and it lists several stories about Kannadeva, each associated with a song he composed.

(1) One day, Kannadeva sat in absolute silence meditating on the river. He emptied his mind of everything except the river. Then he felt a watery hand touch his head, blessing him. It was the spirit of the river that had emerged in bodily form to give him prasad. The hand gently opened his mouth and placed a lump of jaggery on his tongue. Kannadeva sang with his sweetened tongue, *Only you can hold this restless mind still so it can see.*

(2) Once, Kannadeva was walking through the city streets and he saw a rich man beating his servant. The

rich man accused his servant of stealing. Kannadeva stood before them and sang an appeal to the Divine Judge, 'Is there anyone who knows your justice? Is there anyone who knows your mercy?' The rich man stopped beating the servant, realizing that there was One above who would mete out justice as He saw fit. The servant fell to his knees and begged for forgiveness. Kannadeva had taught him honesty through the sight of Divine Mercy for all, from king to servant.

Krishna snorts. He throws the sheets on the floor and frowns. Should he look for more?

His answer comes in the form of Shanta's face. She peeps into the study, sees him there. She looks at the new mess on the floor and says cheerfully, 'Working? I am going to pick up Chitthu from his grandmother's.' Shanta too is Chitthu's grandmother, but she always thinks of her daughter-in-law's mother as the grandmother. As for Shanta, she is simply Chitthu's. He can call her grandmother or anything else he likes.

Krishna gets up, follows Shanta. It's been forty years since they were married and still, all he needs is a smile from her, and he is ready to go where she goes. Besides, he needs a walk.

3

It's Sunday morning. The sun seems to know that too, because it's relaxed, shining cheerfully rather than shining hot.

Asha leaves the hostel building, walks briskly to the gate. She can feel her heart beat fast, as if she is afraid. But really, she is excited, the happiest she's been since she got here. She can't believe it's been only three months since she, Satya and Ravi parted. How can months seem like years?

Then, they were still children in the twelfth standard, junior college, Plus Two, whatever you choose to call it. They were school children trying to vault over the ten plus two public exam, then the college entrance exams, so they could begin another life. The part of life that would begin when they found the answers to a pair of questions stalking them: Which college? What course? For at least a year, these questions had *become* life for Asha, Ravi and Satya, and for each of their families. A college education, especially a professional course, would help Asha, Ravi and Satya find some sort of key. A key that would open doors so they too—child and family, family and community—could go into the big world and be part of it, studying, working, earning, loving, marrying, making families. Living like anyone else.

All three of them were going to be doctors. That's the

promise Asha, Ravi and Satya had made to themselves and to each other. That's the promise that lit a spluttering flame of hope in their families. A child in a medical college! That child could have a future; that child's future could spill over into the family's future. No, wait, it could spread like water in a thirsty field, change things for the likes of them, for their communities. For castes like theirs. For Asha's tailoring mother and her office-going father; for Ravi's parents, daily-wage labourers; and for Satya's mother, her back bent in other people's farms. For that hope to become real, for such a miracle to happen, they would find the money somehow, somewhere. And they did; they worked harder, they borrowed, pawned or sold what little they had. The books Asha, Ravi and Satya had to study for the medical entrance test were different from their school books. Asha's parents bought some of them; Ravi's parents bought a few. They couldn't afford a coaching centre so the three of them studied together, making notes and memory aids for themselves and each other.

It seemed to stretch forever, that time of books and dictionaries and notes and cramming; of learning a new kind of book-English, even worse than the one they already struggled with in school. But though it felt like it, it wasn't forever. It all ended, and so did their promise to each other. That promise is now in the past, part of childhood. Only Satya is going to be a doctor. Asha will be a nurse, a very different thing but, as her mother and father consoled her, close enough. As for Ravi—he is in the limbo of a BSc in zoology. He has no idea where that will take him.

Asha walks briskly; the city has woken up but it is not yet itself. The roads look shabby and pointless while they wait for the usual traffic to come to them. The roadside carts and hole-in-the-wall eateries are already in business though, selling vegetables and fruit, tea and snacks.

Asha wonders how she will describe her nursing course and college to Satya and Ravi. Really, what she wants to ask them is, 'Is it all strange for you too?' The three of them aren't just friends. The last two years in school, and those months of preparing for the entrance test together, they were—she can't find the right word for it—a unit? A family? Satya will know the right word. He's the poet among them though he is studying medicine, not poetry.

She pulls out her cell phone, looks at the time again. She's early as usual. She texts Satya. *Bus reached city?* She stares at the phone till it produces Satya's reply. *Ten mins to bus station. Will take auto.* Satya knows she will be waiting. He knows she will be too restless to wait at the hostel gate or go sit somewhere. He always knows how someone else feels, he's like that. When Asha wants to tease him, she calls him Elder Brother. He is almost a year older than her anyway, and a few months older than Ravi. But though he is their Elder Brother, though he is the only one among them who got a seat in a medical college, Asha and Ravi feel protective toward him.

Asha has been walking fast without knowing where exactly she's headed. She looks around, sees a Barista. But she can't spend money on a coffee there. Will they let her sit inside if she doesn't buy anything? There are a couple of small shops selling clothes nearby. They're not open yet. But there's a man opening the shutter of the bookshop next door. She texts again so Satya and Ravi will know where to find her.

The bookshop has stationery, magazines and textbooks. There is a large shelf with rows of books to prepare people for every sort of entrance test. She picks up a fat one out of habit, opens it. This is for engineering aspirants; but it doesn't matter, she is not reading it. She can't read it, because the words have suddenly lost their place. They're moving out of their straight lines, scattering; some are falling off the edge of the page. Soon there will be nothing left. It will be an empty white page. Asha shudders, puts the fat book back on the shelf.

She picks up another called *English Conversation Made Easy*. The words in this book behave better. They actually bring a smile to her lips, because the book brings back the memory of the three of them trying to practice conversation in English with each other. Satya would be serious, but Ravi liked to make it a drama. What was the point of learning a language if it didn't let you imagine things? Ravi would pretend that they had already got their entrance test results, and that the news was good. He had no idea what people said at the 'counselling' that took place before they would find out which colleges would be allotted to them. But Ravi was good at imagining things so they sounded almost possible. 'You're at the counselling session for the merit list,' he would say. 'You have a good choice of colleges, Miss Asha, congratulations!' What a lovely, foolish dream—and Ravi would put on such a pompous and hearty voice that Asha couldn't help giggling. 'No smiling, no giggling,' Ravi would scold her, but break into a smile himself.

The three of them know a lot of English words. The problem is what to do with them when writing, and even worse, when speaking; how to put them together to make sentences that are not awkward or hesitant, sentences that flow, say what they want to say. Say them aloud. And say them like those other people do, the rich ones, or the upper caste ones who can speak English as if it was as natural as Kannada or Marathi or Tamil. When Asha answers a question in class, she can sense many of the girls smiling at each other. Asha's chin goes up. That's nothing. They can smile or laugh all they like, she at least reads the assigned chapters. And she has a small scholarship, even if some of the girls in her class may think she got one only because she is Scheduled Caste.

Scheduled Caste. SC. All three of them, Asha, Ravi and Satya, were in the science group in school. Physics, Chemistry, Math, Biology. PCMB. Many of the SC students chose the Arts stream rather than Science or Commerce. And of the few science students, Asha, Satya and Ravi were the only three reservation students trying for admission in medicine. Everyone expected the two boys to be together. Asha was the odd girl out. But the three became a trio, first in the eyes of the teachers and classmates, then in their own. The school had miraculously brought them together, small-town Asha, big-town Ravi, and Satya from the village. They found they liked each other. They got to know each other. Only they knew how different each one of them was, though to everyone else, they were the SC trio trying for medical seats. It became a joke among them: they were not reservation students, they were reserved for each other.

Asha's phone pings. It's a text from Ravi. *Come out. Waiting in the auto.* She puts down the book in her hands, runs outside the shop, gets into the auto between Ravi and Satya.

'The beach,' Ravi tells the auto driver who's looking at them disapprovingly.

The driver shrugs; the auto splutters its way down the road, determined to make it hard for the three of them to hear each other. But it doesn't matter. Words can wait. They're not in their new colleges, trying to fit in. They're not at home, waiting for their future to come to them. They're together, huddled like a secret association. They're squashed against each other because it's a holiday, and they're on the road, going somewhere.

Once at the beach, walking away from the gathering Sunday crowd along the shoreline, Asha, Ravi and Satya can finally ask each other, *So what's it like for you?*

As usual, Ravi is the first to speak up.

'A lot of it is the usual nonsense,' says Ravi. 'Most of the teachers are what I expected, and the course too. But I don't care, I'll get the degree.'

Asha looks at his face, searching for hurt. She at least knew she didn't stand a chance once she saw the test results. Her mother, the most practical person in the world, had anyway made Asha apply for nursing as well. But Ravi—he was almost there. Asha knows Ravi hasn't got over how close he came to getting that medical seat. But Ravi's not going to show any sign of his hurt or bitterness.

'There are some students I can talk to,' he says. 'I like my roommates. And Ramesha, that's one of my roommates, says there's a student association called Bhim Shakti. He heard about it from the seniors … But what about you, Asha?'

Asha has plenty to say, but it's all about the rules for the girls in the college, especially the hostel. They have timings for everything: library, leaving the grounds, leaving the hostel building. 'It's all very strict,' she says. 'But I'm getting used to it.'

Satya is the one Ravi and Asha really want to hear from. They want news from their own success story; feeling proud of him is almost like feeling proud of themselves. They turn to him eagerly. But Satya, walking between Ravi and Asha, shrugs. 'I don't know what to tell you,' he says. 'I don't know anybody yet. There's too much to study, that's all I do.'

'And the hostel?' asks Asha.

'It's all right,' says Satya. 'I'm in a small corner room on the top floor. And my roommate—he's from the North. We don't talk much, we have to speak to each other in English. And anyway—but he's all right. I'll get used to it all.'

They look at the horizon receding before them as they walk. Asha can sense there's more. But suddenly she doesn't want this conversation to go on. It's as if they are examining each other for scratches and bruises. They are together after so long, and they are on the beach. Before someone says something nasty, seeing her with two boys, she wants them to have a good time.

'Forget college,' she says cheerfully to the boys. 'Let's go in the water. Then let's get sugarcane juice.'

They stand in the water, looking at the sea. The sea stretches toward the sky, it spreads to left and right. It says to them: 'See how big the world is?' And this sea is never quiet; it doesn't know what it means to stand still, remain the same, or grow stagnant. The waves whoosh and roar as they roll forward, they slap the sand gently as they recede. Always, they do something, say something. Asha feels the joy of the movement the sea is trying to teach them. Their lives will change, they too will move forward. Become doctors, nurses, teachers. Regular people with regular lives, not people with name tags that set them apart—below or behind everyone else. Backward Caste. Other Backward Caste. Scheduled Tribe. BC, OBC, ST. And, of course, SC.

She's never touched either Ravi or Satya before, but now it seems natural to take each by the hand, walk away from the sea.

Asha leads them to the stall selling fresh sugarcane juice. She chooses the cane, then hands the juice to Satya and Ravi. The juice flows down her throat as if the future the sea has promised her will be just as sweet. She turns to the man at the stall to pay. Then she decides she can never have enough of this moment; she wants to hold it a while, stretch it with another glass.

'What about your brothers,' the juice seller asks Asha. 'Do they also want a second glass?' Just because he asks this, Asha gets Ravi and Satya a second round.

Yes, Satya and Ravi are her brothers, not because of blood but something more solid, less easy to spill. The three of them, friends for always though they are now in different places.

But as they leave the beach, she for the college hostel where the week's laundry awaits her, and they for the bus station, Asha feels tears prick her eyes. The visit is drawing to a close. The day they have looked forward to over three months, the peaceful day they have had together: it's not enough to make up for Asha's sense of loss. Already it's hard for them to explain to each other what those days apart have been. Maybe Satya, Ravi and Asha are afraid that if they say it aloud, say 'This is what they said to me,' or 'This is what they did to me, this is what happened to me,' they will all lose heart. It's just the beginning of the battle; the first semester, the first year. Who knows what more they will have to bear? Meanwhile, why burden the other two with the little humiliations Asha has had to brush aside; the disappointment Ravi is trying to take on the chin and move on; or the terrible loneliness of Satya as he plays audacious Dalit, studying to be a doctor?

My body is my boat

1

It's been weeks since the three friends saw each other. They've had text messages, email, a bit of Facebook and the rare phone call keeping them together, but it's not the same. The day at the beach, not one of them could say exactly what the first three months in college was like. Maybe Ravi thought complaining would sound unmanly, and he is in a hurry to be a man. Maybe Asha suspected her college, with its Christian intentions, could not possibly be as bad as the boys' colleges. Maybe Satya didn't want to describe what his experience was because putting it all in words, and to Ravi and Asha, would make it more real.

Asha is in class, the last of the day. It's the most boring class of all—Mrs Kumari drones endlessly about the 'fundamentals' of the nursing profession and how all of them have to become Indian Florence Nightingales. The rest of the time, she reads from the textbook. It's as if she is the student reading aloud, and the real students, bent over their texts, have to check that she doesn't leave out a word. 'Miss Nightingale was the first to mention Holism (treating the whole patient) in nursing, and the first who stated that a unique body of knowledge is required to practice professional nursing.'

Asha stares at her book, head down. The last class, she

had been looking at Mrs Kumari, and their eyes had met between sentences. Mrs Kumari had stopped her droning and asked Asha, 'Let me see if you can remember what we covered in our earlier classes. The word *nurse*. What word does it come from?'

Asha knew the answer. But when she said 'From the Latin word "nutritious", which means nourishing,' several of the girls tittered. Mrs Kumari had smiled too. 'Nut-ri-shius,' she said to Asha, exaggerating every syllable. 'Repeat after me.' Asha had done that, but she wished she had not known the answer. Lots of girls stared blankly at the wall when they were asked a question. Why couldn't she be like them?

Mrs Kumari is now listing the qualities of a professional nurse. It's an awfully long list. The nurse has to be merciful, kind, willing, willing to learn, gentle, patient, understanding, reliable, resourceful, courageous, honest, loyal, observant, cooperative, considerate, clean, self-sacrificing. The list goes on. Mrs Kumari's voice is so devoid of expression that all the qualities sound the same, equally important or unimportant. Asha has been taking a note or two, but she is too tired now to care. Her mind wanders to another room where she heard about why she was fit to be a nurse.

There were two women and one man on the other side of the table. Asha had already got admission; she had submitted all her papers, including an attested copy of her caste certificate after getting the original verified. This was not a real interview, just, as the college put it, a session to familiarise each scholarship student from the 'weaker sections' with the institute and course. It was meant, possibly, to be a Christian act.

The woman who talked all the time gave Asha a lecture

about how the noble profession of nursing needed something called empathy. The other woman said nothing, but she had a fixed smile on her face all through. Maybe she thought she was being kind, encouraging a quota student. Then the man, who had also been quiet, suddenly snapped, 'And why do you think you would make a good nurse?' Asha had hesitated, but the smiling woman nodded vigorously. In a thin syrupy voice meant to reassure Asha, she said, 'But you people are used to serving others, isn't it? Nursing will come naturally to you.'

Still, she is in a good institution, the Sisters of Mercy Nursing College. Asha holds on to this thought for a moment. But then she remembers the empty feeling in her stomach when she looked at the admission chart pinned on the bulletin board the first day, and her triumph gets a little tarnished.

There were many columns in the chart; her eye went first to the 'category' column. General. That was half the students. (General also had subdivisions, quotas for 'management' students. But the word quota sounded different here because all these seats were filled by students with rich parents.) So General as in best because of birth or money; then OBC, then SC. There she was. The tiny Scheduled Tribes list, ST, was below hers. As always, she wondered what it would be like to wake up one morning and find that she too was General. Part of the general public. Not someone who was 'weaker section' or 'backward' or 'depressed' or 'harijan' or 'Scheduled Caste' or even 'Dalit'. It was all true of course. But would she always have a description before or after her name, a name tag that told the world, but more important, told her, that she was not general, but particular, as in particularly handicapped?

Asha pushes this pesky question aside. She's sure she's having a better time of it than Ravi in his big government college, or Satya, a Dalit from a village in a competitive private medical college. Hers is a liberal, enlightened institute. There are strict rules about ragging, though the hostel warden looks the other way when the new students are put through 'innocent' forms of the initiation ritual. From what she has heard of other colleges, Asha knows she's lucky. All she had to do was spread great big gobs of Fair and Lovely cream on her face. When the seniors finally let her wipe the goo off her face, there were hoots of laughter. 'Is she just a little less black?' one of them had asked. At least they didn't say anything about caste, Asha consoled herself. Besides, when the hostel rooms were allocated, it was by alphabetical order, not according to caste or religion or reservation or scholarship. That's how Asha got to share a room with Priya from the General category. Priya is rarely quiet or still; she always has something to say, and something to laugh about. Her family is in the Gulf and her side of their room is cluttered with possessions. She wants to be friends with everyone.

The first Sunday in the hostel, she invited Asha to her local guardian's house for lunch.

Asha had never been in such a smart flat before. It was in a building with a guard at the entrance, and potted plants and colourful children's swings in the compound. Asha felt both excited and nervous as she and Priya went up the lift to the fifth floor. The woman who opened the door and took Priya in her arms looked as smart as the building: short hair, lipstick, a flowery salwar kameez. It was impossible to make out her age, but to Asha, she looked like someone who would always be young and glamorous. Asha hung back. The woman, whom Priya called Auntie, said to Asha, 'Come, come in, are you in Priya's class?'

'She's my roommate,' Priya replied for Asha. 'She doesn't know anyone in the city so I asked her to come for lunch.'

'Of course, please come in,' said Auntie.

Asha sat quietly on the plush orange and brown sofa, happy to listen to Priya and her Auntie talk about people she didn't know and the best mall in town to buy clothes. By lunch time, the rest of the family had joined them—Auntie's husband, Uncle, their son who was as silent as Asha but in a surly way, and an old man, Uncle's father. The old man ate noisily, staring at Priya for a long time. Then he shifted his attention to Asha. Asha could feel his eyes rest on her face; she could feel his look stick to her skin.

He suddenly stopped chewing to ask, 'What caste?'

Everyone fell silent.

He turned to Priya. 'Your friend, this black girl. What caste?' His voice sounded especially loud in the silence.

Auntie got up to get sweets from the kitchen. The moment passed. But when Asha accompanied Priya to the kitchen with the plates from the table, Auntie stopped her. 'No, no, don't come into the kitchen.' Her smile wavered. 'You're a guest, after all.'

Priya is still her roommate, but she spends a lot of time in other people's rooms. She is very polite to Asha when they have to be together. But every word of hers, every look, reminds Asha of the old man's all-important question.

Mrs Kumari has stopped droning. The bell rings; Asha's wandering mind comes back to the class. She shuts her textbook, the one that practically waves a flag to show how casteless this place is. The very first page of the book, there are three bold lines that scream: Untouchability is a sin. Untouchability is a crime. Untouchability is inhuman. It's a sin—for those who believe in that kind of thing, those who live by religion. It's a crime, for those who want to keep on the right side of the law. And inhuman—whose heart does that appeal to?

She wishes she could ask Satya or Ravi what they think. Ravi, especially, who would be less serious about it than Satya. He would know how to make light of it all, make her smile, even laugh at the hypocrisy of it all. *Caste is officially gone.* She can see him act it out, looking for it everywhere, under the table, inside a backpack, in the congealed drain by the roadside. She can hear him playing the fool, calling in a plaintive voice, 'Where are you, where are you? Show us your face, Mr Caste, I know you like to follow us wherever we go …'

Brave Ravi, funny Ravi, who can sing or joke about fear and sadness. Ravi, who can beat his drum when he runs out of words. How is he, what is he doing now?

It's been three months, what's happening? Asha adds an emoji of a puzzled yellow face with hand on chin and finger across the cheek. She clicks the Send arrow by Satya's name then forwards the message to Ravi. Ravi responds immediately: *Busy, lots to tell you. Will email.*

But it's Satya's email that comes first.

Dear Asha,

I am sorry I have not been able to visit as promised. Ravi also seems very busy, we have only spoken once on the phone. He told me all about his roommates, he wants me to come and meet them. Ravi is tempting me, but you know I have to study as much as I can to keep up. My only break is when I take my cycle and explore the surroundings. (Prasad bought me an old cycle. I am lucky to have a brother like him.) I am glad the college is not in the city. If I cycle for about half an hour, I can reach open fields. All the green, the openness, makes me feel fresh and strong again. Watching the women and men at work there, it's almost as if I am home. It makes me feel I am with my mother. I have also found a pond no one seems to use. It's small and not too clean, but I like sitting by it, listening to the breeze and watching the water tremble as if it is trying to tell me something.

Enough about myself. You had asked me to send you a poem for your Facebook page. I tried to write a few lines for you last night but I think I was too tired. This is what I managed:

The field where my ancestors worked
till they dropped dead, turned to earth.
Why does it call me every night,
the field I have left behind?

I don't know where to take it from there. But I read a very good poem, a translation I found of a poem by L.S. Rokade. It starts like this:

Mother, you used to tell me
when I was born
your labour was very long.
The reason, mother,
the reason for your long labour:
I, still in your womb, was wondering
Do I want to be born—
Do I want to be born at all

in this land?
Where all paths raced horizonwards
but to me were barred …

It goes on to describe the mother's life and the land that is hers but never really hers. Then comes the part I like best.

Mother, this is your land
flowing with water
Rivers break their banks
Lakes brim over
And you, one of the human race
must shed blood
struggle and strike
for a palmful of water.
I spit on this great civilization.
Is this land yours, mother,
because you were born here?
Is it mine
because I was born to you?
Must I call this great land mine
love it
sing its glory?
Sorry, mother, but truth to tell
I must confess I wondered
Should I be born
Should I be born into this land?

I can read this poem again and again and imagine that I am speaking to my own mother. It makes me feel sad, but it also makes me feel strong, do you know what I mean?

Your friend,
Satya

But Asha does not feel strong as she reads Satya's email. Instead, it brings back a worrying memory from their school days. Maybe all studious children are unpopular with their classmates. Satya was also serious, quiet, hardworking, kind—and SC. Maybe that's why even his name made him a natural target. In the playground especially, the name made him a girl, more than his lack of interest in cricket and kabaddi.

Asha can see Ravi, who loves sports, his back straight, his face stormy, as he loyally took on anyone who teased Satya in the playground. It only got Ravi into trouble every other week with the teachers. But even Ravi could do nothing in the school assembly where the other boys waited for the part when the Principal saluted the flag then announced solemnly to the standing rows of children, 'Satyameva Jayate!' Several boys would grin meaningfully. Once the Principal left, and the boys started pushing and shoving each other on their way to the classroom, they bullied Satya. '*Satya Jayate! Satya Jayate!*' They circled him, laughing.

Once one of them said, 'It seems your people clean toilets? They lug buckets of shit every day?'

Another boy jeered, 'Did you see the truth in shit today?'

The others loved this question. From then on, Satya was asked 'Did you see the truth in shit today?' every day after the morning assembly. When the teachers were within sight, the voices grew softer, but they could still be heard. 'Satya in shit. What is Satya's motto? Truth in shit.'

Ravi and Asha were teased too, but never in the way Satya was. Why was it worse for Satya? Because he was the better student? After all, for the others, they were the same, all the quotas. They were dark and poorly dressed. They had trouble with English. They could get away with lower pass marks and scholarships. All SCs come from the same dirty place. But actually, the three of them, Asha, Ravi and Satya, were from different places, different families. Did those daily cruelties happen because those boys sensed that even among the quotas, Satya was at a disadvantage? Asha finds it hard to believe they would know the difference. She herself realised how lucky she was only after she got to know Satya.

Asha lets her mind travel home, look once more at the picture of this luck, as if to reassure herself.

She can see her father at his clerical desk in the office, drinking his fifth cup of tea for the day. It's boiling hot, so he has to blow over the glass every time he takes a sip. He can't do this at home, because his wife would be indignant that he's wasting his money on tea and beedis. Asha wishes he could have this small indulgence with a clear conscience—she knows he has been doing the same work for years and years. She knows how he feels about never being promoted though he has been in that grimy government office longer than anyone else.

But then she sees her mother.

As always, her mother is at her sewing machine now that she is alone at home and the cleaning and cooking have been done. 'I could finish three pieces a day earlier, but I am getting old now,' Asha can hear her say. 'My eyes squint, my hands don't run as they used to. Never mind, it just means I have to work an extra hour or two.'

Her mother is always working. Maybe she is afraid that if she stops, she may have to consider her life, and that would be a waste of time. But sometimes, as she pauses to re-thread the machine, does she think of her daughters, Asha and Usha? The younger Usha in high school, sickly but still on a scholarship; and Asha, who's going to get a job as soon as the college says she is a proper nurse?

Asha wants to stroke that face that looks intent on finishing the next piece of work. She knows her mother can look different; she has seen the framed photo of her parents' wedding day. Her father looks ahead into the camera, serious, as if considering the responsibilities he will soon have to bear. But her mother is smiling. She is on the verge of sharing a secret but decides, at the last minute, to tease the camera by withholding it. The strange thing is that it is her mother who rarely smiles now. She has a guarded look on her face, as if she is constantly making a Plan B. But her father—on a Sunday when he can forget about the office and the same desk he has been waiting at for years, he may look at his two girls and say, 'Asha and Usha. Do you know why you are called that?' The girls giggle, having heard this question only a thousand times. 'Asha for Usha,' they recite. His eyes shine every time he hears them say it. Asha for Usha, a hope for dawn.

Asha sees her sister. Usha is thin and sickly, but no one in the world has a sweeter smile. It's impossible to fight with her, because Usha always wants Asha to get the first choice, the better portion of something to eat. All she asks is that she be allowed to follow Asha around like the head of her fan club. She must call home, speak to Usha soon. Asha misses her terribly. She misses all three of them.

2

Krishna and Shanta met as students. She's from Devapura; he came here as a student and never left. He still loves the town despite its recent aspiration to become what is called, patronisingly, a satellite city. He loves the fact that though the town has grown, its university is still its centre, its most important institution, or at least it is in Krishna's eyes. And he loves his set routine in Devapura. For years now, he has gone back and forth between home and university, first by bus, then a scooter, now a modest car. Shanta and Krishna go once a week, usually Sunday evenings, to the Darling Hotel for ice cream. They love the hotel's name; it's a comfortable old joke between them from the day Krishna started his teaching job and they went to Darling to celebrate.

Krishna sets out every morning for the lake where he meets his walking friends, Subbiah, Hasan and Natraj. Not one of them is from the university; they are just people Krishna has known over the years. This makes the walk with them a good start to Krishna's day. Three big rounds, then a five or ten-minute cool-down chat at the green bench, before the lake is taken over by the day's traders and consumers: the man selling peanuts, the man selling balloons, the terrible swan-shaped boats ready to take people on a joyride for a price.

The lake is man-made. It's a placid, well-behaved body of water, tolerant of the polluted strips that mark its body here and there like oily birthmarks. But it manages to create a sense of open space, all the more precious because of the apartment buildings creeping up its sides with impossibly ambitious or cryptic or poetic names. Mount Kailasa, Oyster Opera, Heaven Lake. The lake itself has an unrealistic name, Lake Sagara; a modest lake aspiring to be an ocean. The lake also has a neat little island, thick with trees. It's a bit of a folly, but Krishna is secretly fond of it. What's a lake or a river or a sea without an island, inviting you to go there, learn how to live on land that is the most stable boat of all?

But the lake with an island may soon have a new resident. The Municipal Corporation has plans for a lakeside statue of Raja Sriramadeva, supposedly the king the town is named after. None of the old residents has heard of this before, nor has the history department in the university. But obviously the Corporation, and the party it is trying to please at the moment, know best. Meanwhile, a group called the Devapura Hindu Sene wants the statue to be in the middle of the lake, not at its edge. This apparent disagreement within the same side is useful; many who do not want a statue at all find themselves taking sides in the edge-versus-middle debate. They have been confused into forgetting it's actually a statue-versus-no-statue debate.

Krishna, Subbiah, Hasan and Natraj usually have plenty to talk about on their morning walk. But for quite a few days now, it's been the same—the statue.

Then one morning, Subbiah decides he has had enough. 'I don't want to hear another word about that damn statue,' he says. 'It's bad enough we're going to have to see it every morning, either like a gatekeeper to the lake or a solid mermaid rising out of the water.' Subbiah is the oldest among them and he used to be a math teacher in a school for forty years. It's hard to disobey him.

Natraj helpfully changes the subject. 'You must watch this video, all of you. You will be shocked.' He waves his smartphone at them.

Natraj ran a small printing press for years. He has now "updated", as he likes to call it, to desktop publishing. He has always wanted to be a journalist; at any rate, he is devoted to news, especially breaking news. Ever since his son gave him a smartphone as a sixtieth birthday present, Natraj has become obsessed with news, preferably via Facebook, YouTube and WhatsApp. They have taken to calling him NN for News Natraj, but he thinks this is a compliment.

They ignore the smartphone Natraj is waving at them. They've watched too many videos Natraj claims will shock them or amaze them or make them weep. Besides, it means all four of them have to walk abreast with Natraj holding up the phone.

They refuse Natraj's video offer rudely, as only loving old friends can, and walk in companionable silence. Subbiah's walking stick marks the ground they cover, reminding them that this is for exercise, not conversation. Krishna pulls out his handkerchief once they reach the green bench and wipes his face. He chats with Natraj for a few minutes to make up for the video that was scorned. Then he waves a goodbye and walks home.

Home. There's no gate; Krishna walks in, greets it with affection. It's a small but comfortable house, two rooms downstairs and two upstairs. The best parts of the house are the balcony upstairs and the 'sit-out' facing the small patch of green downstairs. Krishna and Shanta live downstairs. Their son Ram lives upstairs with his wife Leela and their little son Chitthu. Their two married daughters live fifteen minutes away by car, about a half hour's walk. They are in and out of the 'main' house; they are always there on Sunday for lunch, bringing their husbands and children and big bags full of dishes they have cooked at home.

Krishna loves the Sunday lunches he and Shanta host every week. The guests often include writers, students, teachers, occasionally a singer or a music critic. Sometimes it is a special occasion, like the one they just had, a lunch to mark Krishna's new role in the university after retirement. He's now Professor holding the G.G. Anantanarayana chair for poetry. As always, the three children and their spouses were there, along with the grandchildren. Five of them now, three boys and two girls. Once the guests are gone, the late afternoon is usually for the grandchildren. Krishna has taught four of them to read during these afternoons, and he has given two of them advice on their cricket game though he has never played in his life. But it's the fifth and youngest, the baby of the family, who has turned him into a devoted grandfather. Krishna named the baby Chaitanya. This soon became Chitthu. A sage cousin, all of six, explained to Krishna: 'Chaitanya is too big for the baby.' For a while, Krishna insisted on calling the baby Chaitanya, then he too succumbed.

Chitthu is fourteen months old and has just begun walking. He has a few words, but he still uses a unique phrase of repeated sounds when he feels strongly about something.

Gung-gung-gung-gung. He can say this as a wail, a scolding, or just as a way to fill up the time.

Chitthu is now on Krishna's lap. They are in the sit-out, on Krishna's favourite cane chair with the squashed old cushions. Chitthu sits on Krishna's lap, facing him, his legs hanging on either side. Krishna holds Chitthu's hands so he can swing sideways. The little face looks unblinkingly at Krishna all the while. Has there ever been a face as round, as perfect as this? And the almond-shaped eyes quick to sparkle or fill—Krishna could easily drown in them. What words are there for such eyes, such a face, or the love it inspires? But Krishna simply has to say something.

'Gung-gung,' he says to Chitthu.

Chitthu stops his sideways swing to correct Krishna. 'Gung-gung-gung-gung.' He may be only fourteen months old, but Chitthu is a stickler for getting the text right.

'It's a four-syllable poem, Chitthu?'

But the poet is no longer listening. He's leaning back all the way, hanging backward so Krishna has to hold him by the waist. The poet has become a bat.

There's another poet whose words are equally hard to decipher. Krishna has been reading desultorily, in between the pleasures of conversation with Chitthu or Shanta, lectures, long and informal chats with MPhil and PhD and post-doc students, faculty meetings where he is a special invitee, or a bit of Admin with Shiva. Kannadeva floats into the moments in between.

There are several traditions regarding Kannadeva's life and work. Some emphasise the Saint-Poet aspect. Others focus on the Saint-Reformer. In the absence of significant material on his life, many later scholars and commentators have placed him in the 'lesser known bhakti poets' category. A few, more daring, have ventured to speculate. One, for instance, has constructed a timeline to show that the simple poems celebrating the river or the daily life of common people are from Kannadeva's early days. Then there are the struggling poems, the poet in his period of learning bhakti, what it is and how to live it; how to reconcile the need to respond to the injustice and inequality he sees around him with the need to look into the self, seek peace there. On the whole, the passing attention of scholars has preferred to look at just a few of his poems, what they call the 'mature' ones. Kannadeva's life remains opaque. Whatever has been written tends to be a mishmash of the lives of other saint-poets. So Kannadeva's life is full of clichés, making the usual progress from pious parents and precociousness in childhood to initiation into learning and bhakti, followed by saintliness. In between, there are a few predictable anecdotes. It bothers Krishna, this puzzle—of the poems, but also the life—waiting to be solved. He is convinced there is some story here. But how much should he meddle with holes and ambiguities, how much should he read between words and lines?

Krishna has not yet begun chasing Kannadeva in earnest. But he has got the go-ahead signal now from unexpected quarters, people who have little to do with poetry or scholarship. He has got two more hate mails this week—one more from the anonymous hand-delivery correspondent, and another from a Shankar on email.

Krishna begins to sort out his papers. It's not so bad in the department, poor Shiva has suffered Krishna's mess for years, trying to classify books, papers, reports. It's a little harder at home. Shanta is delighted to be invited to 'sort out the study' but unlike Shiva, she is prone to opinions on what should be thrown out and what method he should use to file the rest.

Krishna has found his notes on Kannadeva's death. What he has on Kannadeva has been put into plastic folders and labelled—this is Shanta's idea. She loves pigeonholing and creating order in whatever she touches. Life of. Death of. Early poems? With river. Without river. Named(?) river (calm). Nameless river (moving).

Krishna reads. There seems to have been some crisis toward the end of Kannadeva's life. Possibly to do with his family. The parents may have been part of a group of people who got together regularly to discuss matters of religion, but also their lives as citizens. In the town—what was then the city of Jayapura—people from all walks of life set up a meeting place they called Anandagrama. Kannadeva may have been there as a child; he may have heard discussions and poetry and songs and life stories and ideas for change in this Anandagrama. There is no evidence to show that this place lasted into Kannadeva's adulthood. Like all groups looking for different ways to worship, or challenge a highly stratified society, this group too fell apart. In all likelihood they were unable to withstand the combined power of the king and his officials, the priests of the powerful temples and the rest of the influential Brahmins.

Krishna reads though he doesn't believe he is going to find anything new in these papers beyond the questions he already has. But still he goes over them looking for new clues. Those small questions that came to him as he wrote his lecture for the cultural meet at the Town Hall have suddenly grown and become important. The hate mail that he has been getting over the last few weeks have drawn him back to Kannadeva, so he can pick up the thread of the story with greater concentration. He finds that when he delves into the life and words of Kannadeva, the hate mail recedes. It becomes irrelevant.

Krishna decides to go back to the book which first sparked his questions about Kannadeva. He had donated the book to the library, but he has got it back now.

The book has a faded crimson-red hardcover minus jacket. It's called *Giving Voice to Ananda and Grama: The Mystic Poet Kannadeva* and it was published in 1857. The author, an H.L. Narasimhiah who seems to have published just this one book, has the style of a ponderous Victorian gentleman playing detective.

Krishna reads the book with greater concentration this time, not skipping a word or a footnote or a reference. Every time he turns a brittle page, the edges crumble.

Krishna goes on a clue-hunting journey with Mr Narasimhiah.

There are the sections he remembers, those discussing the variety of signature lines in Kannadeva's poems and the question of authorship. Mr Narasimhiah suggests that there may be at least three or four poets who 'penned these deeply felt lyrical calls to God through the best in nature and the best in human nature'.

Krishna finds the clue, or a cluster of clues, in Notes 85 and 86. How did he miss this last time?

85. It would be an excessively suspicious nature that concludes that the compilation of several poets' work

as Kannadeva's was deliberate. We need to recall, however, that several poets in the period of time before Kannadeva's, and also through his boyhood, were part of one or more groups that spoke to God directly, and that worked for a more equal society, viz. a casteless society. There was, for instance, the brief but powerful flowering of song and poem from those in the fold of the Anandagrama or village of happiness. This group distinguished itself by practising what they preached, and they welcomed to their community men and women from professions as varied as farmers, fishermen, cobblers, weavers, potters etc. In short, the common man and woman. As with several of these attempts to rid Hindu society of caste, this brave village too was dismantled, and its inmates slaughtered or exiled. It is possible, though we may not be able to ascertain this without considerable patience, effort and skill, that some of the poems ascribed to Kannadeva were actually composed by two or more of the members of Anandagrama.

Of course these conclusions are not factual, and the meticulous Mr Narasimhiah is quick to point that out. But despite the scholarly disclaimer, Mr Narasimhiah adds, in Note 86: 'This may too easily be dismissed as folklore, but it is likely to have more than a grain of truth in it. The challenge is to walk a tightrope so as to avoid falling into the pit of treating every legend as fact; while examining why some facts may have been forced to survive only as poems and songs, in bits and pieces, in the larger body of a community's legend and lore.'

Mr Narasimhiah seems to be speaking directly to Krishna, challenging him to sign up for the task. Krishna has a moment of wanting to plead, 'I am not a historian!'

But Mr Narasimhiah is either deaf or relentless. He goes on to say, 'Kannadeva's work was, in all probability, written on palm leaves, possibly by the poet himself who sometimes refers to himself as a scholar in a monastery by a river. This author has not been able to trace such a river. Perhaps it dried up over the years, or changed course and turned into another modest water body, less inspiring to poets. The monastery too cannot be found. But if rivers can be twisted and turned by the hands of time, why be surprised that a mere building no longer stands?'

Then Mr Narasimhiah takes pity on Krishna, or perhaps he decides that Note 86 is long enough.

> Despite these disappointments to the scholar in search of Kannadeva, and those who we may take the liberty of describing as his poet companions (or accomplices in song if their link to Anandagrama is established clearly), let us not forget that bundles of palm leaves, precious old manuscripts, continue to turn up in our country when least expected, and in the unlikeliest of places. It would be a yeoman service indeed if a scholar, or a simple lover of poetry, or a man who seeks reassurance that our countrymen have not always willingly allowed caste and creed to subject them to inferior lives, would embark on a search for these manuscripts and bring them to the light of the modern world. At the very least, such work would enlarge our knowledge of Kannadeva who has, for too long, been reduced to a minor devotional poet.

Krishna exhales. 'Happy to be your yeoman, Mr Narasimhiah,' he mutters to himself. But where to start?

The next week or two, this question burrows its way into Krishna and feeds on him in tiny nibbles. Krishna's lakeside friends are completely involved though they know nothing about Kannadeva or palm leaves or the likes of Anandagrama. News Natraj has been worrying his smartphone and Sage Google, but finds no breaking news on using poetry or songs to challenge caste. Then Subbiah turns to Krishna one morning and asks, 'What about that institute you told me about once? Didn't you say the man running it buys old and rare books and manuscripts and such?'

Krishna nods, thanks Subbiah for the suggestion. He will try the Institute, but it seems an unlikely possibility. He walks home slowly. Should he stop playing the fool? Is he really interested in Kannadeva, or is he doing this only to show the hatemailers that he will not take fright? Both questions dishearten him.

But here's Shanta, cheering him on with words of support, help with files and breaks for ice cream. Here's Chitthu, cheering him up, beating the Made-in-China red drum that Krishna bought him in a weak moment, leading a procession with no followers in and out of every room.

Krishna persists. He tries, for the twentieth time, the telephone number he has for Mr Neeladri Seshadri, offspring of rhyme-loving parents and also director of the Institute of Devotional Culture. Just when Krishna is ready to scream if he has to hear, one more time, the raucous bhajan that serves as Mr Seshadri's ringtone, he gets through.

Mr Seshadri is a very deaf old man. It takes him a while to understand who is calling. But when he does, he becomes effusive. 'Professor Krishna, what an honour. What a pleasure to hear from you. You will not believe it, but I thought of you just the other day.'

Krishna makes polite noises.

'You will not believe it. But let me tell you why I thought of you. Someone has just sold me some old palm leaf manuscripts—quite a pile I might say. A few have stories from the epics, which is why I thought of you immediately.'

'Anything other than the epics?' Krishna asks casually.

'I haven't looked through all of them. Many are falling apart, you understand. But there is poetry, quite a bit of it. Some songs also by the poet Kannadeva.'

3

Chikka is in a boat, crossing a river.

It's the first time he has seen a river. It's the first time he is crossing a river. The first time he is in a snug boat made for four, going he doesn't know where with three strangers. Strangers who call him *brother*. So many firsts on a single day.

Chikka turns back just once. Where is the land he has left so suddenly, so easily? That bank, the village, the jungly no-man's-land dividing high and low, and beyond, the pond, the untouchable settlement, his father's hut, his father: the horizon has swallowed it all up.

Peddi the ferryman is deferential to Elder Brother, friendly with Puttanna, and indulgent to Chikka. Peddi shows off what the boat and he can do together. He slows down, comes to a stop and the boat breathes on its own, moving where the river takes it. Suddenly Peddi pulls back, then pushes and pulls like a demon so the oars beat the water out of the way. The boat runs faster than the river. Peddi looks at Chikka as if to say 'See?' Peddi could be his grandfather, giving him a treat. This is one more miracle in a day of miracles.

It's late in the afternoon. The sun is well past mid-sky, it's slipping down the side of the sky. It's spent the best, or the worst, of its strength. The sun is willing to be benign now. A breeze stirs. It turns cool, so cool. There's gooseflesh on the river's skin. The water ripples. There's gooseflesh on

Chikka's arm too. That thick skin made for humiliation, or flogging, or hopelessness, is losing hold of him. It's peeling off him, falling to the floor of the boat like blood-streaked hide.

This new Chikka, the one who has just been born, hears a humming. It's Peddi.

Puttanna and Elder Brother have heard him too. Elder Brother leans across, taps Peddi on the shoulder. 'Sing, brother. Sing out loud. The river's waiting for you.'

This is all Peddi needs. He throws back his shoulders and sings as vigorously as he rows. His voice is strong, used to straddling the waves.

My body is my boat,
the boat my prayer.

How it sings,
this prayer.
How it sings.

Mid-river or safe on shore,
body and boat
song and prayer
one and the same.

Peddi sings the lines again. This time Puttanna joins him. Their voices blend so they become one. They are showing Chikka what it is to have body, boat, song and prayer become one and the same. Then Puttanna sings on his own:

There's a moonface waiting across the river.
That waiting child—
    whose son is he?

There's a moonface waiting on the other bank.
That child who waits—
    who does he wait for?

Elder Brother chimes in with a response.

He's my son
and I am his,
    he says,
the hungry one done with waiting.

He waits for me
as I wait for him,
    he says,
the thirsty one done with waiting.

It's a concert on the river. Word and song, stage and audience, all fit into one narrow boat. If this is a dream, may he never wake up!

But no, it is not a dream. Chikka can hear the oars slap the water. He can feel the boat bobbing, riding the waves. He can dip his hand over the side and trail the cooling water.

Peddi does not want Chikka to be left out. 'Sing, my little brother. The river likes us to sing. It makes the rowing easier.'

Chikka feels like a fool. But they are all waiting for him, Peddi and Puttanna and Elder Brother, his new friends, as of now his only friends in the world. Chikka whispers the first thing that comes into his head.

Where is that land
where water flows free?

Tell me, *Tell* me.

Where is my land
Where water flows free?

Chikka pauses. He waits for his father to float back to him across the water. He waits for the old misery to swell, take hold of him, swallow him whole. But there's only the river, the day's friends, his new brothers. He sees the drum lying forlorn on the floor of the boat. He doesn't touch it but, as if to placate it, Chikka sings the lines a second time.

Puttanna has seen him looking at the drum. He picks it up, hands it to Chikka. Chikka shakes his head, falls silent. Puttanna looks foolish; there's an awkward moment of silence. All of them are waiting like that moonfaced child in the song. Then Elder Brother breaks the silence and the waiting.

That land is here, and there,
it's everywhere in me.
In me the land
where water flows free.

Elder Brother looks at Puttanna then Peddi. Peddi, who is nothing like Chikka's father, booms those familiar lines into the river air:

Where is that land
where water flows free?

Tell me, *Tell* me.

Where is my land
where water flows free?

And Elder Brother and Puttanna raise triumphant voices together:

That land is here, and there,
it's everywhere in me.
In me the land
where water flows free.

Chikka finds himself joining in. *In me the land where water flows free.* He wants this to last forever, four voices singing to each other, singing with each other. They are the only four people left in the universe. And the universe: it's vast, it's all sky and river.

Their voices fade. Nothing stirs but the steady splish-splash of oars. It's the river's turn to speak. Chikka listens.

This river. It has spread itself wide, wider, as if it has permission to go anywhere it likes. And it has no idea how to stand still. It trembles, ripples, it draws straight lines like arrows, it draws circles that get smaller and smaller then grow large again. It flows, it sways. It reflects sky, tree, hills, bird, boat, even itself. Can a body have so many faces? Will all his life be enough to meet them, get to know them?

But first Chikka has to meet his own life, the one that will unfold on the other side of the river. He can see the land come closer. The trees there are tiny, like toys, then they grow larger, they become real as the boat nears the bank. The day's dream is almost done.

Peddi ties the boat and they get off one by one. Chikka looks around like an explorer making a discovery. The place is an outcrop of land jutting into the water, a lush fat finger covered with every shade of green. The whole world has stretched itself today and got bigger. The sky and the shore, the trees and the walls of creepers, the clumps of shrubs and the fields he can see at a distance—all are open and spacious.

'Let's bathe first,' says Elder Brother. 'Let's keep the river with us for a little longer.'

Chikka scoops handfuls of water and pours the river on his head. He is not sure if the river is blessing him, or he is blessing himself like the song Elder Brother completed so they could sing it together. *In me the land where water flows free.* It's a song that sounds right. But really, what does it mean?

Where is that land where
water flows free?

1

Chikka, Puttanna and Elder Brother have left the river behind. As they walk, the open space shrinks. It becomes the outskirts of the city, then its hem. Then it's there, Jayapura.

Chikka has never seen a city before, but his mood of discovery is wearing thin. There are too many people here; and carts; and roadside hawkers; and temples; and Brahmins, lifting the edges of their dhotis as they walk, as if their clothes are too pure to touch the ground.

Chikka's shoulders slump. He walks as he was taught to, shrunk with humility, weighed down with fear of where the next beating or flogging will come from.

Puttanna takes his hand. 'Don't worry,' he says. 'There are too many like us. And we too have powerful friends.'

Chikka has no idea what this means, though he notices that many people they pass recognise Elder Brother and greet him with respect. But Chikka also sees the others. When they pass a grand temple, one ornamented cone resting on another, Chikka sees a large bare-chested priest sitting outside. His forehead and chest are painted with white stripes; his potbelly hangs like a fleshy curtain down to his knees. The man glares at Elder Brother, turns aside, spits vehemently on the ground. Chikka presses the rough hand in his for reassurance. Elder Brother does not seem to notice, he is walking ahead. Puttanna and Chikka follow, hand in hand.

'That priest. He thinks he's a holy man,' Puttanna says to Chikka, his voice dripping with sarcasm.

Once they are past the crowded streets, Puttanna adds, as if he has been saving up the final verdict: 'That Brahmin doesn't really know who he is. I know who I am. I am Puttanna the ratcatcher, equal to anyone else.'

Chikka gasps, but Puttanna adds with a chuckle, 'Is there a place that doesn't need a ratcatcher?'

A cattle skinner and a ratcatcher, hand in hand! No wonder their hands fit so well together. Chikka gestures with his head at Elder Brother then looks at Puttanna.

'Oh Elder Brother! He was one sort of teacher, now he's another sort. His hands may be smooth unlike ours. But as for his mind—' Puttanna imitates a knife cutting the air to show Chikka how sharp Elder Brother's mind is.

'But what are you doing together? A ratcatcher and a teacher …' Chikka's words trail away, afraid of giving offence, but he simply has to know.

'You think that's strange? That we should be brothers, a teacher and a ratcatcher?' Puttanna swells, about to perform magic, maybe pull a rat out of his hairy ear. 'Wait till you meet my friends. There's Siddha the potter, Chenna the cobbler, Gundanna the toddy tapper. And in Anandagrama, where we're going now—you'll meet weavers and sweepers and shit-carriers and farm workers. But you'll also meet city officials and scholars and poets, other Elder Brothers and Sisters, and our wise Prabhu.'

Chikka's head spins.

'You'll even meet people who used to be Brahmins,' winks Puttanna, 'but are now just people.'

It's too much. Chikka has no more questions. It's best not to ask any more questions. It's best not to make too much of the magic Puttanna is talking of, the miracle no one has ever seen: people coming together as if caste does not matter, as if anyone can be anyone else's neighbour or friend or sister or brother.

Elder Brother slows down, waits for them to catch up. He smiles radiantly at Chikka. 'Welcome,' he says, 'welcome to Anandagrama.' Elder Brother holds out his hand in the air before him as if offering Chikka the world. 'Look,' Elder Brother says.

Chikka looks at the cluster of huts. He trembles; is this a prison too, like the one he has run away from?

Puttanna moves closer to him; he lays a hand, heavy with comfort, on Chikka's shoulder.

Chikka looks at the huts again, sees that though they are modest, they are in an orderly circle. There's plenty of open space around, with people busy at work, conversation or play. And in the middle of the huts, in what appears to be a clearing, there's a larger hut made of beautifully woven thatch held together with bamboo. This hut has no roof, it's open to the sky. Chikka's trembling leaves him. He takes a step forward.

There are people coming out of the huts to greet them. Elder Brother, especially, has people, too many people, men, women, even children who seek his attention. 'Take care of him, Puttanna,' Elder Brother says as he lets himself be carried away into the milling crowd.

Puttanna and Chikka go to the heart of Anandagrama first, the hut with its eye open to the sky. There's so much to take in. There are some people who sit quiet, alone or in a group. Maybe they are praying; or thinking; or simply at peace with themselves. A couple are bent over palm leaves stretched tight and firm, making marks on it, row after row. In one corner, a man is telling the people gathered around him: 'The world belongs to all of us. There's no high, no low. That's what God tells us, the God in me, and the God in you. In Anandagrama, we live what we believe.'

Puttanna nudges Chikka as if to say, 'I told you so.'

They move to the centre of the hut where a discussion is going on—but it's all chant and song, what they are saying. A man is reciting, acting out the words with his voice:

> This water is holy,
> and this, and this,
> they mumble in a foreign tongue,
> sprinkling a few drops on
> stone-faced dolls in the temple,
> the floor of their houses
> and outside.
>
> These men
> even sprinkle water on themselves
> and say they are born again.

A rough-looking old woman with silvery hair nods knowingly then asks a question:

> How much can you teach a man,
> peel skin
> and say Here, See here, and here,
> See how the blood flows,
> how food winds its way down to shit
> washed away by water.

The same, all the same.

Can you teach a man
who thinks hill and stream
mud and leaf
skin and heart
live in worlds apart?

There's a man listening gravely. He's pale, he's so thin he's almost not there. 'That's our wise Prabhu,' Puttanna whispers. Chikka steals another look at him. Prabhu may look grave, but his face flickers with the light of a freshly lit lamp. He glows.

It's raining brothers. Chikka's immediate family grows. First there's Puttanna the ratcatcher, then Siddha the potter, Chenna the cobbler and Gundanna the toddy tapper.

'We're the Fearsome Four,' Puttanna laughs. 'But you're part of us now.'

He takes a deep breath so his chest grows even broader. He lifts his chin and fixes his eyes somewhere up in the air. 'Make way for the Fearsome Five,' he announces, as if he is the king's messenger, walking around each of them. He's so intent on being fearsome that he doesn't see where he's going. He knocks over the toddy Gundanna has brought them in a coconut shell.

'Hey, I'll give you fearsome,' says Chenna, who's been eyeing the toddy. He knocks down Puttanna. They roll over each other in the mud, wrestling and laughing at the same time.

But they can be serious too, this motley family. They discuss the recent showdown in the city square, with Elder Brother and Prabhu on one side, and on the other, some of the senior priests from the Grand Temple. A Brahmin boy refused to wear his sacred thread and ran away to Anandagrama. The priests accused the inmates of Anandagrama of corrupting the young.

'The minute they wear that thread, they start feeling superior,' says Gundanna. 'The thread, all their blessed gods. All that Namo-namaha.'

But Siddha does not join in their laughter. Over the last few days, as he has thrown his pots and spun his wheel, Siddha has been puzzling over something. Why would any god make some people worthy simply because of the family they are born into, while others are born loathsome? Why would any god divide people? And why would any god say to those who suffer day after day, their backs bent with work but their stomachs still empty, 'Suffer now, so your next life is better?'

'It has nothing to do with the gods,' Siddha now tells them. 'Nothing to do with a better life next time round, or the punya and moksha they talk about. This is what I make of it: the gods know nothing, think nothing.'

'They're made of clay and stone and lacquer anyway,' interrupts a scornful Puttanna.

'Yes,' Siddha brushes Puttanna aside. 'Listen. It's the priests. The Brahmins. They tell us what the gods say. They tell us what the palm leaves we can't read say. They butter up the king, tell him the gods have made him the ruler. And why do they do all this? Yes, they want to eat mounds of rice and jaggery and fruit, and pile gold in their houses. But it's more than that. Really, *they* want to be gods, that's what. They want to strut about, more powerful than anyone, be walking, talking gods. They want to be gods in *this* life, *this* world though they say the world is an illusion. They're even less worried about their next lives than I am about mine.'

The others are impressed. So is Chikka, who's acquiring new thoughts and words in one great big rush. He hears the word *equal* often enough in Anandagrama, especially from Elder Brother and the other leaders. But it's Puttanna and his friends who show him what this *equal* means, not only in words, but in how they live with each other.

Chikka loves being part of the Fearsome Five. And there's nothing he likes better than seeing things—the city, the villages, all of the world—through Puttanna's eyes. Puttanna knows every street, every house and barn and mound of garbage where the rats cower in fear of him. He hunts them. He skins them and roasts them so that they are like any other meat, fit for people to eat. The great people of the city may think him a filthy person. But Puttanna's face is like sunrise—bright, waiting for the day to bring a happy surprise. He knows an astonishing number of silly, nonsensical songs, and he often hums them under his breath as if he is testing out their meaning.

The pig, the fly and the lizard
went far in search of a wizard.
They came upon a rubbish heap
they cheered then made a happy leap.

Now and then, when Chikka laughs at something Puttanna says, or sings with him, he can barely recognise his own voice, or the sound of his own laughter.

With the help of his friends, Chikka has slowly learnt the challenges of Anandagrama, and its comforts of brothers, sisters, community. He is admiring, grateful—how could he not be, he has never imagined such a way to live. And the city doesn't scare him anymore. But still—sometimes he feels like a visitor. What is he to do here? Though he has been helping his friends at their work, Chikka is not sure he can ever be a potter or learn to catch rats or tap toddy.

When he thinks of what work he can do, or where he wants to live, he can only think of that river. He longs to go back to it.

Puttanna is gruff and comforting as usual. 'City, forest, village, river—all the same to me. But you—all right—come, let's go.'

It's as simple as that. Chikka is going to his chosen home by the river.

It's late in the evening when they get there. Puttanna leads Chikka to the field nearest the river. There, in a shabby shack, they meet the old man Rangayya. Rangayya is almost done with weaving a basket. It's taken him a while, resting in between to steady his hands. He puts aside the basket when he sees them, looking relieved.

'Rangayya used to be a fisherman,' Puttanna has already told Chikka. 'But then he got sick. No one knows what it is, but Rangayya's arms and legs tremble all the time. His wife Parvatamma works as a labourer in the field.'

'Rangayya,' yells Puttanna though he's sitting close to Rangayya. 'Are you well?'

'I'm very well,' says the frail man. 'How is Elder Brother? And all our friends in Anandagrama?' Rangayya's face turns sunny as he asks these questions.

'They are wonderful,' says Puttanna. 'Here, meet a new one. This is Chikka.'

Rangayya smiles at Chikka, says, 'You're welcome here. Please eat with us.'

Once Parvatamma and her daughter return from the fields, they eat together, men and women.

'He wants to be near the river,' says Puttanna, nodding in Chikka's direction.

Parvatamma doesn't need to be told that Chikka needs work. She is the sort who recognises a problem immediately and has two solutions ready. 'There's that empty shack nearby, the old washerman died last month,' she thinks aloud.

She looks at Chikka. 'Can you wash clothes? Of course you can,' she answers her own question before Chikka can speak.

Chikka hears a giggle. It's the daughter, Mahadevi.

But the washerman's shack is there, it's his for the asking. Parvatamma arranges it all. Chikka learns his new job, washing people's clothes. The river is there for him day and night; so are the open sky and the endless stretch of field and wilderness.

2

Krishna looks at the cell phone lying by his papers. He feels an awful mixture of longing and impatience. What has happened to Neeladri Seshadri? He told Krishna he would be in touch about when he could visit the Institute and see the palm leaves. Seshadri also made it clear that he had to 'make arrangements' for Krishna's visit; in other words, he didn't want Krishna to just turn up.

Krishna gives in, picks up the phone. It's disgusting, he thinks, he has become as devoted to his phone as News Natraj. He taps redial. The phone rings; the same old bhajan plays itself out. A helpful voice tells him that the person he is calling has not answered the call. Would Shanta have better luck? He goes in search of her. She's outside, pulling out weeds from the pots of hibiscus. She's singing softly all the while; the flowers look smug with all the love they're getting. He waits, phone in hand.

But Shanta only gets the message that the number is not reachable.

Krishna takes the phone back, tries again. Yes, Seshadri has taken a step backward, from not answering to not being reachable. Krishna persists. He wills that bhajan ringtone to sing in his ear. Not reachable. What an ominous phrase, how it shuts the door on all conversation, argument, on life itself!

Is there any other way to move ahead?

Krishna drives himself to the university. 'Any luck with the institute landline,' he asks Shiva.

'No, Prof, sorry,' says Shiva, 'It's just ringing, no one is answering.' He offers Krishna the Admin files instead.

Krishna sits at his desk, doing nothing. He frowns at the unopened files. Should he try that damn phone again?

But here's Shiva once more, looking hopeful. 'I have a suggestion, Prof.'

'Tell me.'

'The poems sing of two rivers, right? I mean when they mention rivers.'

'Yes,' says Krishna. It's going to be hard to be his usual patient self with Shiva today. 'So?'

Shiva cannot be hurried. 'I mean,' he says, 'there's a quiet one and a noisy one, isn't it?'

Krishna nods. 'I suppose you could put it like that.'

'Then why not go look at the rivers? I mean there may be some interesting information to be found there.'

'Shiva, what are you talking about? We don't know where those rivers are, even if they are still there. We don't know what they are called either, other than the river of a thousand faces and the river that moves to stillness. Except,' Krishna pulls a face, 'for what that Guru fellow said in his Letter to the Editor. That Kannadeva achieved Samadhi in or near a river called Devika. I've never heard of it.'

But Shiva is beaming at him. 'I've done some research, Prof,' he says. 'I have some info on one of the rivers,' he adds modestly. 'I tracked down that old student of yours, I got some help from him. It seems there's a river,' and now Shiva can no longer look modest—'a couple of hours by car from the institute. It's not a big or famous river, and the place is also not known, must be just villages. But,' Shiva brings it out in a triumphant gush, 'there's a local tradition that Kannadeva was enlightened when he meditated by this river.'

Krishna doesn't have the heart to scoff at Shiva. 'Thank you,' he says kindly. 'Will you find out more?' He doesn't specify what 'more' may mean. In any case, Shiva has dashed out of the room like a man with a mission.

It's Monday evening, the day after their usual overpopulated Sunday lunch. Krishna has decided to give up on the phone and Neeladri Seshadri for a few days. But he feels morose when he looks at the other work he could be making progress with.

Then his son Ram comes downstairs, and says, 'There's something I must show you, Appa. Come, let's go to your computer.'

Krishna is reluctant. He doesn't want one more lecture on how to keep his desktop uncluttered, or update the anti-virus programme. But Ram is waiting; Krishna finds it as hard to say No to Ram as he does to Chitthu, though the reasons are entirely different. Krishna shuffles to the computer, hoping Ram will notice what an old and tired father he has, too old and tired to be nagged about the most efficient way of using a computer, especially an up-to-date one.

But when Ram opens Google, keys in a url, and a site opens, Krishna wakes up.

Not many people know of Kannadeva's work. But here is a whole section of a site devoted to him. 'See?' says Ram, rolling the wheel on the mouse, 'See? This page in the site has been set up very recently.'

Krishna looks. Ram lets him sit down and pick up the mouse, then leaves his father to enjoy the discovery.

Kannadeva and His Holy River, it says on top. Below, there's a painted picture of a man supposed to be Kannadeva, sitting on the bank of a river. On the mud before him is a crimson cloth with a yellow border. On the cloth, a thick book. A few white flowers are scattered on the book, the cloth and the mud. Kannadeva sits in a half-lotus position, a small tanpura on his lap, the right fingers strumming the instrument. The left arm is raised, the hand in the act of keeping time with wooden castanets. He wears a white turban on his head and a—it's hard to say exactly what it is—it can only be described as a robe. Both turban and robe are painted to look wet, as if he has just had a dip before settling down to sing. There are several chains of reddish brown beads hanging round his neck, and he wears white earrings. The face: the eyebrows and moustache are a lush black. His forehead is decorated with kumkum and sandalwood. His eyes look upward, his lips part in a half smile. Maybe he knows, though he is not looking at the back, that there is a bejewelled and crowned blue goddess floating in the misty air behind him. The mist has swallowed the goddess waist down. Below floating goddess and mist is a flat and slim rectangle of blue. That's the river, so holy that there's a goddess coming out of it to bless Kannadeva and inspire him into song. The caption below sums it up: *The holy river Devika purified Kannadeva and made him a saint.* Krishna scrolls down and sees the rest of the text is pretty much like the caption.

The site is run by a Hindu Rashtra Sabha to promote what it calls the most noble cause of all: protecting Indian culture from those who insult, vilify or attack Hindu saints and gods in particular, and 'Hindu civilization' in general. Krishna usually laughs off idiocies like this, but today his sense of the ridiculous deserts him. How did Kannadeva or any of the poets and mystics of the past become *theirs*?

The phone rings. It's Neeladri Seshadri with an explanation about his silence. 'My nephew got married, you see,' he says. Krishna doesn't see, but he lets the man go on.

'Everything is arranged, Professor. When are you coming?'

'In a few days. I thought I would visit the rivers nearby first,' says Krishna, surprising himself. 'Or at least one river.'

Krishna is up early. He walks to the river Shiva has marked on a map as the Quiet River.

It's been a long time since Krishna walked alone in the morning. But it also means he walks briskly, and with a sense of expectation. He is walking to a place that may well bring him closer to Kannadeva, not textually, but, he tells himself, emotionally.

Krishna reaches the river, walks onto the small stone platform with steps that lead into the water. Here it is before him, what could have been Kannadeva's river of stillness. Krishna can't quite see it yet. All he can make out is a glimmer of a narrow ribbon that twists sideways. It's like a sleeping snake, or the ghost of a snake. He's too early, he knows. But he set out well before the sun was up so he could see it rise over the water.

Krishna stands on the platform, waiting in the silence.

He hears a gentle plop. Something has fallen in. A twig from one of the overhanging branches? A frog leaping in, seeing him and taking fright?

The sudden circles spread in the water,
perfect, one within another.
Then they're gone.

The peace that follows tremors,
the peace in the world's noise
waiting deep in your heart.

Show me how it's done, O lord.

It's a little as if Kannadeva is here with him, waiting. Waiting for the lord, or the river, to show him how it's done. And look, slowly, slowly, the sun, still rubbing sleepy eyes, starts its day's work, unpacking its light, pouring it into rays. The river swims into view, just about. The mist makes a long horizontal bar of thick smoke above the river. Then it dissipates. The river reveals itself like a photograph being developed, emerging gently out of the darkness, trying on its daytime appearance.

There isn't much water. The water is thickly bordered with lush foliage on both sides. In the early morning light, as capable of playing tricks as twilight, the river is overshadowed by its borders. It seems a wet body of shrubs, grasses of different colours and textures, weeds that have grown tall and free since no one has called them weeds yet, and trees. The trees are thick green clumps; the trunks can barely be seen. The water is a narrow, wet strip the foliage wears across its body. The water trembles occasionally; but mostly it lies there, having been taken in hand by the surrounding vegetation. This river is never going to be allowed to forget its guardians.

The quiet river. The silent river. In fact, it's not much of a river; it would be more accurate to call this a stream.

The river—or the river dwindling to a stream—sits there, looking at Krishna, unblinking. If it has any secrets to tell, it's not going to share them with him.

Krishna sits down on the top step, feels a crunch under him. He gets up in a hurry. He sees the empty packet of Lays Chips looking crushed and sad. Krishna picks it up fastidiously, but doesn't know what to do with it. He can't possibly add it to the garbage floating quietly in the river as if it belongs there, part of nature. He crushes it some more, makes a small shiny ball of it, and stuffs it into his pocket. He's acting like Shanta, cleaning up, as if removing one empty packet of foil will make a difference. He feels a sharp twinge. It's only been a couple of days since he left home and he misses Shanta already.

Now that he is here, at the river that is supposedly the one that enlightened Kannadeva, he doesn't know what he expected to see. It's a pretty stream, and he can exert his imagination to enlarge it into a full-fledged river, a monastery hugging the side of a low hill nearby. If he returns during the monsoons, he may see the stream restored to its days as a modest river. But what else? Krishna wishes he could talk to someone, not a poet or critic or historian, but a cheerful, teasing sort of friend. He misses his walking gang, Subbiah, Hasan, even News Natraj. He can't wait to get back and have them laugh at his folly, looking for truth and the past in a river.

A voice breaks the silence behind him. 'Swami,' it says.

So much for missing company or wishing for it. Krishna turns, annoyed that his solitude is at an end. It's a man in a dirty dhoti that's been lifted and tied around his waist like a skirt. He's wearing a maroon sweatshirt that says, in fading white letters on his chest, Tantra. His head is covered with a monkey cap; his dark face below is dotted with stubble like white needles.

'Swami, you're from the hotel?' he asks. 'Tourist?'

'No,' says Krishna. 'I am a teacher.' He regrets this immediately. How ungenerous to put himself above both tourist and this man. This man is only hoping to make a few rupees after all. Or maybe he is just being friendly, an old man who's got up too early and is seeking out a kindred soul. As usual, Krishna overdoes it, saying too much to make up for what may have been unkindness. 'I am here to find out more about Kannadeva. He was a poet who may have lived here a long time ago.'

To his shock, the man looks ecstatic. 'Kannadeva. Saint. Yes, his Samadhi is here, not too far away. Come, I will take you there.'

Krishna gives in. He might as well pretend he's doing 'field-work' instead of gaping at a river that is not quite a river, waiting for it to do his research.

It's a longish walk, more than two kilometres. It seems longer because the man, who has introduced himself as Gangiah, can't stop talking. By the time Gangiah says, 'Here, here, we're here,' Krishna has heard the story, mostly the sad story, of Gangiah's numerous children, their lack of jobs and good houses, the loans that need to be repaid, the grandsons that need to be born, and the new wife that needs to be found since old wives have the nasty habit of dying.

Gangiah has just announced triumphantly, as if he is about to show off his own creation, 'Here, here!'

In the middle of nowhere, Krishna sees a square-shaped border of old gray brick, surrounded by stones, garbage, plastic bags and stunted wild bushes. Inside this square is another. At its centre, there's a wooden stool covered by cloth that's held in place with a small finial-shaped object made of brass. Krishna composes his face so his amused disbelief is not visible to Gangiah.

But he need not bother, because Gangiah is in full flow. 'This shrine, this exact spot, is where Kannadeva was buried after he liberated himself from life. (He was too much of a saint to be cremated.) He sat here for a month and a day, completely still and silent, practicing very difficult yoga. Very difficult,' Gangiah emphasizes, looking critically at Krishna, 'not even a teacher like you could have done those things.'

Krishna nods in polite agreement.

But Gangiah goes on to surprise Krishna with a footnote: 'He sat silent. Very silent. He did not even sing though he used to sing all the time. He didn't sing because he was going to the song itself. You know what I am saying? He was going to the first note of all.'

'So he died here?' asks Krishna, impressed despite himself, feeling he must say something.

'No, no. He got ready here. When he was ready for nemmadi, he went into the river—where we have just come from. You know what nemmadi is? That's what we call the river here. He was ready to be content. No desire left. So he could free himself—he attained liberation by drowning. Jal Samadhi, that's the method he chose. It was only his body that was brought back here.'

As they walk away, Krishna plots. How can he escape Gangiah? He pulls out his wallet, thanks Gangiah for his help.

But Gangiah surprises him again. He brings his hands together in a Namaste and says, 'No, no. I look after this

Samadhi, I can't take money.' He smiles beatifically. 'You don't like this Samadhi? I will take you to someone, a very old man who sings like Kannadeva.' He pulls out a scrap of paper and a pen from the pocket of his sweatshirt. He scribbles a telephone number, hands the paper to Krishna. Then he walks away briskly.

Krishna is at the reception of the Institute for Devotional Culture, sitting on a battered single sofa, waiting for Mr Neeladri Seshadri. There's a woman at the reception desk, wearing a brilliant yellow sari with even more brilliant magenta stripes. She has flowers in her hair. She has not neglected other possibilities of ornamentation. Her ears (large and sticking out like Gandhi's) have gold studs on the upper part, shiny dangling earrings, and thin gold chains that link her ears to the hair on the side of her head. Despite her festive appearance, she looks cross. Every now and then she looks around, frowning, as if she would like to give the shabby world a good bath, then dress it up. But she stands up respectfully when Mr Seshadri rushes in, apologising to Krishna for being late.

Mr Seshadri looks like an old manuscript himself, his skin like parchment stretched thin, his forehead and neck covered with code to be deciphered, dots and lines of kumkum, sandalwood and ash.

'As you know, Professor, I don't usually let anyone study what I have just acquired till I have personally classified them and set them on display. But you, of course, are an exception. A devotee of poetry, and also, a friend—?'

Krishna hears the questioning note and hastens to assure Seshadri that he is very grateful, that he is always very careful with such rare finds, and that he, like Seshadri, is anxious that many more generations should get to study them.

Seshadri seems satisfied, but he fusses over the bundles, postponing leaving Krishna alone with them. 'The problem is,' he says, 'the masses are still ignorant or superstitious about palm leaf manuscripts.' He says the word 'masses' with his lips pursed in distaste.

'There are the greedy ones who keep manuscripts to themselves as part of the family property. The ones who think it's all sacred writing are the worst. They think sharing the leaves means exposing them, and that will bring them bad luck. And look at this lot I have kept to one side.' He gestures at the bundles covered with red cloth. 'These had been dumped in the storeroom of some crumbling old house for I don't know how long.'

Seshadri uncovers a bundle. 'See, see where it's been eaten by worms. This is how classics are eternally lost. The government tries to help, but really, they are as foolish as the masses. It's only people like you and me who appreciate these eternal texts.' Just as Seshadri dislikes the word 'masses' and the people the word refers to, he loves the word 'eternal'. He says it so he lengthens the 'ter' and summons the sound of longevity.

Seshadri finally leaves Krishna to it.

Krishna takes a deep breath. With some trepidation, feeling he might be messing with Mr Seshadri's eternity, he uncovers the lot covered with red cloth. He's gentle, as if removing the bandages on hurt bodies. He touches each body carefully, like a surgeon with gloved hands, probing a deep, old wound. Then he finds the soul, a tube-like thing in one of the bodies. Or it finds him, the small collection of leaf paper rolled up tightly. It's waiting for him to unfurl it, separate one leaf sheet from the other, making sure the brittle patches don't give way.

He coaxes a few of them flat, lays them on the table.

The bundle must have as many as fifty sheets, he guesses. All the leaves are worn in a line to the left side. They were probably sewn together at one time. One of the sheets Krishna has unfurled has a drawing. Maybe it was meant to be the first page or the cover. It's damaged. But still, Krishna can see the image: a wave of water, its mouth open, leaping from left to right; a man seated on air, positioned as if he is about to be consumed by the wave any moment; and to the right end of the sheet, the outline of several heads, a whole crowd of heads, watching both the man and the river. It's not as decorative or intricate as the drawings Krishna has seen on palm leaves before. And it's not in multiple colours. This is a simple, childlike image. But its bold strokes give it power.

Then Krishna begins to read—or to try and read what he has found, and make sense of it.

The first sheet or leaf. It's a poem by Kannadeva that he is familiar with. He reads it anyway, making friends with it again.

The second sheet: he doesn't know the poem; and it has two words floating at the bottom in smaller letters. Krishna squints. Puttanna, it says. There's another word next to the name, a word hard to decipher. Surely it can't be *ratcatcher*?

There are other names on other leaves. He decides to list the poets first before getting to the poems. Prabhu. Siddha. Gundanna. Chenna. Chikkiah. Many of the songs commonly ascribed to Kannadeva turn out to be versions of poems by other people. Surely these people were associated with

Anandagrama? But why were these voices drowned, so to speak, submerged into Kannadeva's to make one composite poet?

Krishna thinks of Mr Narasimhiah, author of the book which flagged off his journey of questions. What would Narasimhiah have done if he had found this brave patchwork quilt? One piece of it is incomplete without the other. Often, one does not make sense without the other. He hears Narasimhiah's ponderous voice tell him, 'It would be a yeoman service if someone would read these songs as they were meant to be. The challenge is to separate the strands to understand why they were interwoven, then put them back together, let them remain interwoven …'

Over the coming days, more people emerge from the leaves as Krishna removes each from the roll and gently coaxes it open. Many of the poems are attributed to Chikkiah; several say the poems are by Mahadevi.

Some of the sheets do not have the deliberate and elegant script that is becoming familiar to Krishna. The writing is rather crude, and the leaf itself seems to be of inferior quality, as if the writer was a student and had to make do with less supple material. But here is one which has a postscript in the elegant handwriting. The worms have eaten up some of the words, but Krishna can just about put together the epigram: *These words of Mahadevi were written with attention and downcast sight, straining neck and back. Preserve this, I plead.*

He unfurls more sheets, controlling his excitement so he is careful with them.

Finally he finds a leaf that says, at the bottom, Mahadevi, but also more than the name. The full line is *Mahadevi of field and Anandagrama, wife and friend of Chikkiah, mother of Chandra and Kannappa-Kannadeva.*

Kannappa? Was that another name for Kannadeva?

It's almost dark outside, time to pack up, when he finds a simple but disturbing song. *Where is that land where water flows free?* The leaf has a footnote in small letters. It's a bio line heavy with detail, the kind dictated by love. Krishna peers at it, reads it aloud slowly as if he is learning to read letter by letter. *Cattle skinner and father of Chikkiah of Anandagrama, Chikkiah the washerman and lover of the river and the drum, husband of Mahadevi, father of Chandra and Kannappa-Kannadeva.*

Chikkiah. Mahadevi. Kannappa who seems to be Kannadeva. Krishna recalls the commentaries he has read on Kannadeva, the biographical notes. Not one of them hints at a grandfather who was a cattle skinner or a father who was a washerman. Caste lived then; it still flourishes. But it has been whitewashed so Kannadeva can be a 'saint', a 'Hindu saint'.

Krishna packs up. He can't take in anything more today.

3

Satya is in the corner room that no one wants, especially not the 'Forward caste' students, because the room is next door to the row of shared toilets. It's not that Satya is not grateful for any room in a highly rated medical college; and this room, even if it is second rate for the rest, has a window that frames the thick-leaved heart of a peepal tree.

It's not that Satya is not grateful for his roommate Rahul—they have little in common other than both being quota students—but still, he can try and talk to someone when he's afraid he's forgetting the sound of his own voice.

It's not that Satya is not grateful for the scholarship; he can live on very little and send the rest home to his mother.

It's not that he's not grateful that he can wave that certificate saying Scheduled Caste, force the willing and unwilling to acknowledge the injustice of centuries, agree, in principle at least, that he too can be a doctor. A respected citizen. A real person. It's not that he is not grateful that he was not born a hundred years ago, or even fifty. People in this college like to say that caste is divisive, it stands in the way of progress, no one should talk about it anymore. The college is full of people who don't need to think about their caste because they can take it for granted. If only, if only, Satya too could be allowed to forget who he is for a day or two; or if he could be allowed to decide who he is. If only he could say to them, 'I am only eighteen years old. Can I have a chance to become the person I want to be?'

But those are dreams, the sort he and Ravi and Asha have to plant in the ground, hoping they will take in the soil years and years later, perhaps in time for their sons and daughters. The only dream Satya is going to keep in view now is the immediate goal—surviving, somehow, the four and a half years in college and then the year of internship, so he can get the degree. Meanwhile, all he has to do is work, work, survive the loneliness, and the hundred pinpricks a day.

Satya is at his table, trying to memorise a list of long words. How he misses group study with Ravi and Asha, the occasional laugh about a silly memory aid that made it all lighter for a few moments! How are they, what are they doing? What he would give for Ravi's angry look, or Asha's tender sympathy, if he reeled off another list now, the ugly one he doesn't need to study or revise. He wants to resist this other list, it's out of syllabus and textbook. But it scrolls down a screen in his mind. The screen refuses to be switched off.

Scene 1. The fees, then the hostel. All the students run around with plastic bags full of documents and slips, multi-coloured, original, copies attested by gazetted officer, copies self-attested. They are learning the procedure which has been made as complicated and unreasonable as possible so they will understand how lucky they are to have got a seat in a good medical college. Satya too is running around. There is an especially long queue at the final counter, where the man checks all the papers, then stamps the cashier's slip with a big circular blue ink mark. When it's Satya's turn, he passes his papers through the round hole in the glass window. The man on the other side of the glass spends a long time reading and re-reading the certificates and mark sheets. He spends an inordinate amount of time looking at the caste certificate. Any moment now, he may hold it up against the light, see if it is genuine currency. All the while, he has a stern look on his face, as if he may be examined on what he has read, so he's memorising every word and number on the certificates and mark sheets.

The man finally looks up at Satya. 'Wait at the back,' he says. 'I have to check something.'

The girl behind Satya exhales, as if she has been holding her breath all this time.

Satya doesn't know what to do. He steps out of the line and the girl quickly thrusts her papers through the hole in the glass window. The boys behind her move ahead.

Satya goes to the end of the queue, hesitates then gets in line again. It's 1:20 pm by the time his turn comes again. Satya moves from foot to foot. Is there a problem, he wants to ask, but he doesn't in case asking such a question will make it come true. The man barely looks at him this time. 'It's lunch time,' he barks, though the clock behind him clearly shows there's ten more minutes to lunch. 'Come back at 2.' The man picks up Satya's papers gingerly, as if they are dirty, rolls them up into a pipe and pushes it through the hole. He finally meets Satya's eyes. He looks virtuous, as if he has just done Satya a favour. He's helping Satya learn how hard it all is, how hard it is going to be. He's teaching him now, at the very beginning. How else will Satya appreciate his luck?

Scene 2. The entire batch of hundred new students is heading toward the Orientation Hall. Most of the students have come with someone, a parent, both parents, a brother, an uncle. Satya is, of course, alone.

Scene 3. Satya is in class. The boys are sitting next to each other, the girls form a separate row. Three or four students have broken this unspoken rule and sit next to each other, boy and girl, at the back.

Satya sits in the front, alone. There is an empty seat next to him on one side and the wall on the other, as if he has a contagious disease, or lice, or as if he smells. A lifestyle disease handed down from generation to generation, a disease that hovers over him like a racial memory to become his second skin. A couple of days, he tried sitting at the back like the other Dalit in class, Rahul, so it would be less noticeable, this unofficial and unending quarantine. But he found it hard to pay attention to the lecture from there, to hear every English word he has not heard said before, and to take down notes. So Satya went back to the front row, chose a seat as much to one side as possible, next to the wall so that only one side of him would be empty.

Scene 4. Satya's hand is raised. He knows the answer. He knew it even before the professor finished the question. But his hand has become invisible. The professor doesn't see Satya's arm though the classroom is sunny bright. Satya lowers his arm; it feels so useless, this arm that was once strong enough to dig hard ground in the village, lift sacks and bundles. Now, when all it has to do is lift itself, call attention to the words hanging on the lips of its owner, it can't do a thing. The professor is not looking at him. But Satya can see the professor not looking; he can see the professor thinking, 'Arrogant bastard.' Or 'Not going to waste time on this fellow, probably impossible to educate. Let him go back to the fields where he belongs.' As his arm falls to his side, hangs limp, Satya can hear a soft hiss from behind him: 'Quota.' Then a snigger, not so soft. The professor seems to have turned deaf. The studious ones are never popular. And if they are SC quota students as well …

Scene 5. After class, the students linger in the hallways in groups or pairs. Or they head outside, to the canteen, or the green stretch under the trees, or to town. Many of them have bikes and motorcycles; a few even have cars. Again, there is one student who is not part of any of the groups. Satya has tried. It's no use. By now he has heard it all, he can see and hear their thoughts if their eyes land on his face. *Lazy people living off quotas. It's in their genes. No merit. Taking seats away from merit students. This is a good institution. We care about who we are with.* He could go looking for Rahul, but Rahul spends a lot of time sharing his notes with the girls, anything to help him find a girlfriend.

Satya heads toward the library. When he has read till he sees double of every word, when the illustrations in the book grow ghostly shadows, he gets up, shoulders hunched as if the wind is blowing hard and he has to protect himself. He makes his way back to the hostel, to the corner room.

Scenes 6, 7, 8. Ragging. It's banned, it's illegal. But Satya can still hear the taunts. He can see a body, almost naked, a body that looks so much like his, moving as if dancing. Laughter, shame. Satya doesn't want to think about it. These are not scenes to be re-lived. He is in his room now, alone. He is safe with his books, his study plan for the evening.

But Satya gets up, leaving the list to be memorised on the table. He looks at Rahul's laptop, sitting there invitingly. Rahul has told him he can check email or surf the net anytime. But Satya can't bring himself to do it when Rahul is not in the room.

Satya opens the side of the cupboard that is his. It smells

powerfully of naphthalene balls. He pulls out a bright blue notebook, shuts the cupboard quickly before its fetid air escapes into the room. Satya looks at the notebook. The front and back have been pasted over with blue wrapping paper. On the front, there is a label-shaped rectangle made of small red flowers drawn with a felt tip pen. Inside the label, it says, in celebratory bold letters that look to the future, Dr Satya, MBBS. Satya traces the letters with a wistful finger; he takes out the book only when the need to talk to someone overcomes him. He re-reads the first page now, written in a mixture of Kannada and English.

> I am a medical student. It's still hard to believe. All that work, the permanent worry about money. All of it worth it. Now I have to be worth it all, be worthy of Amma and Prasad and their sacrifices, so I can be the only member of the family who will earn a professional degree.
>
> Then Ravi and Asha. I have to be worth their friendship. Asha gave me this book when we said goodbye to each other the last time we met after the results. I felt bad she didn't pass the entrance test. I felt worse when Ravi didn't make it. Even if we had not got the same college, I would have felt less alone if I knew that they too are studying medicine somewhere.

Satya pauses. How long has it been since he felt he is not alone?

Satya's father left their village a long time back. Satya barely remembers him. Sometimes though, he sees a hazy image of him in his dreams. He's tall; thin, very thin; and he has a permanent look of puzzlement on his face, as if he can't figure out where he is, or why he is there. Did this bewilderment make him forget his wife and sons at home, such as home is?

Before he too left for the city, Satya's brother Prasad said to him, 'Maybe I will bump into the old man on the road one day. Do you think he will recognise me?'

A few months later, working at a car mechanic shop, learning on the job, Prasad said to Satya on the phone, 'I don't know what I was thinking, imagining I would bump into the old man here.' He laughed at himself. 'This city is as big as the universe, and has as many people.'

Satya was quiet.

'He must be dead,' added Prasad, then changed the topic. He never spoke of their father again.

As for Satya, he does not speak of his father, or think of him. He only thinks of his mother.

His mother, back bent. Sari lifted high above her knees, tucked into her waist. Her head covered with one end of the sari to protect her from the sun. Her feet in water, soaking in watery mud all day long. Working, working. Is there anything else he has seen her doing? Is there anything else life has given her? She has two children whose stomachs needed to be filled, children who needed to be removed from the fields and sent to school. Now they are grown up; she has only her own stomach to feed. But still she works, because how else will she live? How else will she keep the moneylender away from her, make sure Satya becomes a doctor?

This is how Satya likes to remember his mother when he is away from her. She is singing. She is working, of course, but she is also singing. It's been some years since he has heard her sing. She has no energy to sing now, she says. And in any case, there's been less and less work in the fields. But Satya can clearly remember her deep voice singing, then the other women joining in the refrain. The women sang of all sorts of things: the sky above them, the land they loved and slaved at but didn't belong to them, the rain they coaxed into pouring with their voices, the greedy or lecherous eye of the man who owned the fields they were working on. They sang their wish for prosperity, even if they had never seen it in the face; they sang their hope for a good crop. They sang to cranes and bulls, asking them to keep the crop safe, to make it grow tall and strong. But most of all, they sang about work. *Bele.*

> Come, everyone, come on.
> O-bele.
> Come step into the fields,
> O-bele.
> The children of ten mothers,
> O-bele.
> Let's sing together,
> O-bele.

O-bele. O-bele, O-bele, bela, bela. Oh work, Oh work, Oh work, work, work. Words repeated to make their own bodies repeat their movement. Words, songs to make it easier to do what they had to do, to keep moving, to forget about hunger, the ache in the lower back, the sore in the foot, the empty cooking pot at home, the unlit fire. Forget as much as you can. Remember only how to move: to bend, move sideways like a crab, keep going till all the transplanting is done. At least there is work now. What when the season is over? Best not to think of that yet.

Satya chases that thought away as she must have. He bends over the diary and writes instead:

> Amma, singing as she pounds the rice. Lots of rice, none of it ours.

I don't want pearls,
I don't want rubies.
Just a piece of land
O mother,
and the songs we sing on that land.

Father searched for a groom
and sent me away from home.
Mother wept.
But look!
Look, my friends,
how quickly the flowers in my hair
have wilted.
How quickly my hennaed feet
sink in slushy mud.

Satya shuts the diary, looks out of the small window. He's grateful for the window, which he has opened all the way so he can see a small patch of sky above and the part of the peepal tree that has spread its branches close to the building wall. He rations his time at the window. Ten more pages, one more chapter, he tells himself, and I will take a five-minute break, stretch, go to the window to see what is happening. There are birds there, and bees, hornets, squirrels; Satya is making friends with all of them, though they don't know about it yet.

The patch of sky has grown a deep blue, edging its way to the dark face it wears every night. The peepal's branches lose detail, turn into silhouettes. The crows, loyal evening visitors, arrive, and begin their usual clamour: *Night is almost here, night is almost here*. Satya sighs. A few more pages, then it's time to go down to the hostel mess, eat alone, come back upstairs for his night shift.

How it sings, this prayer

1

Ravi is restless. At first, he did not want to be where he is, a government science college, or studying what he is, zoology. But he's getting used to it; it helps that he likes his two roommates. There's Harisha, a first year botany student, as quiet and pleasant as the plants and flowers he draws and labels neatly in his notebooks. Then there's Ramesha, a loud-voiced firecracker. Every sentence of his is a mini-explosion, a challenge that cannot be ignored. He is in Ravi's zoology batch. The room the three of them share is a tiny reflection of home—it's crowded; they talk late into the night; they eat together; they borrow each other's clothes. And the room is a mess, but it's theirs. They watch out for each other. Ravi and Ramesha are from different Scheduled Castes; Harisha is ST. Really, in the eyes of the upper caste or rich students in the college, all three are the same. For Ravi, it's almost like being back with Satya and Asha, only better because the three boys live together. Besides, they are in college, trying to become men. What they want is to be men whose choices have not already been made by others.

For now, Ravi and Ramesha are working on their assignment, trying to be as conscientious as Harisha. It's still early days in the course; there's still a lot of the basic classification business to go over. This introductory section is not that different from what they studied in school. But still, how dull to take hold of those names again, possess all those lists all over again! Ravi hates memorising. He doesn't want to do it aloud because Harisha will be disturbed; he has a way of making his large soulful eyes look terribly hurt. Luckily Ramesha has no such inhibitions. He also feels the need to comment on everything he reads.

'India is one of the twelve countries identified as mega centres of biological diversity,' he reads, then adds an annotation. 'They forgot to add the usual bit about diversity among people.' He skips a couple of paragraphs, gets to the part about how important classification is. 'Differentiating, grouping and giving names to living things has been an ancient activity of every human culture. Without proper classification it would be impossible to deal with the enormous diversity of life forms.' Ramesha suddenly looks less bored. 'Hah,' he says, 'they should add that Indians are even better at classifying human beings than animals. Let's see—according to Simpson, zoological classification is the "ordering of animals into groups on the basis of their relationships".'

Ravi puts down his notes, more than ready to be distracted. Harisha rolls his eyes, exasperated.

'Okay, Ravi,' says Ramesha, 'here's a lesson better than Simpson's. Harisha, don't look so pained, put down your book. We have domain, kingdom, phylum, class, order, family, genus, species, all in a nice ladder from top rung to lowest rung. So where do we begin? You can't just say the usual Brahmins, Kshatriyas, Vaishyas, Shudras. That makes it all too simple, not looking at jati. So let's look at ourselves, the outcastes. Where do we fit into Manu's *taxonomy*?'

It's all nonsense, Ravi knows, but it's late at night, and he's done with reading and memorising what seems to have nothing to do with him.

Ramesha begins listing all the possible names he has heard to describe those who don't belong in the acceptable list, those who are humiliated through names specially made up for them, those who pollute with their bodies and spit and shadows, those who do the shit work, those who are not entirely human. 'Antyaja, Chandala, Panchama, Asprushya—what else, Ravi?'

Ravi is happy to join in. 'Let's see—there's Madiga, Mala, Relli, Chindu, Mashitla, Pariah, Parayan …'

'Don't leave out the tribes,' Harisha suddenly pipes up. 'Gaudalu, Hakkipikki, Irula, Jenu Kuruba, Malaikud, Malikudi, Bhil, Gond, Chenchu, Koya, Yerava, Haleya, Korama—do you want more?' Ramesha and Ravi look at him, awe-struck. No wonder he can remember what he reads word for word.

'No, no, just a long list doesn't work,' says Ravi, warming up to the task. 'We have to explain why all these are at the bottom steps of the ladder—no, why they are off the ladder. We are protozoa—the only cell we have is caste or tribe, official names SC and ST.'

'So I can grow a new head or a leg when it gets cut off?' Ramesha laughs. For some reason, the three of them find this hilarious. Ravi laughs till his stomach hurts and his eyes fill. But when they finally switch off the lights and get into their beds, it does not seem one bit funny.

That damn entrance test—now a thing of the past—has come back to his head to sit there like a mocking ghost. Maybe he lost the seat even before the results, even before the test? Maybe he lost it the moment he ticked the SC box in the application form. Did they look at anything other than that box with its fat black tick sitting like a straight-backed snake? He was so sure all three of them, he, Satya and Asha, would get into medicine. Asha, at least, seems to have learnt to be happy with nursing. It's hard to say; Asha is always afraid to complain, something Ravi has never quite understood. Ravi learnt early that life would be even harder if he didn't complain, shout, cry, make some noise or the other. Of course Asha's family is small, just the four of them living in one house. He, Ravi, grew up in a crowd, a large family in a Dalit settlement where everyone knows each other's children and business. All their neighbours knew he was trying to become a doctor. Maybe the whole colony knew, because his father spread the news like feast food to be shared with everyone, giving each one their share of the dream.

Then the results came; the dream broke; it had to be repaired with the backup plan, the one made of brass instead of gold. His family was disappointed. But he would catch his father or one of the old men in the neighbourhood stealing a worried look at him now and then, wanting to help. 'You're going to college, my boy,' an old man told him. 'It's more, much more than your grandfather or father or I got.'

Ravi never let them see how angry he was. Maybe that's why his brightness as the family star, one of the settlement's stars, did not lose its shine so easily. They adjusted their fantasy a little, that's all. In their newly adjusted dream, Ravi was moving ahead, he was going to college with a scholarship, and it was for all of them. If he could become a college professor or a scientist, maybe they too could dream of better lives for their children.

Ravi listens to his two roommates snore. Harisha's is a gentle monotone, like a bee humming to itself. Ramesha snores like a plane taking off every few minutes. Maybe when Ramesha gets older, he too will snore like Ravi's grandfather, the champion of snorers. Ravi smiles in the dark, shuts his eyes. He sees home, scene by scene, but from the time when his grandfather was still alive.

There it is, home, as crowded as it always has been. There are his parents, daily-wage labourers, out all day. There are his two sisters and his brother. And there is the bare-chested old man, his grandfather, supposedly in charge of the house and children in the day, but who spends most of his time sitting at the entrance of the house, chewing tobacco with his gang of old men.

Mother, father, grandfather and four children in two rooms, made into three rooms with an old sari dividing the children's room into boys' and girls' sections. His grandfather slept outside. 'The sky and stars are my night time companions,' he liked to say. The relatives are nearby. At any rate, everyone in the congested Dalit locality is related in the sense that they are all Dalit. They all have houses like matchboxes. They are related because everyone knows what is going on in each family, in the house next door, and all down the street. They are related by the age-old practice that dictates that the lowest of castes will live together, away from all other castes. Related by blood, related by caste.

It's always been like this. This could be said sadly, or with anger or bitterness or resignation. Whatever the tone, Ravi has lost count of the number of times he has heard this said.

Ravi would be playing with his brother or sisters, or

he would, as the youngest, be sitting on his grandfather's bony lap at the entrance of the house. As usual the old man would have at least two or three of his friends sitting with him, smoking beedis or chewing tobacco, saying something now and then. What they said to each other was in a kind of shorthand. That seemed to be enough. Maybe—since *it's always been like this*—they knew how to fill in the gaps, hear the unsaid. Or maybe they had heard these stories far too many times before.

'Remember that old man who couldn't walk straight?'

'Oh yes, the one who sat on a horse once? He was beaten so badly, he was lucky he was not killed.'

Or: 'Yes, that was the time all the women in the village got raped. Even the little girls.'

Set on fire. Stripped and paraded. Stripped and flogged. Going into a sewer, drunk to bear it. Houses set on fire. Burnt to death. Then a long silence, till an old man broke it: 'Once I got so angry because no barber would cut my hair. I let it grow for months. Everyone teased me that I had turned into a woman.'

All of them laughed, including the storyteller. But even the child Ravi felt the disgusting aftertaste of that laughter.

Once his grandfather told them: 'You know, all his life my father would take his drum and go when he was called to one of their funeral processions. He would sling the drum on his shoulder and drag me along. He said we would get into trouble if we didn't follow tradition. Tradition—' and his grandfather fell silent for a while, chewing the word with his tobacco. 'They need us for all the degrading jobs. Carrying carcasses of dead cows, shovelling shit and carrying basketfuls of it. Burying dead bodies.' He paused then mused aloud, 'Death is as important as birth. I know that, but there's something I don't understand. Why should your brother's body or your father's body become something polluting?'

It's always been like this. No, thinks Ravi now, as if making a promise to his grandfather. It should not always be like this. It will not always be like this. Will it?

When Ravi falls asleep, his grandfather and friends are nowhere in his dream. It takes Ravi just a few seconds of dream time to walk through the house. He goes to what should be a balcony at the back, but is actually a narrow cement ledge overhanging the canal that flows behind their row of houses. The canal is usually congealed and stinky with every possible kind of garbage and shit. But as Ravi stands there, looking at the canal, it begins to pour. It rains so hard that the canal becomes a bubbly stream. It becomes playful, running past him, carrying all sorts of things on its back. Leaves, twigs, plastic bags of all colours and sizes; an old slipper looking for its twin; a dead kitten and a half-eaten bandicoot floating close together, best friends. Then Ravi sees a small twiggy nest bobbing up and down the water. Even from a distance, he can see there's something in it. He gets off the ledge, wades into the canal. He grabs the nest. He has never seen anything so beautiful. It's made of braided twigs and bits of leaves, and it holds three perfect grey eggs.

He is about to wade back to the ledge, but suddenly the canal has grown. It's no longer a sewage canal or a drain; it's no longer a stream; it's become a river. The miserable houses on either side have disappeared from view. Ravi is being carried as if he too is flotsam, except this flotsam of bone and muscle has a nest in his hand, three smooth eggs in his care. He loves the fact that the canal is really a river, and that it is flowing, moving fast. But did it have to happen just now, when he has to keep the nest and the eggs safe? Then there's a bang, and the nest, the river, home, all of it disappears. Ramesha has not shut the door of their room properly. A stray wind has just taken hold of the door and shut it with a bang. Ravi jumps up, wide awake. What a silly dream! But still, though it made no sense, it's made him feel refreshed, as if he has just had a dip in a river.

The next day, Ramesha sits next to Ravi in the back row, his face shining with news. He leans toward Ravi, says to him, 'The students' association we heard about, Bhim Shakti? They're going to have a meeting this evening. I just found out.'

'We must go,' says Ravi. Ramesha looks pleased with Ravi's reaction. The class which will begin in a minute or two, the classification of animals and human beings, what do they care about it now? This evening promises to be nothing like the one before.

2

Krishna has spent weeks with the palm leaves, deciphering words which have been gobbled up by worms, or lines that have frayed. But the story that emerges is, surprisingly, almost coherent.

There are the poems he recognises, the ones he now 'confirms' as Kannadeva's because they do not have another name below or the epigram to indicate that it has been written by a copyist. There are poems he is entirely unfamiliar with. Krishna does not know the names below these poems either; nor does he know how they are linked with Kannadeva, except, perhaps, through Anandagrama. Then there are poems he thought were Kannadeva's but here they are somewhat different, more direct, less 'learned' than Kannadeva's usual style. Some of them are ascribed to others.

Krishna the professor of poetry is wide awake. He can't sleep without Shanta next to him. But sleep doesn't matter, and, besides, he has company. Every night, alone in bed, he sees Kannadeva in the film running a loop in his head.

Here is Kannadeva, perhaps close to the end of his life, sitting night after night by the light of a spluttering oil lamp, taking a sheaf of processed palm leaves—reddish leaf paper—meant for the writing of mantras or his own devotional poems. He painstakingly inscribes letter after letter on the palm leaves with his kanta, a thick metal needle with a sharp point. Since he cannot correct or overwrite, he has to take great pains to make each leaf error-free. He takes the coal powder that is ready in a casket and applies it; he makes sure the letters are conspicuous enough to be read easily. He makes holes in the wide margins of the leaves; or maybe the leaves have these already. Kannadeva passes silken thread through the holes, ties the leaves carefully to make a book. Maybe he places thin boards, like wooden folders, above and below so the leaves do not get crumpled. What he has ready now, what will be passed on, hidden, bought and sold, lost, hidden then found again, is the Book of Kannadeva.

The Book of Kannadeva, which turns out to be the book of many people—Kannappa who became Kannadeva, his mother Mahadevi, his father Chikkiah, and many others. All related by their association with Anandagrama.

Krishna recalls a poem by Kannadeva that leaked through the palm leaf and got under his skin. The sense of loss in that poem: it was palpable though it hid behind the usual abstractions. Did Kannadeva see that what he was copying was more deeply felt, more *connected* than his own words? How did he feel when he copied onto a fresh leaf, one more poem that pulled him down to the hard ground of work, challenged him to find meaning in actual living?

What is this mystery,
that one asks, looking into the distance.
This one looks for life in his navel.

What mystery is this?

Find a heap of rice,
    peel the husk of each grain.

That fish:
    remove all its fine bones.

That god playing hide and seek.
    Make him your friend.

The rice and fish to be grown and caught,
    cooked,
    the children fed.
That friend of friends
    to be held close.

There,
and in the cloth to be woven
    the fields to be planted
    the goats to be slaughtered
    the cows to be skinned
    the rats to be caught
    the shit to be carried away
    the bodies to be loved
    the songs to be sung
    the stories to be told.

You'll find it there,
    Your mystery.

You'll find it there,
    my lord's mystery.

This homely wisdom, this philosophy born out of living: how it must have struck learned Kannadeva, how it hits Krishna the professor like a well-aimed blow! And this is not the only connection between Kannadeva and himself. There's another link, a painful one.

Why did Anandagrama have to happen? There had to be a place where fishermen, cattle skinners, ratcatchers, shit carriers, all those who were considered low, lower, lowest, had to come together. Why was Anandagrama killed? The people's combined strength had to be met with force, crushed. Their self-respect, their insistence that they too be real people, was a threat to those who have always held power in their closed fists.

Hundreds of years later, how much has changed? Krishna lives in a time when there is a Constitution; he lives in a country where there is a promise of equality, rights for all its citizens. But how often does he hear of cattle skinners and manual scavengers, forced to do what they do, despised for what they do? Krishna feels a dull anger grow in him at the thought of this unchanging eternal India.

Suddenly he wants to get away from it all: from the written copies, Kannadeva's palm leaves and his own paper copies. From reading. He wants to get away from Mr Seshadri and the Institute. He wants to *hear* words, and he wants to hear them sung.

He finds the scrap of paper with a telephone number and calls Gangiah.

'I made enquiries for you,' Gangiah announces, as if he has been expecting Krishna's call. 'There are some singers who have come here from the Chaitanya area. That's the big river a few hours away, I'm sure you will want to go there too. But first, come and hear these singers? The old man is here, the one I told you about.'

Krishna thinks of the palm leaves, feels like a truant schoolboy; but he takes up Gangiah's offer.

'You won't regret it, I promise,' says Gangiah. 'Tomorrow night?'

It's a glorious night, cool, breezy. There's a small fire outside the modest little house in the fields off the main road. There are four singers, and all appear to be related to each other in some way. Krishna is sure of one relationship. The youngest is a grandson; his grandfather is the oldest of the four singers. He has a face that looks like history personified. He sits close to the fire which lights up every line and wrinkle on his face. He lights a beedi every now and then, coughs. The others sing; he listens, nods now and then in approval.

When they fall silent, Gangiah moves closer to the old man, whispers conspiratorially, 'The professor was asking about Kannadeva. That song I heard before—would you sing it again?'

The old man is silent. Then he throws his beedi into the fire and gestures for the drum. His grandson hangs the drum around the old man's neck gently, hands over the two sticks.

The old man beats a slow, gentle rhythm; he sings in a soft but surprisingly clear voice.

Kannadeva, messenger of peace.
You left everything behind.

Desire, memory,
the father who sang to the river,
the name which was yours,
the home which was yours,
a home with people talking songs to each other.
Mahadevi, Puttanna, Gundanna, Siddha,
the Elder Brothers and Sisters,
a new world flowing out of people's voices.

Kannadeva, messenger of peace.
How heavy your empty heart!

Kannadeva, Kannappa, your home is gone.
Your Anandagrama is gone.

How will you find it again?
How will you go there again?

Don't be sad, Kannadeva.
Don't be sad, Kannappa.
The river remembers them,
the river with a thousand faces.

The river, sad messenger of peace,
the people's flowing river.

And that is how Krishna hears what he will later think of as the Ballad of Kannadeva.

The old man hands over his drum to one of the others and lights up again. He holds out the beedi packet. Krishna doesn't smoke, but it seems churlish to refuse. The smoke tickles his tongue and throat. Krishna coughs, and the old man smiles, as if to say, 'Now we are brothers.' Gangiah looks smug, having brought together two people meant for each other.

Krishna asks the old man what else he knows about Kannappa, his parents, and the others mentioned in the song.

The old man's reply is brief and cryptic. 'I know the song. The song of Kannadeva. It's an old song.'

Krishna doesn't give up. He asks about the Samadhi that Gangiah showed him earlier. Does the old man know anything about it?

'Go to the Chaitanya,' the old man says, 'there's another one there. Foolish—all of it is foolish.' He coughs then spits into the fire.

Gangiah looks crestfallen.

'My father used to say,' continues the old man, 'what does it matter how anyone dies, it's how he lives that matters. It's his words that matter. Those words of Kannadeva's. They flow like a river with many tributaries, all flowing into the same mouth. That's the mouth that speaks. It speaks a language that lives, not like your English. Or Sanskrit.'

The old man spits again though he has nothing left to spit. 'Your Sanskrit,' he says to Krishna, almost accusingly, 'it refused to live, that's why it's a dead language.'

Having said his piece, the old man falls silent. Krishna can't get another word out of him.

But it's not till he is done with Seshadri's Institute and Kannadeva's palm-leaf book that he makes his way to the Chaitanya River. And maybe it wouldn't have happened if he had not got news about the river from his old morning-walk friend, Natraj.

News Natraj called him, breathless as usual. 'Krishna! It seems you are not far from the Chaitanya River. And there's some breaking news you should hear …'

'There's a sadhvi called Mata Nikhila,' Natraj told Krishna, 'she's demanding that the Chaitanya should be declared a living person. Wait, I have jotted it down here—"a living legal entity with its own rights and values". And there's a government official's reaction too. Wait—here it is. "All Hindus have deep faith in the sanctity of the ancient Chaitanya. Their connection with the river goes back over generations and its waters are central to the material and spiritual well being of the community, indeed the entire Hindu population of India." '

The living Chaitanya. How differently this word *living* can be used or understood! What would his newly discovered friend Chikkiah say about his beloved river being declared alive by a court, by a government? There are those words of Chikkiah's he has recently discovered in Kannadeva's palm-leaf book:

> My river, generous as always,
> gurgles as it laughs.
>
> Only those who have sweated day after day
> know what it is to be soaked, O friend.

The river or mountain or land that is part of people's daily lives—their work, their source of food and drink, the intimacy they have with it, makes a different living 'entity' altogether. Chikkiah's river is no legal being. It's something more subtle, part friend, part brother, part lover, part god. Chikkiah's songs tell this story of lived experience, a living relationship.

Krishna packs his bags, calls Shanta to tell her he will be home soon. He's got just the one small detour to make.

The noisy river before him has a grand name: Chaitanya. A namesake of the sixteenth-century spiritual leader who built a bhakti movement. A namesake of his own little Chitthu. Chaitanya, Consciousness. Universal Self or Soul. Spirit. Intelligence, energy, enthusiasm, sensation. Vitality, fire, knowledge, living force, life. Can a river hold everything Chaitanya means?

Krishna considers the river that has not yet spoken to him, though judging by its turbulence, it has much to say. He walks by the shore. He would like to imagine that this riverbank is where Chikkiah washed clothes as a washerman. Maybe his wife Mahadevi helped him, and so did their children, running off to play in between. This is where, perhaps, their son Kannappa came back as the venerable Kannadeva, a saint who didn't want to be a saint once he discovered—through his lost family—that asking questions may be the best virtue of all.

But it's not easy to see the living past as he walks on a shore littered by the present. Krishna sidesteps the garbage that lies around, the empty Bisleri bottles, the shiny colourful packets that once held chips (Magic Masala and Sour Cream and Onion), cigarette butts, used condoms, dog shit, and, to assert the holiness of the place, fresh as well as dry cow dung. The past, imaginary or otherwise, remains elusive.

But the river has its own ways of demanding attention.

The sky begins to darken though it is still day, as if someone has abruptly switched off the sun. The heavy clouds sag over the water; the river rises to meet the challenge.

The sky thunders, throws a quick and flashy bolt at the water.

The river spreads itself in all directions. Its waves flow hard, slap the shore. The river works itself into a rage; it leaps into the air.

The rising river, the glowering sky, their old duets and battles, awe Krishna into submission as it has others in the past. What's some quarrel about living and dead rivers, saintly poets and people's poets, when the universe is stirring itself to show its power?

3

Chikka is no longer Chikka the skinner of dead animals. He is now Chikkiah the washerman.

He still makes his way to the city once in a while. It has become less strange and frightening, now that Puttanna has shown him all the streets, or at least the places he needs to know. But Chikkiah has not been anywhere near the king's palace. 'That's asking for trouble,' Puttanna told him. 'Those whoresons,' Puttanna began with relish then broke off, looking sheepish. He had suddenly remembered the few prostitutes who had also found refuge in Anandagrama, every one of them as good as himself.

But Chikkiah doesn't care about the palace anyway, having discovered his own open-air palace. Chikkiah knows where the mansions of the nobles and wealthy merchants are, and where the medium-size-but-still-too-big houses of the Brahmins and army officials. He has seen those houses at a distance and that is enough. Chikkiah also knows where the big temples are, including the Grand Temple. The cows roam free on these streets, garlanded with marigold and rolled up leaves. The holy cows feed at the heaps of rubbish thrown behind the temples every day. Chikkiah carefully avoids these areas where the air smells of fresh and rancid flowers, spilt milk and ghee, sugary prasad, cow dung, camphor and vibhuti.

Once in the city, Chikkiah is happy to go directly to Anandagrama and listen to what is being said. He likes hearing calm and low-voiced Elder Brother and the wisest of them all, Prabhu, though Chikkiah doesn't always understand what they say. Maybe they are less wise, but Chikkiah loves hearing the fiery ones too. Wise, fiery, or both, he always waits to hear that word spoken. Equal. Chikkiah loves this word no matter how many times he hears it. He thinks he knows it better now. He thinks it's almost his own.

Chikkiah himself doesn't have much to say while in Anandagrama, or even when he is with Puttanna and his friends, Siddha, Chenna and Gundanna. But slowly, very slowly, the words that have been simmering inside Chikkiah are rising to the surface. He is discovering words of his own. The words make better sense when they come together.

They come together when he is at work by the river, beating cloth against stone, rinsing it, then beating and rinsing again before he spreads it out to dry. Some clothes he hangs on the ropes he has tied from tree to tree. The maps of clothes, mostly white, but some in orange, maroon, yellow or green, sway in the breeze; or embrace, tightly, their stony resting place. They make him hum as he works, even sing aloud. He sings what he has recently learnt in Anandagrama, or from Puttanna and other friends.

But when he sits alone by the river at night, these songs do not seem enough. Their words are not enough for what the river does to him, or what the nights by the river do to him. Sometimes, on a night when the reddish moon hangs full, pregnant with hints, the sky and the always-moving river seem to be there only for him. They're his teachers, his father and mother. That's when Chikkiah remembers Chikka. He remembers him almost without suffering.

The old drum sometimes sits by him, keeping him company. His father comes back to him a few of these nights.

He sees his father and himself.

Chikka sulks in one corner of the little hut. He has just refused to go with his father to skin a dead calf their neighbours have brought there on their shoulders. His father shouts at him. 'Who's going to feed you if you don't work? What else can you do? What else can I do? Your mother died giving birth to you. I've fed you till you can feed yourself. And now you're too good to do what I do? What the likes of us have always done? Get up, you ingrate, you sonofabitch, come and help.'

Chikka does not move.

'You'll be there, won't you, when we get our share of the meat? You'll be hungry, you'll be one of us then!'

Chikka tries to shut out his father's voice, but his idiot mouth fills with saliva. His father storms out. Chikka's stomach growls. He gets up, defeated.

But later, after they have eaten, and he has drunk as much as he can out of the dented lota, his father sings a different tune. 'They hate us, the miserable cunts. They love their cows. But can they love a cow like we do, use every bit of it once it's dead, eat it so it lets us live another day?' His father reaches for his drum; he reaches for the stick to beat the drum to death.

His father beats the drum as if it holds everything he knows—hunger, humiliation, the grinding repetition of it day after day. Then he throws the stick aside and holds the drum to his chest, looking remorseful. He strokes it, as if a caress will put it in a good mood. Then he beats it gently.

'Where's that land …' he begins his plaint, the question he asks every night though it remains unanswered.

But one night, he stops after the first line. 'Chikka,' he whispers, 'You're right. Don't do it. Do something else. Find a river, go to the sea. Become a fisherman.' His father begins to sob; he spits on the drum, throws it across the hut. Then he slumps against the wall, defeated. The only possible escape is a fitful sleep.

Chikkiah feels those old wounds gingerly. Are they still tender to the touch?

'It's here, father,' Chikkiah whispers to the river. 'It's flowing here, the water. My lord, my friend, is here. Your drum is here too. Stay with me.'

Chikkiah picks up the drum, beats a tentative rhythm. He sings what he has recently learnt to the river:

This water is holy,
and this, and this,
they mumble in a foreign tongue,
sprinkling a few drops on
stone-faced dolls in the temple,
the floor of their houses
and outside.

These men
even sprinkle water on themselves
and say they are born again.

But he wants to say more; Chikkiah adds to the verses he has heard in Anandagrama. He adds words of his own that have come out of the night sky; lines that have come to him from the murmuring river.

My river, generous as always,
gurgles as it laughs.

Only those who have sweated day after day
know what it is to be soaked, O friend.

The river teems with life in and around it. Even when Chikkiah is solitary, he is not alone. There are fish that let themselves be seen only when the river lies flat and quiet at low tide. There are tiny crabs that scurry up and down the cleft of the rock with a hundred holes as if it is made of cork. The egrets, white fluff on black sticks, walk in the shallow pools between rocks. One takes off, glides just above the water. There are trees that turn every colour; the trees house residents of every colour. Some are as black as Chikkiah.

How black this crow,
every feather merging into
the safety of night.

How black this crow,
sitting silent on the branch.

But how its grey beak points.
How its red eye looks and looks,
O river of a thousand faces.

Chikkiah's the crow, looking and looking. At the river with a thousand faces, *his* river. His lord and friend. In the depths of this river, his father's anger, his own memory and sadness, can turn into hope. Death can become life. And the river may tell him, it must tell him, how this is to be done.

Should I stay here,
look at you,
pray?
Or come to you?

Tell me what to do,
O river of a thousand faces.

Sometimes Chikkiah goes to the shack in the fields, spends an hour or two with Rangayya, helping him weave his baskets, or keeping him company. When Parvatamma returns from the field, she invariably says, 'Mahadevi, bring Chikkiah something to eat.' Mahadevi obeys; but when her mother is not looking, she grins mischievously at Chikka, the smile-equivalent of sticking out her tongue.

Once Mahadevi makes her way to the river bank, a large bundle of clothes hung over a shoulder. She reaches the thick wall of creepers, densely pink with trails of tiny, delicate flowers. Past the creepers and the whip-like roots hanging from trees, there's a tall muddy slope. She always runs down this slope. Always she feels the rush and thrill of that downward run, then the magical reward of the river coming into view. Now, before she can tackle the slope, she hears a voice. It's a man singing. The voice rises like a light wind and fills the air. Mahadevi stands behind the curtain of creeper, listening.

This potter hums with spinning wheel,
that cobbler drones a note for each nail ...

Mahadevi takes one step then another. She negotiates the muddy slope cautiously, afraid any noise, even her breath, will stop his singing. She sees a spiny clump of a bush at the bottom of the slope. She crouches behind it, looks.

Chikkiah is on his haunches, squeezing out one wet cloth after another. On a slab of stone to his side, there's a pile of clothes, each squeezed out and twisted into a thick rope, waiting to be untwisted and dried. There are other people in the distance, but Chikkiah looks like he is all alone in the world, with no one to speak to but the river.

Mahadevi shivers. Then she hears his voice again and she makes herself go still. She looks. She can hear better if she looks hard at the naked back, the bare shoulders and arms. They glisten wet-black in the sunshine. Can she see his muscles rippling even at this distance, or the sweat on his skin glinting like silver? If only she could see his throat too, and the face above it. If he would turn around she would be able to see his singing mouth. But he doesn't turn around, he doesn't look up. He opens another bundle, pulls out more clothes. He sings to himself, or to the river, as he beats cloth against rock like a steady drumbeat.

This potter hums with spinning wheel,
that cobbler drones a note for each nail.
The weaver's song twines thread
  with thread.
I too sing when cloth slaps stone.

But you, you don't raise your voice.

My lord, my friend:
You're the song,
the song that sings itself,
O river of a thousand faces.

Chikkiah gets up, spreads the smaller pieces of clothing on stones and rocks. Then he stretches out several yards of red cloth and hangs it on a rope tied between two trees. The red curtain flutters as Chikkiah hums,

You're the song,
the song that sings itself,
O river of a thousand faces.

Mahadevi waits till he walks away. Then she runs across, drops her bundle near the first cloth-covered stone and runs back up the slope, afraid he will see her, afraid he will find out she has been there all this time, listening to him.

Chikkiah smiles when he finds the bundle. He knew there was someone behind the bush. He goes there now, looks at it to see what it can tell him. He sees a strip of yellow cloth, carelessly dropped on the ground. He recognises it as Mahadevi's, feels a sharp thirst. He picks up the cloth, takes it to his throat, holds it there. His sweat turns cool. Who would have thought a scrap of cloth, bright as sunshine, could quench his thirst so easily?

The river unfolds songs, prayers and stories all the time. But for now, Chikkiah can only hear the stories that are peopled by one small person. Chikkiah makes his way to Rangayya's shack, the fresh bundle of clothes cradled tenderly in his arms.

He loves Rangayya and Parvatamma, but today he is happy to see that Mahadevi is outside the shack. Before he goes in to sit with Rangayya, he can talk to her. Look at her.

Mahadevi is tending to the small patch of greens she is growing, scolding the hen and two new chicks running helter-skelter, getting in her way. She chases them away, laughing, then kneels at her patch again. The chicks seem to know the scolding is part of the fun. They return, tumble in between the sprouting bursts of green. She chases the chicks again, laughs again. She finally looks at him, as if she has only just noticed his standing there with the bundle in his arms, staring at her.

'I heard you sing,' she says, coming to the point like a quick arrow.

'I know.' Where has his voice gone, why is he whispering as if he is telling her a secret?

'I have a—I too have one for you,' she says.

'You have one?' he asks, wanting to smack himself for sounding like a silly echo.

'A song.' She pulls out a weed from the patch and throws it aside with a flourish.

'Sing it for me?' There, his voice has come back, she won't think he is an idiot.

'I can't sing.' She picks up one of the chicks and strokes it. The other chick is happy to be ignored; it's pecking at the seedlings.

Chikkiah waits.

'But this is what I have for you.' She says in a sing-song voice,

The seed pierces the land,
travels to its heart.

(The chick is struggling to jump off her palm, join the other. She keeps it prisoner, stroking it firmly.)

That's where it sprouts,
The lord's burst of green,

(She kisses the chick and sets it down. It scurries away into the patch.)

Mahadevi looks at Chikkiah, then adds meaningfully, 'O river of a thousand faces.'

'The river and the line don't belong to me,' he tells her. 'They're yours too.'

The river holds every colour, it is nothing but colour. So is the cloth Chikkiah beats with passion, squeezes out till his heart races, then stretches out wide, wider. There's a red curtain, its edges marked by mustard lines. There's a blue blue one, the sky's faithful mirror. And here, here is Mahadevi's cloth, clean and fresh, exactly the colour of saplings. It's a field. No, it's a river, a green river. No, it's not. It's neither field nor river, it's Mahadevi. He moves closer to the hanging cloth. He shuts his eyes, feels the fluttering on his face, his stomach, his thighs. He can see the cloth draped on her. No, he can see it unwrapping itself. The bit over her shoulder slips. It bares her neck first, then the meeting point of tender hillocks, then the belly. It hangs there for a moment, but it knows the way it has to unravel, this cloth, how to uncover field, mud, reveal the skin underneath. Can skin be so smooth, can it glisten like this? This deep brown land waiting for him to discover it, inch by inch. Her land of skin. A river of skin, a thousand lamps lit on the bed in its depths.

That thing you do
when wet cloth
is stretched tight in air,
a sheet of field
to lie on.

That thing you do then.
Will you do it again?

Chikkiah runs to the river, plunges into its arms, swims hard as if swimming for his life.

He has to talk to someone. Not one of the wise ones, certainly not Elder Brother, whom he loves, but whose love he doesn't want to test with his little troubles. How can he talk about Mahadevi, his mind clogged with Mahadevi, to men whose minds roam free, see nothing but spirit in every tree and pot and spear and body?

Chikkiah seeks out Puttanna. Earthbound Puttanna, who curses, spits *and* prays like a man who always drinks deep.

'Brother,' says Chikkiah, 'I can't think straight. I see her everywhere, in every bit of cloth, every stone, every field, every face of the river.' His voice dips. 'I—I see her skin. Bare. Waiting for me.'

Chikkiah looks at Puttanna, silent for once, then hangs his head. 'Is this wrong? How do I heal myself, Brother?'

Puttanna puts his arms around him. Chikkiah can smell his sour sweat; it's an infinitely comforting smell.

'No,' says Puttanna. 'No, no, no, Chikkiah.'

Chikkiah tries to pull away. He doesn't know what he expected, but he feels a sharp twinge of disappointment.

Puttanna will not let him go. 'Come here. Hold fast. No, my boy, it's not wrong. It's not wrong. Skin, bare or clothed. Youth, beauty, enjoyment. And lust, and fucking—' he grins at Chikkiah, 'are all part of the same thing. How can it be wrong? How can anything that breeds only enjoyment, only love and friendship, be wrong?'

Chikkiah is almost weeping with relief. He's close to tears, but he's also laughing. So is Puttanna. They walk to the river. The water is lit a mysterious pink in memory of the sun that has just drowned. They wade into the water, splash each other like children.

'Skin, eh, skin!' teases Puttanna, slapping a wide arc of water so it flies sideways onto Chikkiah's face.

'Yes. Yes,' shouts Chikkiah, grabbing Puttanna by the head and dunking him in the water, then pulling him up and kissing the spluttering face. 'Yes! Puttanna, my beloved fool, skin.' He stops, turns solemn. 'Mahadevi,' he says under his breath like a secret prayer. Puttanna hears him and he too turns solemn. He holds Chikkiah tight. The indulgent river watches them, used to keeping a friendly eye on all couples, men or women.

> The branches hanging over your wet body:
> they have gazed at you for so long.
> Do they strain
>   Downward,
> Do they long to
> float, swim,
>   flow,
>   move,
> O river of a thousand faces?

Chikkiah can feel the light spreading itself across his face. There's an arm resting lightly across his chest. He can feel the warmth by his side. It's firm and shapely, this warmth called Mahadevi. Even before he opens his eyes, Chikkiah knows what the morning will bring: a day like a tender leaf, still damp with its afterbirth. A day with a husband and a wife. Mahadevi, his wife. He, her husband! Chikkiah opens his eyes wide. She is still asleep. Later she will be annoyed he did not wake her, but how can he? She looks as if she is dreaming of the child who is curled up, quiet and peaceful, in her swelling stomach. He kisses the stomach lightly, slips out of her embrace.

He makes his way to Rangayya's shack to check if there are any morning chores before he collects today's wash. Outside the shack, Parvatamma is already at work. He takes the broom from her. She nods; she took some time to get used to the idea of Mahadevi marrying Chikkiah, but Rangayya had no doubt from the beginning. He looked pleased when Puttanna spoke for Chikkiah, as if this was one more test he would pass to get closer to heaven. Parvatamma wanted to ask about Chikkiah's family, the village he had left behind, what relatives he had. But Rangayya stopped her. 'We are his relatives, all of us in Anandagrama. Who else do we need?'

It was as simple as that. Chikkiah, washerman by the river, regular at Anandagrama, maker of homely lines, singer of humble songs, guardian of his father's drum, was now a son-in-law. He and Mahadevi had a shack of their own, not too near but not too far from her parents. Chikkiah's drum played a new beat of four syllables: Ma-ha-de-vi. The drum may have got stuck there, but Chikkiah and Mahadevi were learning new beats, new words, new ideas, all the time.

The coucal repeats
    over and over
the same one-syllable argument.

Green and yellow leaf
    damp with night
see light at the same moment.

The slim-lighted sky has seen
and heard it all before.

But how new
this breaking of dawn,
the first morning every morning,
O river of a thousand faces.

The river with a thousand faces

1

Ramesha and Ravi are at the Bhim Shakti meeting. They hear several students speak at the meeting, but it's a young teacher who impresses Ravi the most. Senthil teaches physics; but everyone calls him just Senthil, not Professor. He is dark, tall and painfully thin; Ravi can see a hard knob moving up and down his neck as Senthil speaks. His voice is not loud, but every word is clear. 'We are not here because of someone's kindness, or some god, or some quota. We are here because we have the right to be here.'

Ravi feels a twinge of gladness. It's like feeling he's in the right place after all.

'Remember how hard it was for people like us—for Bahujan—to even go to schools. Now that we are here, in colleges and universities, or in the professions, can we forget what Babasaheb Ambedkar told us to do? To educate, agitate, organise?'

This word *Bahujan*: it sounds bigger than Dalit. Ravi is not clear how many people it has to make room for. He is going to find out though, he's going to learn all about it.

At the end of the meeting, Senthil takes centre stage again, but this time, he doesn't speak. He sings.

Just yesterday I read their history
and found I was missing.

My grandfather in his soiled dhoti,
my mother working on all fours,
my brother beaten to death.
I couldn't find them.

All I found were words like walls.

Today I tell you:
Your history has too many missing people.
My words, my history, will break your walls.
My people will break your walls.

The man can speak *and* sing. Ravi is mesmerised. At the end of the song, Senthil holds up his arm like a flag and shouts: *Jai Bhim!* Everyone takes up the call. The room fills; it resounds with many voices, but oh, how it sounds like just one big voice to Ravi!

At night, Ravi lies in bed, wide awake. The words and ideas he has heard fill him with energy rather than anger. It's a good feeling; Senthil's song plays in his mind, keeping him awake and ready.

Suddenly he thinks of Satya, the poet among the three of them. The poet and the medical student. For the last few months, Ravi has almost wished he could be jealous of Satya. But how can anyone know Satya and not like him? Not admire him? Ravi reaches for his phone so he can email Senthil's song to Satya.

The narrow light seeps in shyly through the window. An early bird whistles sharply: *anatomy class today*. Not just a class, but a test. Satya jumps up, grabs his towel, soap, toothpaste and toothbrush. It's better this way. It's barely dawn, but at least he won't have to hang around outside the common bathrooms, hear a snide remark behind him in the queue—*So SCs have started bathing every day?*

He may be the only person awake in the world. Rahul has not even stirred—he's fast asleep, though he has travelled all over his bed in the course of the night. He lies diagonally across the bed, his face as well as his body covered with a thin sheet.

Bathed, dressed, Satya sits at his table, revising the portion for the test, the muscles of the face. He has learnt every word of it the night before; it's just that he doesn't want to take a chance with Dr Sharma, the anatomy professor who likes to pretend there is a blank space where Satya sits.

Half an hour later, Satya can't sit still. A new day is unfolding itself outside the window. He can refuse to go to the window, but he can see the trembling slab of light on the floor, teasing him. He can hear the birds calling to each other. Satya can't bear it. He's filled with energy. His heart is racing, telling him to live, *live*. He gets up and races downstairs, unlocks his cycle, and sails down the road.

He reaches the pond. As usual, there is no one there, just a couple of white egrets feeding intently at its edge. Satya lays the cycle on the ground, then lies down nearby, gazing at the cloudless sky. How clear it is, this blue hood of emptiness! He hears a cock crow somewhere. It tells him the world is vast enough for him to find a place in it. But first he must do really well in the test today, get past the hurdles Dr Sharma scatters in his path; he must make sure he passes all his papers in the midterm exam, even the anatomy paper.

He can do it. He can find that place patiently waiting for him to come claim it. Satya gets to his feet, picks up the cycle. A light breeze rustles leaves, stirs the water in the pond.

Satya takes one last look, then pedals as if his life depends on it. He can do it; he *will* do it.

He hangs on to this feeling in class as he answers the questions. Luckily he does not have to speak. He can write, and the words, the longest of English and Latin words, medical words, come to him though he knows Dr Sharma's cold eyes are resting on him a little too often. He's midway into the test paper when Dr Sharma walks up to his desk. 'This is not a good place for you to sit,' he says. He never uses Satya's name, only *you* or *he*. 'Go to the back row. That's empty. There's less chance of copying if you're sitting there.' Satya picks up his papers, makes his way to the last row. His face is aflame. But he's not going to let shame—or Dr Sharma—stop him from answering the rest of the paper. He sits down, bends over the paper.

The next day, he sees that all his efforts were wasted. When he goes forward to collect his corrected paper, Dr Sharma gives him a quick look of triumph. 'You may think you have brains,' the look says. 'But I know better. You've just about passed this time. Next time, you will fail.'

What can he do now, who can he speak to? Satya picks up his phone, keys in Ravi's name. He longs to hear Ravi's cheerful, confident voice, telling him, 'Of course you can complain. We aren't going to get a thing without fighting for it.' But Ravi doesn't know what it feels like here. What it feels like to be told, in so many ways, that he's strayed into the wrong place.

Satya puts away his phone, walks to the library.

He does not have the words to speak to Ravi or Asha. Or wait, he has the words. More than enough words. But these words—the ones that do not come out of his textbooks—make a heavy burden when they come together. How can he take them off his shoulders, shift them to someone else? And that too someone he cares about, who cares about him? Someone who may have his or her own unspoken burden of words?

How can he, for instance, describe Dr (Professor) Sharma? He would have to explain to Ravi and Asha why nightmares do not live only in the dark, when the mind may travel to dangerous places. Dr Sharma stalks Satya's days, in the anatomy class and out of it. Satya's nightmare is a thin-lipped man; every now and then, he purses his lips fastidiously as if everything around him is dirty and he is afraid of being infected. He looks completely lipless in those moments.

Satya can't describe Dr Sharma to Ravi or Asha, but he can write to the diary Asha has given him. Satya has to speak to *someone*. Later that evening, he opens the diary, writes on a fresh page.

> The muscles of the face are unique. Most of the other muscles connect to bones, move only bones. But facial muscles mostly connect bones to skin. *Zygomaticus major. Orbicularis oris.* (There is unexplored poetry in the names of these muscles.) When muscles like these pull on the skin, they can create what appears to be an infinite number of facial expressions.
>
> Dr Sharma's muscles, the muscles on his face. What do they do when he looks at my face? What does his *levator labii superioris alaeque nasi* do? It raises his upper lip. It dilates his nostril. When I answer a question in class, or when he reads my assignment, his *levator anguli oris* also begins to work. His *nasolabial* furrow, from the side of the nose to the upper lip, deepens. That's when I can see disdain on his face; contempt. He doesn't

> have to speak to say: 'Let me see how you get your MBBS.'

Ravi has forgotten, for the time being, both the MBBS that escaped him and the zoology that he has in hand. He is studying with an English dictionary by his side, but what he is reading with such concentration is what the physics professor, Senthil, has told him to read.

> On coming into effect in 1950, the Indian Constitution addressed the needs of large sections of the Indian population who had been traditionally marginalized. The Constitution described these as Scheduled Castes (SCs) and Scheduled Tribes (STs). The terms are from the time when these communities were enumerated in schedules prepared for the Colonial India Act of 1935.

Strange, that place where his second name was born, well before he was. Ravi can't quite take this in.

> The Constitution abolished untouchability. It also provided measures to protect and develop these communities. One of these measures was the policy of reservation for SCs and STs—a fixed percentage of openings for them in government-funded educational institutions and state employment.

Ravi's attention wanders. He turns pages. Then his eyes light on a quotation from Ambedkar's *Annihilation of Caste*: 'Turn in any direction you like, caste is the monster that crosses your path. You cannot have political reform, you cannot have economic reform, unless you kill this monster.'

A monster. The monster that walls in Ravi, Satya, Asha, thousands and thousands of people like them, in settlements, colonies, quotas, 'traditional' occupations; the monster that walls them out of their own lives. To have it spoken like this, to name the monster, fills Ravi with strange elation. It is a monster, yes; he knows how ugly it is, how violent, how cunning. But if he learns everything he can about the monster, won't that make him a better fighter?

Ravi turns back to the book.

The very next day, he is called to battle. There have been a couple of abusive messages posted on social media questioning Senthil's qualifications as a professor. The first of the messages is by a student of the university.

So-called professor Senthil does everything but physics. Supposed to have a doctorate in physics. How did he get degree? Tricks and bribery? Misusing quota? Shows how merit is dying, our jobs taken away.

The student's post was promptly shared by a person who calls himself Shankar@hindupatriot. He also added some abuse of his own.

This casteist bastard Senthil talks about caste all the time, or blames Hindus. Covering up his ignorance about physics, what he is supposed to be teaching. Talking about caste instead, dividing Hindu family.

There's to be a meeting, maybe a protest march. Ravi is too new to the cause to do more than help make placards and post messages on social media. But this is the right time for him to take out his drum.

He pulls the suitcase out from under his cot, and takes out the two sticks, one long, one short, and the sturdy flat drum that used to belong to his great grandfather.

Ravi remembers his grandfather telling him in his wheezing breathless voice, 'My father used to carry it with him when he would get called to a funeral. Only our people beat the drum at funerals.' His grandfather had stopped to cough; Ravi knew the old man was very sick, so he waited patiently for him to go on. 'See, you hold it between your hands, like this, and you can rest it on the left arm. Do you want to try?'

Ravi had taken the drum. The minute he took stick to cowhide, he had fallen in love with the bold sound the drum made. His grandfather had smiled at him. 'Do you want it? You can have it when I am dead.'

Ravi was ecstatic.

'But remember, my boy, the drum doesn't make us who we are. I refused to do what my father did. I was ready to do anything else, break stones, carry them like a donkey. But I was not going to play the drum. My father—he didn't say anything but he must have felt bad. But now I can tell you: there's nothing wrong with the drum. It's not something to be ashamed of. You can chase birds away from the fields with it; you can make the work go faster. You can call people to gather where you want when you beat this drum.'

His grandfather had taught Ravi how to play it. And, as promised, when the old man died, the drum had become Ravi's.

Ravi now wipes the drum carefully, hits it with the two sticks. Yes, it sounds just as he remembers it. Even though he has not hit hard, it speaks clearly. Its voice is strong. It speaks of power, not shame.

All day Asha has felt troubled. Is she imagining things? Why, of all the students in her class, was she singled out, chosen to clean what Mrs Kumari calls the sanitary annex?

The class had settled down for a boring dictation of the text. But today, Mrs Kumari had other plans. 'We will practise the Fundamentals of Nursing today, not just talk about it,' she announced. 'I will choose ten of you. Please follow me to the ward. The others, please read the next chapter, your turn will come tomorrow.'

Once they were at the ward, she had divided the ten of them—or nine of them, leaving out Asha—into three groups. 'Every woman,' she said, 'should learn the art of cleaning. She has to learn to keep a home clean. Just like that, every nurse should know how to keep her ward clean. We must practise this so we can learn how to do it properly.'

She had distributed tasks to the three groups: 'Three of you check on the linen. You three, go inspect the kitchen. And the last three, clean the ward.' The girls had melted away. Mrs Kumari looked at Asha, the only one left, as if surprised to see her there. Then she said in a thin voice, 'The care of the sanitary annexe is very important. Wash all the bedpans and urinals thoroughly, then the walls and floors of the bathroom.'

Asha had worked alone for hours. The bedpans and urinals smelt no matter how many times she cleaned them, but it wasn't the cleaning Asha minded so much. Why did she have to be a group by herself and why did she get the dirtiest of the jobs? Was this a quiet way to let her know that caste lived even here, among the sisters of mercy?

Now, as she heads to her hostel room, all she wants is to be alone and quiet. Hopefully Priya will be, as she usually is these days, in someone else's room.

But when she lets herself into the room, Priya is there

in bed, the sheet drawn all the way to the top of her head. Should she mind her own business? Asha hesitates, then goes up to the bed, lifts the top of the sheet gently. Priya is awake. She looks at Asha with such misery that she doesn't need to say anything. Asha can see she is trying to stop herself from shivering.

'Do you want me to call your guardian?' Asha asks Priya.

'No, I don't want to go there.'

Asha waits. How can anyone prefer being sick in the hostel room to being looked after in that comfortable flat?

'The old man,' Priya whispers. 'Auntie's father-in-law. He looks at me in a strange way. He brushes my arm or my shoulder every time he walks past. I'm scared of him.'

It's the same man who had asked Asha what caste she was the time she went with Priya to her guardian's home for lunch.

For the rest of the evening, Asha has some more nursing practice. She bathes Priya's head with a cold wet towel; once the fever breaks, she changes Priya's sweaty nightie for a fresh one. At one point, Priya takes hold of Asha's hand. 'Asha, I am—.' She doesn't know what she is, but her eyes speak a silent word or two.

'Just go to sleep, I'm here if you need anything,' says Asha. Priya nods and tries a watery smile.

It's been a bad day. But by the time she stretches out in bed, Asha feels, strangely enough, that she is not always alone when she's away from home.

2

Kannadeva, who was a minor saint-poet just a year back, has suddenly grown. There's every possibility that he may keep growing, at least the saintly part of him, and become larger than life.

Krishna has been speaking here and there on Kannadeva, at a seminar, a conference, in universities and in 'public meetings'. His monograph, based on his findings at the Institute of Devotional Culture, is almost done. In a week or two, he can send it to his usual publisher.

The Kannadeva site set up to protect Hindu saints from 'Hindu-haters such as P.S. Krishna' is flourishing, calling for a celebration of Kannadeva's alleged 900th birth anniversary.

And the Sagara lake statue controversy has taken a new turn. The Devapura Hindu Sene has decided that the statue of King Sriramadeva should stand on the walker's trail round the lake. Their energies have shifted to a new plan for the middle of the lake: a statue of Kannadeva rising out of the water. The Municipal Corporation, still eager to please its current masters, is pushing for a budget of 18.5 crores. The pedestal has already been sanctioned.

'Not bad for a saint,' says Natraj to Krishna as they walk with Subbiah and Hasan round the lake.

But Krishna's own resurrection of Kannadeva is not so

easily sanctioned. The editor at the publishing house he has been associated with for many years used to be Krishna's student. He visits Krishna at home now, looking sheepish. 'Professor, there may be a problem with the book,' he says, unable to meet Krishna's eyes. He is making believe his coffee needs to be examined, very closely, before he drinks it.

'A problem?' asks Krishna, though he is already preparing himself to hear the worst. Preparing for the worst doesn't help when he actually hears it.

'We have been advised to hold off publishing,' the editor says. He doesn't say who the advice is coming from.

'Hold off? Does that mean you will publish it after a few months? When all this nonsense has died down?'

The young man has finished his coffee. He is forced to look up. He looks miserable; in a few minutes, he may burst into tears. 'I don't know. It depends—' he ends lamely.

There's no point losing his temper with this fellow. There's no point asking him, 'What is so dangerous about my little book? Why are you so afraid?'

Subbiah, Hasan and Natraj have forgotten all about statues, whether of kings or saints. Their morning walks with Krishna have become meetings for action. Hasan comes up with the simple answer. 'Self-publish,' he says. 'Who's to stop us?'

The 'us' warms Krishna; he turns to Hasan with affection.

Hasan grins, pointing at Natraj. 'Have you forgotten our own publishing and printing baron?'

Natraj is annoyed with himself for not thinking of it first. He makes up for being slow with being thorough. He goes into the smallest details he can think of. He displays fonts and page styles on his phone for Krishna to choose from.

By the time they get to the green bench to take a post-walk breather, it's all decided. Only one question remains, and Natraj is too kind to bring it up. Who will pay the costs?

Krishna has already thought of this. There's the money that has just come in post-retirement, his life savings through the public provident fund.

But Shanta will not hear of it. 'Your PPF is more than mine,' she says. 'You've taught longer. Let's save yours and use up mine. Please—I want to back your book. I want to be a proper part of it.'

She refuses to listen to any arguments from Krishna. 'Go do your work,' she says. 'Go take a last look at the manuscript before sending it off to Natraj.' They both agree they won't discuss this with the children, especially not Ram.

Krishna goes back to the manuscript. As always, it's the songs that give him the most pleasure. Framed as they are now, as many people's voices singing the Anandagrama aspiration to be caste-free, they move him almost to tears. Their literary quality, or the lack of it, does not matter. What apology is required when passion and hope bring words, lines and voices together?

He pauses at a page with a cautionary poem by Mahadevi. It asks a sharp question he has to acknowledge, and it has nothing to do with literary merit.

It's the firefly season.
A week or two
before worms crawl to naked earth.

But look, O lord,
Look, beloved friend.

These children
chase flitting stars,
jump, run this way then that,
grabbing fistfuls of air,
O river of a thousand faces.

Is he grabbing fistfuls of air like those children? Krishna's closest friends, starting with Shanta, will support him in whatever he does. In a way, that makes it more difficult because it is his decision alone. His decision. But the truth is he can no longer separate all the strands. They have got glued together in such a way they cannot be unravelled. Chikkiah, Mahadevi, Kannadeva, all of Anandagrama's poets. Krishna and his little book. Krishna's fear of what the self-appointed guardians of saints and poets, of all Hindus, might do. And Krishna's certainty that he can no longer teach or write or read poetry, that the university can no longer run, that all of them, his students and colleagues, his friends, his children and grandchildren, cannot live in a country where they are told when to be silent, when to speak and what to say.

What's to be done but grab what fistfuls of air he can?

Krishna goes back to the first page. He reads the monograph carefully, checking for typos, sequence and flow, infelicities, any overreach by way of linkage and speculation.

Someone else is collecting bits and pieces of the Book of Kannadeva, not the palm leaves or the 'original text', but Krishna's comments in seminars and lectures.

Guru (Sri Sri Sri) Santosh is in a state that combines, in equal measure, anger and excitement. The charges against Krishna are clear. The so-called professor has described Kannadeva's glorious choice of Jal Samadhi as suicide.

This is a minor offense compared to what Krishna has said about some palm leaves he claims to have found. Krishna has brazenly claimed that Kannadeva was called Kannappa in his earlier life, and that he was the son of a washerman whose father skinned cattle. Santosh feels a rumbling in his stomach. Is there no end to this distortion of saints' lives? Of Hindu history? The arrogance of these Hindu-bashers! Of course those padris and mullahs will do anything to disrupt the march to a glorious Hindu nation. That goes without saying. But these rats at home, the rats within the Hindu fold, are the worst of all. This man's name is Krishna. He teaches epics like the Mahabharata, the body of wisdom with the shining soul of the Bhagavad Gita. Isn't he ashamed to foul it like this? Shit in the most sacred room of his own house?

This is an open challenge. He, Santosh, Guru to so many, cannot ignore it. It is also a chance to make an example. Traitors, like rakshasas, must be suitably dealt with.

Santosh runs a mental eye down a list of dependable allies. Should he have a word with Pramod or Rishikant? Both have been involved in a training camp. Or any of the other groups in the network? Santosh surfs the net as he thinks about this. He comes across a piece written by a leading light from one of the groups he has been considering. The piece discusses Kannadeva's poems, word for word, to show that he came from a simple but upper caste family that fed poor Brahmins and worshipped all cows.

Santosh's nostrils flare. It's all very well to write an article, but is that enough? Analysing poetry, finding the truth behind a song! It's just not enough. No, he has to find better allies. As for these talkers, they will help create the right climate. Let them make their noise. That's groundwork.

For real seva that will take the country a foot closer to Hindu nationhood, no word, no poem or song is enough.

He inhales sharply, feels his stomach muscles tighten. This Kannadeva-Krishna business proves what he has been saying for a long time. The Hindu man is slowly becoming soft; he's turning into a woman. He talks when he should act.

For now Santosh needs to keep his own counsel. His is the head; that's what matters. How hard can it be, finding the right body, spurring it to action?

He will plant the seed. The sevaks, his disciples, the allies, named and unnamed, will do the rest. One sevak is all they need to do the job.

But first there is the editorial team waiting to meet him. Santosh joins the four young men waiting with their laptops at the conference table. They stand, heads bowed, as he approaches; one by one, they touch his feet. One of them pulls out the larger chair at the head of the table.

They get to the day's business. All the laptops have been opened to the home page of the Hindu Rashtra Sabha. The Guru has to be shown proof of the Sabha's power, *his* power, before they get approval for the new posts they have in mind. They show Guruji a new photo they posted yesterday. The title is 'Swami Sivaganga showering flowers on the Blessed Guruji (Sri Sri Sri) Santosh'.

The photo: the wet orange tilak bisects Santosh's forehead. Sadly, he's balding. There's only so much Photoshop can do. The wisps of hair, dyed black, have been bravely combed so as to make a fragile bridge across the top of his head. (When the wind blows, this bridge flutters like a banner. That's why fans are forbidden in Guruji's reception chamber.) In this picture taken yesterday, Guruji is seated on a chair—his knees no longer let him sit on the floor though he often writes about the benefits of yoga. His head is bent at a modest (but not humble) angle, his hands come together in a Namaste. He's wearing a garland of jasmine and red roses; a disciple is pouring red, yellow and white petals on his head.

One member of the team, the art director, describes his idea for another image, an imaginative one to go with an article that has just come in. 'Guruji,' he says, 'we would like to have your exalted self standing in rosy early morning light by the river.'

'What river,' asks Santosh. He believes in keeping track of detail.

'Well, maybe not a river, that's not important. But we thought there could be some suggestion of water, a lot of it behind you to match the sky above. This will suggest the vast universe in your care.'

Santosh nods; he has a quick imagination, it's not hard for him to see things described to him. The art director, encouraged, goes on, 'There's a wide spotlight pouring light on you. There are flowers floating inside the beam of light, they're falling from the hands of the crowned gods and goddesses standing in the sky.'

Santosh nods again. 'Make it six. Four gods and two goddesses. And the article? The one that goes with this picture?'

The editor reads out the piece entitled *Guru (Sri Sri Sri) Santosh's five central principles of a good Hindu life.*

'1. Live every day by the truth. Where is the truth? In the Vedas. Who will show you how to find it? The Guru. The Vedas are the truth. The Guru is the truth.

'2. Keep close to the centre of the universe. If it is true that the earth has both land and water; if it is true that gods and saints stand around all the land and water, encircling it with their rules and laws; then it is true that Guru (Sri Sri Sri) Santosh is in the centre of it all, between land and water.

'3. Make sure positive energy defeats negative energy. How to release the positive energies of a true Hindu life? By worshipping the gods, performing regular pujas, donating to the temples, and staying pure. Where do negative energies come from? From unclean Hindus. From those who offend the gods, saints and gurus. From those who pray to Allah or Christ. All these release terrible negative energy. It is the sacred duty of every Hindu to combat negative energy with the power he gains from his Guru's positive energy.

'4. Learn the fighting power of positive energy. The Guru is the incarnation of Hindu energy. He holds positive energy in his breath. He is the fountain of wisdom on how to conduct warfare on negative energies.

'5. Direct all spiritual efforts at the obstacles in the path of the glorious Hindu Nation. Guru (Sri Sri Sri) Santosh, a spiritual authority on positive energy, has proved that our goal on earth is Hindu Rashtra. Guruji has described this Rashtra as a land with no borders, a spiritual experience that will overcome all enemies and take over the land and water, not just in India but the whole world. Every Hindu must march toward this glorious nation, led by the truth that never changes, the Vedas and the Guru.'

'There must be some drawings of good Hindu men, women and children in the text,' Santosh says.

'Of course, Guruji,' says the art director, furiously keying in notes.

Santosh's day is full. His disciples, old and new, need constant guidance before they can become full-fledged servitors of the cause; real sevaks of Hindu Rashtra. There's so much for him to do. Santosh sighs, but then he considers the rewards of all this labour. He becomes more than Santosh in an instant, he becomes Guruji and Sri Sri Sri again. He can never do enough for his beloved sevaks, or for the glorious nation they are travelling to day by day.

Before he knows it, it's evening, that time when the light streaming in through the windows declares it is neither day nor night and anything is possible. Santosh sits with a small group of sevaks who have proved their devotion. His eyes move slowly from one to the other, then settle on Srikumar, the young man in the first row.

Srikumar wears a spotless white kurta pyjama. But though he is completely covered, Santosh can see the flat firm stomach, the straight back, the wide shoulders, the healthy muscles on the upper arms and thighs. He must be what, twenty-nine? Thirty? This is what a man should look like. This is how a man's body should be, waiting like a tightly wound snake, ready to uncoil when the time is ripe. But his mind? Is there strength there? Control? Can he be taken to the next stage of service?

He will concentrate on the Guru-disciple relationship today, Santosh decides. 'What is the difference between a student and a disciple?' he asks.

Srikumar listens intently.

'A student pays his fees then carries on his life away

from his teacher. The Guru is more than a teacher. A Guru is like a mother or a father. He's more. He cannot be paid or repaid in this life or the next. The disciple serves the Guru with love. Still, it's not enough. He has to do more. More. Even more.'

The word *more*, the more Santosh repeats it, mesmerises the sevaks in the room. Srikumar feels a flutter in his lower back then it disappears. He sits even more straight; *he* will do whatever the Guruji says, he will do more.

'What is the most sacred relationship? What is the only true relationship in the world?' Santosh looks at the silent disciples, one by one, saving Srikumar for last.

Santosh waits.

Srikumar says calmly—though his heart beats fast at being singled out—'The relationship between guru and disciple.' How those six words stretch between them, make a whole conversation, a spiritual exchange, augur a lifetime's worth of upliftment!

'Come to me, son,' says Santosh.

Srikumar gets up, goes to him. He bows, then falls at Santosh's feet.

It is strange, Srikumar thinks, this pride that fills him even as he lies flat on the floor near a pair of feet. He takes in the elegantly shaped feet, the marked arches, the sprig of hair on the big toes. His eyes have always been good at looking at the microscopic detail. Then he hears the Guru's voice, so low he could be whispering. 'May you build your strength and march ahead,' the Guru blesses him softly; so softly that the words are almost a secret between them.

3

Chikkiah carries baby Chandra, his and Mahadevi's piece of the moon, their firstborn. He cannot believe his luck. Can anyone have so much luck? Can he bear so much joy?

The days are full; there's plenty of work. He has clothes to wash, farm work to help with, and the whole world to show Chandra. He and Mahadevi line up a parade for Chandra, saying *See, see!* The world we have for you, every sprout and seed, every star and cloud in the sky, the tallest of tall trees, birds, cows, dogs, pigs, dragonflies, red and black ants racing between hills of their own making, insects that count every blade of grass in their way. The drum. The river. Their lord and friend. Words, words whispered, chanted, recited, sung. Chikkiah's words, Mahadevi's words. No wonder Chandra learns to sway on her unsteady legs, to dance even before she can walk.

Their piece-of-moon needs someone of her own to dance with. Chikkiah and Mahadevi oblige, provide her with a brother with equally chubby legs, always ready to move, crawl, walk, run, dance. Kannappa.

Their own Anandagrama is full. Mahadevi makes up songs for all of them. Chikkiah sings by day as he works, sings with his drum at night. Some of the words in his songs are his, some are Mahadevi's—he no longer knows which is whose. They complete each other's lines all the time, even when they are talking to each other about mundane things or tending to Chandra and Kannappa.

When they teach the children to swim, Mahadevi says to Chandra or Kannappa, whichever of the two is wriggling in her arms, 'There's a moon, little one, a silver face playing hide and seek in the water.' Chikkiah takes the baby from her, makes a steady raft under the little body with his arm, and croons, '*You're* the moon, little one. You're the moon the river has brought me.'

The days they can put aside work, he, Mahadevi, little Chandra, Kannappa the baby, proud grandparents Rangayya and Parvatamma, boastful uncle Puttanna, and the rest of the Fearsome Five, Siddha, Chenna and Gundanna, meet their brothers and sisters at Anandagrama. They speak, they listen to discussion, song, poetry, sometimes a debate. They cook and eat together.

Once Chikkiah saw an ex-Brahmin among them, still fat from his days of privilege, considering them. The ex-Brahmin had one eyebrow raised as if amused by their visible happiness. That night Chikkiah had a dream: the river was calm, too calm. It was asleep; it had stopped flowing so it could sleep. Then a spear rose out of the still waters. It was long and fierce; the spear seemed endless, it rose so high. Its sharp tip glinted red. And it dripped. Surely that is blood, thought Chikkiah in his dream, surely this spear has hurt someone. Who has it hurt? Whose blood is that? Then he woke. The night air was calm, though a sleepless crow cawed in the distance. Mahadevi slept facing him, her face bland and untroubled. Chandra was a little clinging spoon behind her mother. Kannappa was a happy frog between him and

Mahadevi, his knees bent to make a chubby bracket, his arms thrown up without a care. All was well. Chikkiah drifted back to sleep.

The days are full. There's work, song, prayer, talk, listening to talk in Anandagrama. The grandparents are there of course, Rangayya and Parvatamma; their shack is not too far from theirs. But most days, Chikkiah, Mahadevi, Chandra and Kannappa, and the land and trees and river, make up an almost complete universe. It's a murmuring, rustling universe that is never quiet, never still. There's the pair of hornbills that fly from tree to tree, flapping their heavy wings; they always fly together, this couple. There's the mongoose that moves through the tall grass; it moves sleekly though it looks like an overweight rat. There are the winding snakes, the cautious turtles. And all this teeming life is never quiet, they all have something to say: the rushing sound of the waterfall; the coucal's insistent call, as long drawn out as its tail; the consensual choruses of frogs and crickets; the sudden thud when a coconut falls to the ground.

In this place and time when the world says *life, life*, with every breath it takes, there's a cloudless day they will always remember. Or Chikkiah and Mahadevi will, and even Kannappa, though he is only seven years old at the time; except this day can only be remembered along with the week that will follow.

It's a cloudless day though it's the monsoon. The sun is at peace. A warm but not too warm light spreads itself on the river, the muddy bank, the coconut and mango trees and pink bauhinia. Chikkiah and Mahadevi dry the clothes that have been waiting for the rain to stop. Chandra and

Kannappa run around them. When chased away, they run along the riverside, shouting, laughing.

Chikkiah and Mahadevi can hear them. Chandra is making believe she can recite lines like the women in Anandagrama, sing like Mahadevi, play the drum like Chikkiah. She hits an imaginary drum in the air. She shrieks, 'O river! O river of a thousand faces.' Kannappa is behind her like a tail. He's not to be left behind, he's yelling, 'Faces, faces. Thousand faces.' It becomes a game, this repetition of a line. A competition to see who can say it more times, and faster. Chandra whirls to 'O river of a thousand faces, O river of a thousand faces.' The trees, the river in high tide, Kannappa, Mahadevi and Chikkiah are just quick flashes, images racing round and round Chandra as she chants, 'Oriverofathousandfaces, Oriverofathousandfaces.'

Kannappa can't do it. He bursts into tears, runs to Mahadevi.

The next day, the clouds are back in the sky. It pours. Chandra is burning with a fever. It does its work fast, this fever. It won't let her get up. It won't let her sleep or eat. In a week, she can't say a word, leave alone O river of a thousand faces, slow or fast.

It only takes a week. Every day the unending downpour adds to the rising water around their shack; it brings them a new, unfriendly river. Chikkiah does not leave the shack. He sits by Chandra in case she opens her eyes, says something, wants anything that will make her feel better.

It's the evening of the seventh day when Chandra goes. She dies as evening slips into night, though because it's raining so hard, afternoon, evening and night are the same. They all look like night. A stormy night.

'Is she sleeping?' whispers Kannappa.

'No,' says Mahadevi, dry-eyed and exhausted, taking Kannappa onto her lap.

Chikkiah can't bear to sit all night by a Chandra so unnaturally still. A look passes between Chikkiah and Mahadevi. Wordlessly they wrap up Chandra in a cloth. Outside, the water, the rain, the slushy mud, make sure they cannot go far. Chikkiah carries Chandra. Mahadevi and Kannappa follow, hand in hand. They trudge through the mud. By the time they get to the bauhinia tree, they are soaked. Rain, tears, they are one and the same. Mahadevi takes her limp piece-of-moon in her arms one last time while Chikkiah digs a small grave, not too deep. He wants Chandra to see the sky and the sun when it stops raining. He wants her to see the pink of the flowers when the bauhinia blooms again.

The next morning, the rain quietens down, settles into a respectful, soft-spoken drizzle. Chikkiah and Mahadevi are quiet. So quiet that Kannappa is afraid to speak. It's no use saying words aloud if Chandra can't hear them. It takes many weeks, many visits from Puttanna, consolation from Rangayya and Parvatamma, visits to Anandagrama, for the words to come back, to be spoken. At first the words are spoken only in their minds.

Chikkiah sits by the river at night, the drum silent by his side. The past floods his mind. Not the recent past—no, that's too raw. The generous river before him, the loving drum by him, help him go further, all the way back.

In a past life I was untouchable.
In a past life they smelt my shadow and fled.

In a past life the meat I ate was rotten.
In a past life I bathed in a stagnant pond.

That was the past.
Tie me, tether me so I don't stray there again.

Keep me here, in current and whirlpool,
O river of a thousand faces.

Mahadevi remains in the present. All her life is here, only now there's one unfillable hole. She goes past the bauhinia every day. She tracks each new flower that begins as a fleshy, purple-pink tube in the morning, unfurls stickily by the afternoon and, by late evening, is an over-large butterfly, the tips of its wings drooping delicately, making all kinds of promises. Will it be there the next morning? Or will it lie limp on the ground?

More and more, Mahadevi looks at sky and trees. She sings of the river but spends less time by its side. There are two trees near Chandra's bauhinia, one teak, the other, mango. Mahadevi watches them as the season turns. The leaves of the teak die a slow death. The large leaves turn brown; then they lose patches of skin. The leaves look ugly in the daytime, as if diseased. But as night arrives, they look like fine lace against the deepening blue of the sky. How tenacious they are, holding onto beauty and the last murmur of life. When they fall, the leaves slap the ground gently. They rustle when the wind kicks them around; they crunch when Mahadevi steps on them.

All this while, the mango tree stands nearby, flourishing. The mangoes are ripening; the tree looks smug. But Mahadevi can see the flying blue-black beetles, their wings whirring; she can hear them drone nonstop. They're drilling holes in the trunk, marking the days left to the tree. That's the time Mahadevi sings a new song for Kannappa.

It's the firefly season.
A week or two
before worms crawl to naked earth.

But look, O lord,
Look, beloved friend.

These children
chase flitting stars,
jump, run this way then that,
grabbing fistfuls of air,
O river of a thousand faces.

Grabbing fistfuls of air

1

Kannappa has grown. He looks older than his years, a child with a grown up face. He's too serious for a boy, but he also has all of Mahadevi's tender ways. When his grandmother Parvatamma sickens, he is her nurse. He moves to his grandparents' shack and insists on sleeping by Parvatamma. He sleeps little; mostly he sits by her, wiping her fevered face and limbs with a soft wet rag. She takes her last breath in his arms; it is he who plays the funereal role of the son. Rangayya, Chikkiah and Mahadevi weep, but Kannappa is dry-eyed. He leads them to the burial ground, a young messenger to death. On their return from the burial ground, he consoles the adults as if he is the adult, they his children.

Kannappa likes these good works. He likes helping Rangayya make his baskets, Mahadevi with her work in the field, and Chikkiah with his washing clothes by the river. But there is a little distance between Kannappa and this work, or between him and the people who perform it day after day. It's like he is only visiting them and is a well-behaved guest.

What Kannappa likes best is words. He collects them, stores them, examines them in secret, probing them for sounds and multiple meanings. Kannappa is taciturn, but he can surprise them by suddenly reciting lines Chikkiah has forgotten though he made them up. It's not just his prodigious memory. Sometimes, Kannappa takes a word or a phrase of Chikkiah's, or Mahadevi's, and returns ten for one, lines weighed with ideas. He makes riddles of their simple songs; he makes poetry out of them that they can barely understand.

Chikkiah and Mahadevi overflow with love. But there's an edge to their love for this wonder they have made between them. He is no longer a piece-of-moon they can hold in their arms, a body they can wash, cuddle, kiss. That other piece of the moon went first, it's buried under the bauhinia tree; it has become the bauhinia. Kannappa, no longer a piece, has the full moon to himself. More and more Kannappa is the moon in the sky that his parents can only admire from afar.

What can they do, how can they make Kannappa what he should be, *better* than them?

As usual, Chikkiah seeks out Puttanna.

Puttanna is greying. He looks as strong as ever, he is as loud as ever. But sometimes he sighs, or coughs, as if he knows the old Puttanna sneaked away when he was not looking. Mahadevi piles his plate with rice, pours a thin fish gravy over it and places a lota of water nearby.

'Puttanna,' says Chikkiah, 'Mahadevi and I want some advice.'

'Oh advice,' chortles Puttanna, rolling up the rice and gravy into great big dripping balls. 'That's cheap and easy. Ask, and I will give it to you without a fuss.'

'We have a dream,' begins Chikkiah. 'Or at least we have one for Kannappa.' He hesitates.

'Ah, a dream. What does the boy want now?' Puttanna slurps the last of the gravy off his hand, turns his wrist to see if he has missed a few drops. 'Bring it on, don't be afraid. I know all about dreams.'

'We want him to learn how to read and write,' Mahadevi interrupts.

Chikkiah nods. He looks a little alarmed, as if he has to convince himself that a son of his, however clever, can do such a thing.

'Yes, he's old enough, isn't he? Older than the other children in the monk-school, but he's a bright boy. He'll catch up in no time. Give me a week or two,' says Puttanna. He burps enthusiastically. 'Ah, Mahadevi, no one feeds me like you do.'

Three weeks pass by; they think he has forgotten. But has Puttanna ever failed them? Puttanna is, after all, the sort of hunter who can track down the most cunning of rats, catch hold of them. Is there anyone Puttanna does not know, anyone who does not owe him a favour for some mysterious good turn he has done them? He can talk to any man and make him believe Puttanna is his equal.

When he returns, Puttanna asks them to walk to the river with him. Chikkiah, Mahadevi and Kannappa follow him. Puttanna has not told them what or who waits for them at the river. But they sense it's something important, some big change is coming. They link hands for comfort.

There, at the bank, they see a tall man waiting for them. Puttanna greets him with folded hands. Standing next to Puttanna, the tall man's skin seems terribly pale. Maybe it's all the hours he spends indoors in study. Maybe the sun is afraid of touching him, he's so learned. He looks upper caste, but his chest has no sacred thread. Chikkiah feels reassured then tells himself not to be silly. Thread or no thread, of course he is upper caste. Did he think a cobbler would teach Kannappa how to read and write?

The tall man takes Kannappa to a rock some distance away, asks him questions. The child answers; his voice is like a flute playing softly. Sitting with Mahadevi and Puttanna, Chikkiah is too far away to make out every word. And what words he can hear merge into each other so they make no sense. But he can tell that Kannappa speaks with confidence. Kannappa can look into this great man's face and pass any test he sets. Why then does Chikkiah feel so sad, why are Mahadevi's shoulders drooping?

The tall man gestures to them. 'Pack his bundle,' he says, pointing to Kannappa. 'Get him ready early in the morning. Puttanna will bring him to me tomorrow.'

Chikkiah and Mahadevi thank him humbly. They have little to offer him other than thanks. Kannappa's quick answers, his precocious memory for words, his quickness to perform good works—all these will have to make up the gurudakshina. (Later, they will learn that Puttanna paid the gurudakshina. He refuses to tell them what it was, laughing off their questions.)

Puttanna is the only one to sleep that night. Chikkiah and Mahadevi lie awake, listening to Puttanna snore outside the shack. They have heard this cacophonous lullaby many times before and it has never bothered them. But tonight it keeps them awake. When the snoring pauses, they are on tenterhooks, waiting for it to begin again. That's the only way they are sure Puttanna is there, that morning will come, that Kannappa will get what he wants and what they want for him.

Kannappa is too excited to sleep. He lies between his parents, though he has forgotten how to cuddle. He fidgets every time his mother's arm steals around him. But he must have dozed sometime. By the time Mahadevi packs his bundle, Kannappa is fast asleep. She has to shake him awake, feed him with her fingers, making believe he is a baby one last time. Chikkiah looks as if he does not know what to do with himself. He sits there, watching them.

Then they are back at the river, Puttanna, Chikkiah, Mahadevi and Kannappa. Kannappa's bundle is small but they take turns carrying it, as if it's too heavy for one of them to carry it all the way. They go to the part of the bank Chikkiah and Mahadevi know best, the part with her slope, his stones; his trees with the lines of rope marrying them forever.

There's a boat there today though; and there's a ferryman in it. Chikkiah remembers Peddi, his own ferryman from long back. If only Peddi were here again, in charge of rowing Kannappa into the unknown. If only Elder Brother was in the boat too, ready to sing to Kannappa, see to his first crossing of the river. But this ferryman is a stranger. He sits in the boat, waiting for their goodbyes to end, trying not to let his impatience show.

Kannappa, impatient and fidgety all night, suddenly seems reluctant to get into the boat. He stands behind Mahadevi, hiding himself from the ferryman.

Puttanna goes around Mahadevi, peers into Kannappa's face. 'What's the matter, young man?' he asks, pretend-firm. 'Do you want to learn to read and write?'

'Yes,' mumbles Kannappa. Puttanna waves his hand in the air, as if amplifying the word for all of them. Father, mother and son stay where they are. Puttanna shakes his head at all three of them in mock exasperation. 'So?' he asks Kannappa, 'you don't want to leave your mother?'

The child's eyes overflow. Puttanna suddenly looks lost.

It's Mahadevi who decides it's time to let go.

She gently pushes Kannappa away from her. Her eyes are wet too, but her voice is decided. 'Kannappa, my son. Go, learn as much as you can. Learn everything we can't teach you.' The firm voice turns sweet, coaxing. 'Reading and writing! Wonders your father and I do not know, or your grandfather, or grandmother, or Puttanna here. Maybe you can write down your father's songs, maybe you can write down mine. Our words, our songs. Read them aloud and you won't be lonely. Maybe you can write your own and send them to us. Someone will read them out to us. We'll sing to each other even if we are far away from each other.'

Kannappa sniffs, turns away from her. He ignores Chikkiah and Puttanna, gets into the boat with the stranger. He does not look back.

2

All the pages have been edited. The manuscript is ready. It has remained untitled all this while though. Krishna has consulted Shanta and the walking group. He remains torn between the top two of the shortlist, *The People's Voice: The Singers of Anandagrama* and *Kannadeva's Family: The Poets of Anandagrama*. He finally decides on the latter in a somewhat unscholarly fashion. He's watching Shanta teach Chitthu how to re-pot a lush palm that has grown so well its roots have cracked the old pot. Shanta is in charge of the mud, Chitthu the sand. Chitthu looks solemn; he waits patiently for his turn then scoops up the sand with his hand, lets it pour through his fingers. Krishna thinks he has his answer. Could Kannadeva get to the 'people' before he got to his family? And were the people not his family?

It's as if the title has made the book real; it has brought home Chikkiah and his earthbound songs via Kannappa-Kannadeva to Krishna's own times. And the home, or the times, are not Krishna's alone. There's Shiva in the department, putting all other work on hold so he can help Prof sir. Shiva has already keyed in various versions for Krishna; some of it was painful because Prof really knows too many languages. But just keying it in has made Shiva feel he is part of Prof's project. The walking group is equally involved and excited. News Natraj refers to himself, Hasan and Subbiah as the 'publishing group'.

The publishing group's morning walk is now a meeting on the move. Natraj is constantly breathless from talking too much as he walks. Subbiah tries to calm him down every now and then in his usual gruff way. 'This is only the beginning,' he says, 'the book—and we—have a way to go.' Nobody is sure what exactly this means, but it only excites Natraj more, and it makes Hasan nervous. His friends have not remembered he is *Hasan*, but he knows, of course, that his fellow citizens will notice. He has only to look at what's been happening in the last couple of weeks in Sagara Lake.

There's a monster slowly pushing its way out of the lake at its very centre. Sagara is giving birth to a solid cement platform. The Devapura Hindu Sene has been appeased by the authorities. A press release has announced that in view of 'the people's sentiments', a solution to the lake-statue controversy has been found. A royal figure will come up near the lake by and by. But meanwhile, Saint Kannadeva, whom the Sene has recently claimed as one of their ancestors from the 'hoary past', will, over the coming months, emerge stony and voiceless from the lake. Two fountains are planned, one on either side of the statue; the water spouting from the fountains will be coloured saffron with electric illumination. For now, only the platform has been finalised by the design and execution team. The commissioned sculptor and his assistants are delaying the saint's statue, trying to make sense of the variety of Kannadeva portraits they have been given as models.

It disturbs Hasan, this concrete evidence of a rival to

Krishna's Kannadeva. Why aren't the others looking at what's happening in the lake, why aren't they connecting it to what they are doing with Krishna's manuscript? Krishna has told them about the occasional hate mail and threats, and they have all admired and encouraged his apparent disregard for 'unscholarly criticism'. (Hasan is also a teacher, though he teaches chemistry to large classes of first-year students in a small 'minority college'. Luckily, it has not occurred to anyone to critique, in a scholarly way or otherwise, how molecules bond with each other, or how compounds are made.) Natraj and Subbiah seem so preoccupied with Krishna's new, improved Kannadeva that they barely respond to the birth throes in the lake beyond a few disapproving noises. Hasan forces himself to turn away from the lake, listen to News Natraj.

'It's happening like clockwork,' Natraj reports. He has not looked at the updates from his WhatsApp groups for weeks. He wants to make sure all his attention is on the Plan of Action. The bills have been paid in advance thanks to Shanta's PPF withdrawal. There isn't enough money for a designer or artist, so the cover will make do with Natraj's typographic artistry with the words *Kannadeva's Family*.

'The proofs are due any day now,' Natraj tells Krishna.

Krishna looks childishly pleased. 'I'll read them carefully, and I'm sure Shanta will want to double-check,' he says.

The proofs come and go; the binder is at work. Then Hasan surprises them all by striking a deal with a distributor, and making a list of places to send the book for review. The reviews will take a while, they know, given that the book is not exactly bestselling material. As for a 'launch', Krishna insists it be a private one, at one of his home-on-Sunday lunches, with the guest list just a little bigger than usual.

It is a memorable occasion. As usual, Krishna's daughters and daughter-in-law have outdone themselves with the food. There's all kinds of conversation; it makes Krishna happy when he overhears a mildly argumentative discussion about university matters that have nothing to do with Kannadeva.

It's Shanta who brings Kannadeva back to the lunch. Or Kannappa's Chikkiah and Mahadevi. In a surprise performance, she sings two poems from Krishna's book, one by Chikkiah and one by Mahadevi. She sings both in Carnatic style, Chikkiah's in Kalyani ragam and Mahadevi's in Krishna's favourite ragam, Sahana. How strange, thinks Krishna, but what a marvel too—Shanta's voice brings together a music that has become identified with Brahmins with those words of longing for a better, more equal life! He looks tenderly at Shanta's throat, trembling with effort. That's the place, he thinks, where this kind of magic can happen; the throat that can only pray by singing of friendship and love. Even Chitthu has put aside his drum and is trying to climb onto his grandmother's lap. Krishna swallows the lump in his throat, takes Chitthu onto his own lap.

That evening, before they set out for Darling Ice Cream Parlour on their regular Sunday date, Shanta takes Krishna to the study, hands him a copy of the book.

'Hold it close to your heart,' says Shanta.

Krishna obediently holds the little book to his body, lets it rest for a minute on his gentle heartbeat.

'Now let it go,' says Shanta.

He puts the book back on the shelf.

'Now we are just us again,' she says, leading him out of the study to the sit-out. Chitthu is there, supervising the orderly commute of big black ants by the wall. He sees Krishna and Shanta, jumps up, picks up his red drum, and beats a powerful note to welcome them back to real life.

Krishna goes back to his usual life in the university, with the feeling that he has just finished a race or passed an exam. Soon he's in that hazy period of looking around, waiting to be surprised, puzzled, then deeply involved in the next project, whether it is a writer, a language, a story, or a new PhD student. He feels a bit like young Chitthu who is done with his red drum. He has hit it so hard for weeks that the plastic has caved in. But Chitthu is unfazed. He has discovered that a steel plate and spoon make a lovely high-pitched ringing sound when brought together. And there is an unending supply of plates and spoons in his grandmother's kitchen.

Only Ram is not happy. He doesn't like Chitthu being allowed to make so much noise of course. But what he is really unhappy about is the reaction to the book. He's had another look at the Hindu Rashtra Sabha website. He has found a small but disturbing piece. 'P.S. Krishna besmirches Saint Kannadeva's spiritual life and profound work by needlessly bringing caste into his book,' it says. 'Krishna is typical of people who say they oppose caste but use it for their own ends. Is it not a disgrace to create a controversy by saying Kannadeva's father was a washerman and used to be a cattle skinner? To link the evolved soul Kannadeva with cruelty to the holy cow is nothing but mischief.'

Ram has also heard from one of the other professors at the university—one or two PhD students have asked to change their guides. Ram knows this must be a first. He's never heard of a student who would willingly give up Krishna as a guide.

Ram goes downstairs, speaks sternly to his parents.

Krishna and Shanta sit silently like children in disgrace getting scolded by an elderly uncle. Krishna feels extra chastened because he has not told Ram (or Shanta) about the calls he is getting regularly. Usually the person at the other end is silent. But once, a menacing voice called at the university department and said, 'Leave our Hindu saints alone, Professor, or else …' Krishna had not thought the word *Professor* could be made to sound so ugly, so filled with scorn. Krishna had hung up and gone out with a delighted Shiva, honoured to be invited for a coffee alone with Prof sir. But luckily, since then, a wonderfully deviant story-song about Draupadi has come to Krishna's attention. This means he can get back to the life he knows best.

Srikumar's life is about to be changed forever. It is his lucky day. He's one of the few chosen for a private audience with his Guruji.

When he goes in, Santosh asks him to sit, not at his feet but in the chair across him. They sit there, one facing the other, silent.

The silence grows. Guruji's gaze never leaves his face. Those eyes—glistening pools, the pupils growing larger and more radiant till they threaten to swallow up everything!

Srikumar looks. He looks more and goes limp. He cannot look any more. He cannot sit. He gets up, seeks the Guru's feet.

Santosh looks down at the man grasping his feet, washing

them with tears. He bends, lifts up Srikumar gently, takes him in his arms. He whispers in Srikumar's ear, 'You are one with your Guru. You are the Guru's holy arm.' Santosh can feel the man tremble. Having felt the divine, even for a moment, he is tender to the touch. A man can take a while to recover from such an intense spiritual experience.

Santosh lets him go. Srikumar is completely calm now, sitting on the floor, looking at Santosh's face as if hypnotised.

'Surrender yourself,' Srikumar hears Guruji say. 'Surrender your body, your wealth, your wife and children, even your life. Then you will be my true disciple.' Guruji holds out his hands, palms facing upward as if waiting for Srikumar's alms. 'Surrender.'

Surrender. Seva. Sevak. Dharma. Surrender. Surrender. What luxury this is, to let his mind float out of his body, find Guruji's hands, rest on his open receiving palms a while, then return to himself charged, strong as never before!

'You are now liberated,' says Santosh. He smiles at Srikumar's surprise. 'You have received initiation at my hands. The old Srikumar, the one your mother gave birth to, the one your parents reared, is gone. You are now a hundred per cent sevak of the Hindu Rashtra. Now you are my disciple only in name. You are ready and you are on your own.'

Santosh watches him go, his face a bland mask. Once Srikumar is out of the room, Santosh's mind moves on. There are others who will take care of Srikumar now; take care of Srikumar, his mission, and the rakshasa.

3

It's bad enough to live every single day in the shadow of caste. But to have someone mock you when you fight with that shadow, or emerge from it—how can you bear it? The Bhim Shakti students in the college are enraged by the abuse heaped on Senthil. Caste humiliates them in a hundred quiet ways even on good days, in times of "peace". If the subtle humiliation becomes open, public, if it becomes acceptable to speak hatred for someone who has struggled to reach where he is, what will happen to the college? What will happen to all of them?

Ravi and Ramesha join the students sitting with Senthil over glasses of sweet hot tea. How should the student who abused Senthil on social media be punished? The most vocal of them is a final year student, Kiccha. Kiccha is a burly young man with a thick mop of hair, a lush beard and moustache. Everything about him is a little excessive, whether it is all the hair, the booming voice, or the muscles not fully covered by his tight half-sleeved shirt.

'See, he can be booked under the SC-ST prevention of atrocities act,' he says.

'That doesn't always work,' says Deepak, soberly.

Divya, the quiet girl sitting by Kiccha, speaks up. Senthil has to hush Kiccha so they can hear her. Her voice may be soft, but she knows what she wants. 'Now that the university has set up a committee to decide what to do, we could demand that the student be expelled.'

Senthil drains his glass of tea in one long gulp, puts down the glass. 'Look, each of us has a story to tell. I know how hard it was for me to get a supervisor when I was doing my PhD. But I don't want that to make me bitter. Ruining one student's career is not going to solve the problem.'

'But we should send a clear message,' Kiccha argues. 'This kind of thing has happened in the past also. And what about the posts this Shankar@hindupatriot has put up? He's not a student, we don't even know who he is or where he is. How will the college punish him?'

'Yes, of course, it's a problem in and out of the college. And this time it's the saffron lot leading the abuse. They talk about the Hindu family while every bone and muscle in their bodies is casteist.' Senthil looks around as if counting numbers. 'Let's use our anger well. Let's start with the college. We decide what each of us will do, and how we will work together.'

Ravi does not take his eyes off Senthil's face. He has never seen a face so full of intelligence, but with enough room for compassion. It makes Ravi feel humble; but it also makes him want to *do* something. He feels a little shy about speaking up, the others seem to know so much. But he says, almost as softly as Divya, 'I can work regularly, every day, on the Bhim Shakti Facebook page.' Ravi can already see himself, giving voice to the mess of questions choking him. And when he picks up his drum, when he beats it hard as they march down the street, those questions will come together, become one big, clear one. His voice grows stronger. 'And Ramesha and I will mobilize among the freshman science students for the march.' Ramesha nods; he has been surprisingly quiet but that doesn't mean he is not taking it all in. Maybe there's something happening at home he's not sharing with Ravi and Harisha? Maybe it's a girl—Ramesha always looks wistful when he sees couples walking close together, heading toward the quieter part of the college ground?

'Good,' says Senthil Anna, smiling at Ravi. 'I know you'll work hard.' He turns to the others, several of whom speak at the same time.

Ravi spends more and more time in a cyber café, or in the library, not with its books on four-legged animals, his list of recommended readings, but at the computer. He doesn't have a laptop like many of the students; Ramesha has a second-hand one that he is happy to share with Ravi, but Ravi now likes going on his own to the library. He finds there are some things he has to learn alone. *How did this caste become the air we breathe? When did this happen?* Ravi is making up a course and syllabus that may explain how he became who he is.

Ravi struggles through what the books tell him. It's easier when Senthil explains it all to him, but he wants to show Senthil that he is doing his homework. He borrows one book at a time, from the library, from Senthil, waits till he is alone in his room, and reads aloud so he can understand better.

> In the medieval period, caste was completely oppressive. It governed every aspect of life, and it was almost impossible to challenge the all-pervasive Hindu religious ideology.

Ravi stumbles over the word 'all-pervasive,' stops to think about what it really means. There are details he has heard from Senthil, but also from his grandfather and his tobacco-chewing buddies. Their occupation was decided for them; it was whatever the upper castes decided was too dirty for them to do. 'Skin carcasses, work with hide and leather. Carry shit. Catch rats. Weave baskets. Hunt.' And if they worked in fields, the fields were never theirs. Their work polluted forever, the pollution was handed down from mother to child, father to child, like an inescapable legacy. They had to work, but they had to be invisible. If one of them came out of their untouchable colony, he had to ring a bell, to warn anyone who might see him or pass him on the road and get polluted.

Still, Senthil had told Ravi, there were people, cattle skinners and cobblers and ratcatchers and those who worked with dead bodies or shit or iron or rope or meat, men and women, who had challenged such a living hell of a system. They did it through a different sort of god, a religion that allowed a different sort of god and devotee. This is a source of puzzlement to Ravi. He is suspicious of all gods because of the god he has heard most about, the one who allows people to say the sins of their past lives are being visited on them now.

There were movements in South India between the seventh and twelfth centuries, Ravi reads. They were devotional, which is why they were called bhakti movements. But their gods were different because they didn't need any middlemen—priests and Brahmins who kept gods locked up in temples. Or maybe it is the devotees who made all the difference. If they refused temple and ritual, if they cared about others simply because they are fellowmen or fellow women, couldn't they melt that iron net that made them less than human?

Mystics, Senthil Anna called these people. Ravi has a hard time understanding them. Mystic, sufi, it all sounds like some myth or dream to him. But he didn't say anything aloud, and he took the books Senthil lent him respectfully. He has tried hard to make sense of what he has read. *A protest against caste oppression and the excessive ritualism of the Brahmin priesthood. Universal equality in the eyes of God. Medieval mysticism independent of sectarian or orthodox practice. Disavowed caste customs and their tyranny.*

He will be bold and ask Senthil Anna, Ravi decides. What difference did they really make? Did the casteist monsters understand all this god and love and spirit? Were they about to give up their power, talk equality?

Asha is sitting alone in the mess. She has got a glass of coffee, smiled at three girls sitting together a few tables away—all SC of course—but Asha sits by herself. She pulls her phone out of the pocket of her white coat. There's an invitation from Ravi to follow the Facebook page of the Bhim Shakti Students Association. She clicks, skims through the posts. It makes her feel a little guilty. Her own FB page has been neglected for days. And she has been sharing silly things like pictures of flowers and cute animal videos. Her mother has been sounding tired on the phone; she's always tired, but she's been sounding more tired than usual. Asha is counting the days to the midterms and the visit home afterward. Meanwhile, she wants to do nothing for a while, not even chase Ravi and Satya for news.

Asha puts away her phone, takes the hot coffee to her lips, shuts her eyes.

'Sleeping?' says a loud voice near her. Asha almost spills the coffee on herself. The three girls who were at the table across now stand by her, laughing.

'Sleeping?' the girl repeats.

'No, she's dreaming of a boy she likes,' says another.

'We're going to a movie. Come with us, no?'

Asha goes with them to see the latest romance. It's set in an engineering college where two young men fall in love with the same girl. The girl, whose nickname in the college is 'Textbook', has to understand that no textbook or exam or career is as important as love. Everyone breaks into song and dance every fifteen minutes, and wears clothes that Asha has never seen in real life. But she quite enjoys it; it's a relief to be part of the crowd in the dark, laughing with the other girls. But once she is out of the theatre, there's a niggling question in her mind. She has never had a boyfriend. But she doesn't know any girl other than herself who has two best friends who are boys. What does this mean? She expects to get married—sometime. There's so much to do before that; she has never applied those fantasies on the screen to herself before. But she wonders now as she lies in her bed in the dark: who would she marry, Ravi? Teasing, laughing, drumming Ravi? She smiles to herself, it's such a funny thought. Satya, then? For some reason, the smile vanishes and her eyes tear up. Why is she feeling sad at the thought of her and Satya, why can't they have a future together?

Satya, unaware that he may one day be part of a romance, heads to the library. For now, this is what he loves. He loves the rows and rows of bookshelves from ceiling to floor, the line of tables with computers, all waiting like gift boxes to be opened, or windows to look out of, discover places far away from this college. Then Satya can almost make believe he is just like everyone else, a student. Or a seeker. Before he pulls out the books he needs to read today, he seats himself at one of the computers, double clicks on Chrome, opens his email. On Facebook he sees an invitation from Ravi to like the page Bhim Shakti. Satya likes it immediately then reads the latest post.

> National Science College today issued a press release on the decision taken by the Committee examining charges of abusive messages against a Dalit professor on social media. The student has been fined and reprimanded. The College has clarified that it will not tolerate any abuse, physical or otherwise, of any member of the college community.
>
> The press release does not mention names or the nature of the abuse, or the political affiliation of the student. The Dalit professor, Dr Senthil, is from the Department of Physics, and has been very supportive of students, especially Dalits and those at a disadvantage in the college because of their caste or community. The student, Venkat Rao, put up an abusive post on his Facebook page, casting aspersions on Professor Senthil's doctorate and his fitness to teach.
>
> The post was shared by many who are not students in the university, but are, clearly, of the same political persuasion. For example, a Shankar@hindupatriot posted that 'This casteist bastard Senthil talks about caste all the time, or blames Hindus. Covering up his ignorance about physics, what he is supposed to be teaching. Talking about caste instead, dividing Hindu family.'

> Such abuse is serious enough to call for use of the Scheduled Castes-Scheduled Tribes Prevention of Atrocities Act (1989). But when asked about punishment for the student Venkat Rao, Professor Senthil said 'I don't want to spoil a student's career and prospects. It is a serious offence, no doubt about that. It's not just what he has said about me. It's also what he has implied about other Dalits in academics, and the intolerable way he seeks to divide people on the basis of caste. I am not surprised he is from the right wing group on campus.'
>
> The Bhim Shakti group would like to state that while we appreciate the response of the College authorities to our demand for action, the punishment should have included rustication of the student. Our group also condemns the abusive posts on the Facebook page of the person who calls himself Shankar@hindupatriot. It's clear to us that his idea of patriotism is undemocratic and vicious.

Satya takes a look at the large clock hanging in the library. He feels a sharp pang. The clock is uncompromising in its obedience to time. He exits the page and gets up reluctantly. Just for a while, he got to see that the world is not the shrunken, sparsely populated place he lives in: the place of learning that has no room for people, only textbooks and dictionary, class, library, room, window, the peepal tree and its small inhabitants.

Satya goes to the first shelf, A for anatomy. Ravi's Bhim Shakti is still with him; Satya is going to show Professor Sharma what he is capable of. He reaches out for a copy of the fat *Gray's Anatomy for Students*. He would like a copy of his own, but even the portable concise edition costs almost two thousand rupees. He carries the book to a table, opens it to the first page of the introductory section on the spinal cord.

Satya is deep in the section, going back and forth between Gray and the dictionary, and in between, his own notes. He finds it helps to write out the words, especially those that are as long as trains and almost impossible to fit into a mere mouth.

There's another student at the same table, his head bent over another copy of Gray. And one of the girls in their class—she's the pretty one called Malini—is at the table across from them. Her eyes are directed at their table; she looks impatient. Is she waiting for the book? He feels uncomfortable because he can't ask her; he's never spoken to any of the girls in the class, not that there's been much conversation between him and the boys either. He wills himself to concentrate. An hour later, he shuts the book, gets up. He goes toward the girl. 'I'm done with the book if you're waiting for it,' he says. She looks uncomfortable. 'It's all right,' she says. Her eyes do not meet his. She speaks to a point in the air an inch or two from his face. 'There's the other copy, I'll wait for him to finish.' She now looks the other way, as if he has disappeared completely.

A day later, he receives a summons. Dr Sharma wants to meet him in his cabin.

Satya looks at the closed door with the forbidding nameplate: Dr (Professor) Sharma, MBBS, MD (Lond). He takes a deep breath, knocks on the door, then pushes it open.

Satya stands near the chair, waiting to be asked to sit down. Across the table, Dr Sharma ignores him for several minutes; he is re-reading Satya's latest test papers. It's a pile of them, so it can't be just the anatomy tests. How did he get hold of all his subject papers? Satya shifts from foot to foot. Then it strikes him; it must be Murthy, the man in the office who has access to everything, from attendance sheets to test papers.

Dr Sharma finally looks up; his face is blank, as if he has not summoned Satya there. 'Yes?'

'Sir, Professor, you asked—you asked me to meet you.' Satya hates the soft stammering voice saying this, a voice he does not recognise as his own.

Dr Sharma has lost his blank look. His face fills with mock puzzlement. 'Oh yes, I remember now. There's something I don't understand, and I need you to explain it to me.'

'Professor? Explain—what should I explain, sir?'

'Your test marks in the other subjects. I know how badly you are doing in anatomy.' Sharma is having a hard time keeping up the puzzled look; there's a smirk peeping through.

'Yes, Professor, I want to talk to you about the last test paper. I compared it with the answers in the text.'

Sharma ignores this. Instead he says, thoughtfully, 'How did your marks improve so suddenly in the other subjects? No one has noticed your copying?'

Satya is flabbergasted. Before he can say anything, Dr Sharma leans forward, asks in a perfectly reasonable tone, 'All this trouble for what? Suppose you get your MBBS—just in case you do manage to get your degree from here,'—he emphasises the *here*—'how many people would agree to be treated by you?'

His face hardens; his eyes bore holes in Satya's face.

Sharma has stopped playing. He holds up his right hand, makes a fist of it. It's such a tight fist that whatever empty space remains inside must be airless. 'See this fist? Take a good look at it because that's where your future is.'

Where is my story,
my own history?

1

Satya wakes up, sweating. He looks around wildly, then remembers where he is. What a relief—he is in the room he shares with Rahul in the hostel, in a medical college, private and deemed, and he has his scholarship. He is not in that awful time when he, Ravi and Asha were preparing for the entrance tests, when his money ran out despite the best efforts of his mother and brother, and he had to depend on Ravi and Asha for books. He made up, of course; he made the notes for all three of them, handwritten in blue ink, the important points underlined in red. Then he got the seat, began his journey to this room, to the class, to the library. The moneylender was his companion all through; his, and his mother's. That man is still with them. His hunger grows every day, as if he will only be satisfied when he has fed on their flesh and blood.

Satya can't go back to sleep. But he must—he can't afford to be sleepy in class tomorrow, especially in Dr Sharma's class. He switches on the lamp, waits to see if the light will wake up Rahul. They've both studied late into the night. In the lamplight he sees Rahul lying on his back, sleeping with his mouth sagging open, his arms thrown up in surrender. Satya picks up the diary on the table by his bed, looks for a pen.

> Don't sit like you belong nowhere, my mother liked to say to me. She was always sure I belong somewhere. She was very sure—she is still sure—I will find that place. Why else does she slave like she does, starting before the sun rises, and stretching out on her mat late at night when everyone else is fast asleep?

No, Satya can't write about his mother tonight. It's not her face the words picture but the moneylender's.

He gets up, goes to the window. The peepal tree looks at him, bland and uncaring. In the light of day, alive with birds and squirrels on its branches, it knows Satya, almost. But in the dark, no tree or bird, no field or sky can offer him any comfort. If he is an outcaste, what do they have to do with it? Satya picks up the diary again and writes.

> We have gone beyond caste, says one.
>
> Another says: we have to stop looking backward, caste is history.
>
> The good man among them says: Yes, I agree all people are the same and we must not say these are high, those are low. But caste has been there for so many years. It can't change overnight, can it?

Satya can't continue with this list. What 'they' say. They say too much anyway, he has to listen to them all the time. This book is for himself; for his words. He has to let his own words take him down the page, flow like a stream.

> Did I, and others like me, invent the word caste? I too hate the word caste. I too want to be free of it. The word has become part of my skin, my blood. But when can I stop using it, or even thinking about it? When can I say I am just me, Satya, not a Dalit? That's the cruelty of it: it's not up to me.

That last line brings his pen to an abrupt halt. Words, words. Prose or poetry, anger or heartbreak, what's the use? Satya pushes the diary under his mattress, switches off the lamp. He shuts his eyes tight.

Ravi is wide awake. He does not have a moment to waste. This college, second-best choice, is becoming home—at least if home is the place where you have to raise your voice every single day, make yourself heard. He wants to share this place he is making his own with Satya and Asha, though he is not sure how. At least he has convinced Satya that he can take a day off from his studies; Satya has promised to visit Ravi this weekend.

Ravi wets his hair, combs it as neatly as he can. His hair is so thick that this is not an easy task. He combs the narrow strip of a moustache as well. Ravi smiles at his reflection then pulls a face. He decides he looks decent enough for his host, Senthil Anna.

Ravi now calls Professor Senthil, Elder Brother. It makes his heart ache with pride, this being able to call a physics professor, a Dalit professor, *Senthil Anna*. Senthil has given him so much to read; thanks to him, Ravi is learning human science side by side with animal science.

It's the first time he has been invited to Senthil Anna's place. He puts together the books he has to return in his backpack. On an impulse, he stops on the way, and buys a bar of chocolate. He's been told Senthil has a little child.

Many of the faculty members live on the campus, but Senthil Anna lives in a congested part of the city. Ravi gets to the area with the help of the GPS, but once his phone tells him he is three minutes away from his destination, he is lost. This place where Senthil Anna lives: it's better than Ravi's own colony at home. But like his colony, this area is crowded. Little houses have been divided into pretend flats. The few balconies that are not enclosed overflow with all kinds of things, from cycles and buckets and clothes hanging out to dry, to a couple of unhappy potted plants struggling to stay alive. Ravi looks for the usual statue of Ambedkar in his blue suit holding a book to symbolise the Constitution he helped write. He doesn't find Constitution, book or Ambedkar; nor can he find Senthil's house.

Ravi asks a man sitting outside one of the houses for 7th Cross. 'Turn right there,' the man says, pointing down the street. 'Whose house are you looking for?'

'Professor Senthil's,' says Ravi.

The man looks at Ravi carefully. He asks sharply, 'What do you want? Who are you?'

'I am his student,' says Ravi, taken aback by these questions. 'He has invited me to meet him at his place.'

'What caste?' asks the man. Ravi is astonished, but he says, puffing out his chest, 'I am Dalit. And proud of it.'

The man looks both relieved and amused. 'That's okay then. He's been married for some years now, but still—some of us like to watch out for him. She's not Dalit, you see.'

'She's upper caste?' The words come out before Ravi can hold himself back, he's so surprised. Is he going to hear one more version of that tired old story? The plot has been around too long—or the fight has been around too long. The human impulse to love versus the need to keep castes apart, keep outcastes out.

But the man says, 'No, thank goodness, that would have

made it worse. But for us, even the other low castes are upper, no? Come, I'll take you to the house.'

Sunday arrives quickly; Ravi is waiting for Satya at the bus station. He sees Satya before Satya sees him. How tired Satya looks, how his shoulders hunch as if he has shrunk in a few months! Then Satya sees Ravi, and his face breaks into the old sunny smile, showing rows of perfect white teeth.

They make their way to a tea stall. Ravi doesn't want to take Satya to his room yet, he wants to have Satya to himself for a while. Eating two vadais, drinking a glass of tea: that's all the time it takes to see there is something troubling Satya. Ravi wishes Asha were here too. She's good at getting Satya to talk about himself. But the past few weeks, Asha has not been saying much to either Ravi or Satya. And she seems to have been infected by her roommate Priya's enthusiasm for selfies. Asha has been sending Ravi and Satya photos of herself in the hostel room; one in the ward; one in the beach, captioned *Remember? When do we meet next?* Neither Ravi nor Satya has answered her question yet. As it is, thinks Ravi, it's been hard to get Satya to come here today.

By the time they walk to Ravi's hostel, Satya has thawed a little. 'I want to meet all your friends. I want to hear all about Bhim Shakti,' he says. Ravi offers him a guided tour of the college, his room, his new friends, his new ideas. If only Ravi could also offer him the best gift of all—he so wants Satya to meet Senthil Anna. But Senthil Anna is out of town for a couple of days. As if to make up, Ravi spreads out the fresh batch of books Senthil Anna has lent him on the bed. He picks up a slim one and holds it out. 'This is all about a Dalit poet, about many poets who fought against caste,' he tells Satya. 'I haven't read it yet, just glanced through it. You can always send it back to me after you've read it. I'm sure Senthil Anna won't mind. I've told him about you, about how you write poems yourself.'

'I don't know if what I write is poetry,' Satya smiles.

'If you think it's poetry, it's poetry,' Ravi says airily. 'Who's anyone to tell us how to write what we think and feel?' Ravi's arm sweeps aside all literary experts with one wave. Then without warning, he changes the subject. 'You don't look so well, Satya,' he says. 'What's happening?'

'The usual,' says Satya, caught off guard. 'Money, what else? I haven't got my scholarship yet, and I have to send Amma money.'

Ravi waits; there must be more.

'And there's a professor who—' Satya hesitates—'I am worried about passing his course.'

Ravi looks at him closely. 'Caste?' he asks. Satya nods. That word is shorthand; it's enough for them to understand each other. The rest of it is detail.

Ravi racks his brains for advice. Sometimes he feels he is slowly becoming an activist; but face to face with Satya, everything he has read and heard, or learnt from Senthil Anna, dissipates. He really does not know what to suggest. There's no student group in Satya's college, at least nothing that will fight for Satya. 'You'll have to fight it,' Ravi finally says. Even as he says the words, he knows they are not enough. He adds, his voice dipping a little, 'I'm going to ask Senthil Anna what we can do from here.'

Ravi posts, shares, tags. He re-reads what he has just put up on the Bhim Shakti page. It's a list he has compiled from newspaper headlines over a few months. The list ranges from humiliation to injustice to brutality, and it's far from complete.

Uttar Pradesh: Twenty-two-year-old Dalit woman found dead.

Andhra Pradesh: Dalit woman assaulted and stripped.

Bihar: Dalit couple killed, daughter injured.

Maharashtra: All nine men accused in Dalit youth's murder case acquitted.

Gujarat: Dalit woman, three kids stabbed to death.

Uttar Pradesh: Pregnant Dalit woman killed for touching upper caste woman's bucket.

Gujarat: Dalit man beaten to death for attending an evening of garba dancing.

Gujarat: Law student beaten up for sporting a moustache.

Kerala: Dalit priest stabbed.

Telangana: Dalit activist escapes attack.

Gujarat: Twenty-four-year-old beaten up for sporting a moustache.

Punjab: Dalit women accuse upper caste men of thrashing them.

Madhya Pradesh: Dalit man beaten to death for allegedly stealing lentils.

Uttar Pradesh: Dalits flee homes after Thakurs threaten them.

Punjab: Dalit man tied to tree, thrashed by landlord for stealing fan.

Karnataka: Water poisoned in well used by Dalits.

Odisha: Dalit family ostracized in village.

Uttar Pradesh: Dalits barred from entering temple.

Madhya Pradesh: Dalit girl forced to lift excreta by upper caste man.

Madhya Pradesh: Dalit woman's nose cut.

Gujarat: Twenty-four-year-old Dalit man beaten up.

Rajasthan: Dalit woman branded witch, stripped and beaten up.

Gujarat: Dalit man, mother thrashed for skinning dead cow.

Uttar Pradesh: Dalit woman lynched in Agra.

Karnataka: Dalits stopped from offering prayers by upper caste.

Andhra Pradesh: Dalits face boycott in village.

Kerala: Dalits in village on Kerala-Tamilnadu border claim they are subject to untouchability.

Uttar Pradesh: Dalits attacked by Thakurs after rally.

Uttar Pradesh: One Dalit killed, sixty Dalit houses set ablaze.

Madhya Pradesh: Upper caste men pour kerosene in Dalits' well.

Rajasthan: Dalit groom attacked with beer bottles for riding mare in village.

Rajasthan: Dalit writer threatened.

Karnataka: Three Dalits assaulted for allegedly eating beef.

Uttar Pradesh: Boycotted for killing a calf, Dalit kills self.

Rajasthan: Rajputs attack Dalit wedding group, assault women.

Tamil Nadu: Six Dalit men beaten up.

Gujarat: Eight Dalits thrashed during cricket match.

Haryana: Dalit groom thrashed for riding mare.

Tamil Nadu: Huts of five Dalits set on fire.

Jharkhand: Cops beat Dalit to death for applying Holi colours on upper caste.

Karnataka: No haircut for Dalits in village.

Haryana: Six Dalits injured in clashes, forty families want to flee.

Uttar Pradesh: Dalit man thrashed, house burnt for not saying 'Ram Ram'.

Gujarat: Seventeen-year-old Dalit attacked for sporting a moustache.

Ravi touches his upper lip. He decides he is going to let that thin moustache grow. *Here's a Dalit with a full proud moustache, asserting his manhood on his face. What are you going to do about it?* But the rest of the list challenges Ravi: how is a moustache on his face going to help those already killed, or those beaten or humiliated, or those who live in fear? Ravi's heart feels empty. No, it's filling up, it's too full. All these people he doesn't know want room there because they are his extended family. It's all too much, this jostling, and the scale of the battle. He's just one man. One boy. He breathes deep, exhales; the crowds leave his heart. But it's still full, though there is only one person left there. A boy like him, but unlike him, he has a sweet, sad face. Satya.

Ravi calls Satya again. The phone rings and rings; or a recorded voice tells him, as if he has not noticed, that this phone number is not answering. He texts Satya. *You ok? Call or msg?* Then, for good measure, he texts Asha. *Spoken to Satya? Was very quiet and worried when he came here.*

Those few hours with Ravi, meeting new people, talking: how quickly Satya shed loneliness. And now, back in the room waiting patiently for him, how quickly real life wraps itself around him again. Satya shakes his head, irritated with himself. He cycles to the pond, races back to his books. He listens to music with Rahul; this is one thing they can do together since it doesn't require too many words between them. He goes back to the blue notebook. Asha and Ravi are in it, so is his mother. The real Satya is in it. And Dr Sharma … What if Satya had a teacher like Ravi's Senthil? Would that make Dr Sharma more bearable? But he won't think of Sharma tonight. Satya picks up the book Ravi gave him. It's a slim book in Kannada, called *Kannadeva's Family: The Poets of Anandagrama*. He opens it, begins to read.

The more he reads, the more he feels as if he has been put into a time machine. The book is showing him his ancestors; it's letting him eavesdrop on their most hidden dreams and hopes and fears. Their struggle. But wait, he can't make those times and these times identical. Satya recalls his mother saying once to their neighbour, her friend Suja, 'When I was young, hardly any of our people went to school for more than a few years. Now, so many finish at least up to the tenth standard. And my Satya, look at him, he wants to make something of himself. A doctor, he says.' His mother wiped her face with her sari, smiling through her tears. 'Silly me, to cry about it. I'll do anything, you know, to make his dream come true.'

No, the times are not exactly the same. But there have been hundreds of years in between. Shouldn't they be more different?

It's late at night but Satya is still reading. He can't stop midway. Rahul looks surprised that Satya is not at his notes or textbooks. But for once Satya doesn't care about the next morning's classes.

There are so many people, so many voices in this book. Poets. Poets who work, suffer in ways Satya can understand immediately. Poets who don't care if others don't think they are poets. Satya is especially struck by this. There are poems he doesn't understand though he is not going to give up on them—he is going to read those again. And best of all, there is a poet here called Chikkiah, whose words do not need a second reading. Every word of his speaks to Satya. Speaks for him. How is that possible? Chikkiah, a man from long ago, a man who may or may not have actually lived, putting together words in lines, singing them just for Satya?

Where is that land where water flows free? How the line pierces Satya, how it pins his own pain! It doesn't matter that this book cannot tell him every fact about Chikkiah's life. No book can. But the few poems are enough; hearing Chikkiah in them is like getting to know himself, Satya, all over again.

Satya opens the book to that page again, copies the lines in his diary, saying the words aloud as he writes them down.

Where is that land
where water flows free?

Tell me, *Tell* me.

Where is my land
Where water flows free?

And that response, though the question remains sharp despite the brave answer:

That land is here, and there,
it's everywhere in me.
In me the land
where water flows free.

It's almost dawn when Satya puts away both books, switches off the light. His eyes are shut, he is fast asleep, but still the song has not left him. It sings clear and true in his dreams.

The next day, as he leaves the anatomy class, Dr Sharma gestures for him to wait. 'Your attendance is not what it should be,' he says.

Satya is shocked. 'I've never missed a single anatomy class, sir,' he says.

Dr Sharma lifts his eyebrows. 'That's what you say, but my attendance sheet tells a different story. At this rate, who knows if you can sit for your exams? But there's time for that. For now, let me give you a friendly warning.' The word 'friendly' has never sounded so unfriendly before. 'Murthy in the office was telling me your scholarship may be held up because of poor attendance. There are rules, you know. You can't escape the rules.'

2

Srikumar parks his bike at his usual spot within sight of the shop. He used up most of his savings to buy the bike just a couple of months back. There was the small loan he had to take from his cousin Vinay as well, but it's worth it. It's a Honda CBR 25OR sports bike, Gray Metallic with strips of Mars Orange, and it has a four-stroke 249.60 cc engine. Srikumar is in love with it.

He locks the bike, looks around to see if anyone is watching. Then he unlocks the shutter of the shop, rolls it up halfway. It's still early; the shop opens an hour later. The shutter rolls up with an assertive clang he enjoys. It signals the start of his day, the hour when he is completely alone, something he can't be sure of at home or later in the day in the shop.

Srikumar goes behind the counter past the curtain to the small area at the back of the shop. It's almost a room. The place is full of boxes on the rows of shelves that jut out, eating up the space. But what Srikumar thinks of as *his* wall is bare, except for a large picture, a small shelf and a hook. The room may be small, but it's impeccably neat, everything in place. Srikumar is fussy about cleanliness, especially about dusting and sweeping this part of the shop. He flicks a switch so the small lights garlanding the picture on the wall come on. He hangs his backpack on the hook. He wipes yesterday's ash off the small shelf and lights a fresh pair of agarbatti. Then he gets to his morning ritual before the glossy picture pasted on the wall.

He draws the curtain, strips down to his briefs. He stands straight, pulling himself up to his five feet seven inches, and inhales deeply. He looks at the picture. He looks *into* the picture as he does his breathing exercises.

The picture: it is a neon lemon yellow. Out of this solid-toned background springs a dark figure from the bottom left to the top right. The figure is a man; a youngish man, naked except for a cloth tied around his lower hips. Beads encircle his torso and his bare arms. A curvaceous snake hangs upside down round his neck; its mouth is almost near his belly button. His right hand holds a brave trident, its tip pushing the top of the frame. In his left hand is a small drum. Muscle defines his lithe body, but what makes the image so powerful is the suggestion of controlled movement. This control is intense. The man is moving, but his muscles, the trident, his long matted hair flying in snake-shaped banners behind his head, the rattling drum, are all in his control. And the control signals that the decisive moment is imminent.

Srikumar breathes in and out, the inward and outward rush of air keeping his chest and abdomen taut. He can hear a voice, firm despite its gentle tone. It says to him, 'May this sight never be erased from your mind. The decisive moment is coming. Surrender, surrender. Watch—now, any moment, he will spring out of the yellow frame.'

Srikumar echoes silently: 'He will come, hard flesh and harder blood, challenging me. Surrender. I will be ready for him. I am ready.'

Once he is done with the morning exercise, with the prayer and promise to the picture hanging on the wall and the Guru sitting in his head, Srikumar becomes an ordinary shopkeeper. Raju and the boy arrive; the shutter is now open all the way.

Srikumar has two assistants at the shop; or one and a half assistants. The half is a twelve-year-old boy whose mother begged Srikumar to employ him. He is always hungry, this boy, but the food seems to go nowhere. He's skinny; he speaks rarely; and he seems to understand only one in ten sentences spoken to him. But he is completely obedient. He lifts packages, fetches and carries, sweeps inside and outside, any number of times and without a murmur. Srikumar often thinks of him as a nameless dog, and as dogs go, this one is useful to have around. The other assistant, Raju, is by no means stupid. But he is in awe of Srikumar because of his devotion to God and gym and bike, and his rare but unforgettable displays of temper.

The shop sells a variety of things depending on market demand and the price of bulk supplies. There are children's books, a few video games at a discount since they are not new. There are also cordless phones and mobile phones, new and used, as well as accessories. Srikumar has an agreement with his cousin Vinay who runs a mobile repair shop down the street. They send each other customers, depending on whether a phone needs to be repaired or bought. This evening, Srikumar will go see Vinay, not to return his bike loan, not to talk about their business arrangement, but about something more important.

Vinay is a few years younger than Srikumar and hero-worships his elder cousin. Vinay failed his tenth standard.

But Srikumar not only finished school, he also did a B.Com. correspondence course. He knows his own mind; he knows what he wants and is always working on getting it. The only time Vinay feels he is Srikumar's equal is when he repairs something for Srikumar; a mobile, or a bike, or almost anything that can be taken apart and put back together again.

Srikumar and his cousin Vinay are practically brothers. Better than brothers, because Vinay too has been coming to the meetings of the Sabha. Vinay knows he will never be chosen to do anything important, but he doesn't mind that. He likes having a leader like Srikumar telling him what to do. He likes being a good follower. This is good, because Srikumar may need his help with any mission he is assigned—transport may need to be arranged, a motorcycle may need to be kept in good repair; or he may need multiple SIM cards and mobile handsets.

The next evening, Srikumar is at a sevak session again. This time Guruji is not there. He is either travelling or busy. But one of the second-rung leaders, Vivek, takes the group of sevaks who have just been initiated, four of them, through their paces. The session is on rakshasas—'How to Defeat Demons'.

The session leader, Vivek, is quick and to the point. 'Training,' he says. The way he says it, 'Try-ning,' with the 'r' rolled thoroughly, underlines how critical this first step is in any battle. 'Physical try-ning. You may or may not have other weapons in our struggle against the rakshasas. But remember, your body must be ready for anything. It must not let you down at the critical moment.'

Vivek lists the ways the sevaks can train their bodies. He

adds, 'Obviously a trained sevak's body is not just a well-exercised body. It has to be made capable of union with the glorious cause.' He goes through a longish and detailed list of do's and don'ts. 'Bathe in the morning before sunrise with lukewarm water, chanting slokas all the while. A river is the best place to bathe, but a well, or at least flowing water, will do.'

(Srikumar feels frustrated; he has bathed out of a bucket of still water all his life.)

Vivek adds a cautionary note: 'A head bath is essential if you have vomited, or had a haircut, or a nightmare, or sex; or if you have come into contact with a menstruating woman, a dog, a corpse, a rakshasa, or a scavenger.'

(That he already follows; Srikumar recovers himself.)

'The second step is complete and utter loyalty to all of us who believe in the cause, and,' the doctor pauses respectfully, 'to Hindu Rashtra.'

What magic there is in these words, just the two of them, just four syllables that hold the promise of a better India, a purer world. Srikumar can see it almost as well as he sees the neon yellow image of the man of action waiting for the right moment on the wall of his shop. The air itself will be pure in Hindu Rashtra, filled with the chanting of slokas. The fragrance of the crackling homa fire, the sweet prasad of bananas, milk and honey. The rivers will flow, being holy again. Cows will be garlanded, their foreheads streaked with red and yellow, gladdening the heart of every decent citizen. As for citizens, the people, and the way they live: every one of them, but everyone, will be part of the same family. They will all be the same. What else can there be then but peace, holiness and harmony?

Vivek holds up his hand. Srikumar leaves his sweet dream in the future, comes back to the present.

'The third step is the most critical. That's when we kill the demons, just as our gods did when they came down to earth to help mortals. Remember: no man is a man, no God is a God, unless he kills the demons, whether rakshasas or rakshasis. Remembering this, we must undertake the most important task a man can perform on earth: rid our motherland of rakshasas and rakshasis. Cut down those who sully our noble cause. Those who are obstacles in the path that leads to our goal.'

(Srikumar feels he is at his morning prayer. His fists are clenched tight. But Vivek has gone on to the charges against the rakshasas. Srikumar loosens his fists, pays close attention.)

Vivek thunders, 'What do they do? They say our gods are not real. They are *stories*, they are legends and myths. They distort our rich history, deliberately leaving out our glorious achievements in science and culture, and the making of our civilization. They insult everything that is ours. They spread terrible lies about our priests and saints. They encourage Muslims and Christians to marry or abduct or rape our women so our women and children are no longer pure. They go on and on about caste as if there is any place on earth where all are born equal. They run after Western medicine and clothes and ideas. They kill and eat our holy mother, the cow. They eat its tender child, the innocent calf. They eat all kinds of unclean things.'

Vivek is sweating. But he has to shout out one more sentence before he gets down to business. 'Free the whole earth from these enemies of the gods, enemies of the devoted servants of gods.'

Vivek pauses, catches his breath. These are unforgiveable charges against the enemy, and the list is long, though he has been selective. This is what they are up against. The full effect of this message has to spread in the room like the fumes of potent incense. It has to enter each of these sevaks' bodies through his nostrils as he breathes, it has to fuel his lungs and heart.

The air is thick; the room is silent.

Then Vivek's hand goes up again. He stretches it as far as it can go; his right hand forms a fist. But his voice is almost a whisper. A choked, powerful whisper. 'The demons will not stop us. We will stop them—with a bullet.'

Srikumar is looking at that fist, at the hole it's making in the air. It's got just a little purer already, the air that's going to be completely free of rakshasa stink. Already his lungs are inhaling more air than usual, his heart is beating hard, saying *I am here, I am here*. For a moment Srikumar feels what it is like to be a god who walks the earth—or at least a demi-god. One shot. That's all it takes. Shouldn't one shot do it? Vivek seems to know what Srikumar is thinking because he adds, 'If the first bullet does not kill the enemy immediately, fire another, and another, all the while chanting in your mind the mantra for the destruction of the enemy.'

Vivek winds up by telling them to expect smaller, more focused meetings to 'finalise preparation and try-ning'.

'You will receive the support you need. Go bravely and fulfil your mission. Remember—always begin your work on a good day…'

The meeting happens in a place Srikumar is a little surprised by. He gets an invitation to a birthday party.

He doesn't know the birthday boy—all of two years old—or the parents, or anyone else in the crowd that is eating its fill of eggless chocolate cake, samosa and chips. Once he has handed over his present, he sits alone, sipping a glass of coke. He's been there almost an hour when the birthday boy's grandfather walks up to him and says, casually, 'We can talk in the room upstairs.'

There are two men already in the room. They break off their conversation when Srikumar and the grandfather enter. The grandfather introduces them to Srikumar as Sirish Mama and Dr Rajesh. They seem to know him though Srikumar has not seen them before. Grandfather passes two boxes around, one sweet, one savoury. Srikumar refuses both politely. The door is shut, but they can hear the party downstairs, the shrieks of the children who are now playing passing the parcel. *Jai Jagadeesh Hare* is playing as accompaniment to the game.

There's something about Sirish Mama that makes Srikumar think of an army general. He is quick, quiet. Everything he says is said in a kind of telegraphic language as if he has just deciphered a series of coded messages. Dr Rajesh seems an echo but, like a doctor with a good bedside manner, he provides content and explanation of Mama's staccato bursts. Grandfather is the host.

Sirish Mama says: 'Strategy. Personality-specific. Eliminate anti-Hindus.'

Dr Rajesh echoes, 'We already have a hit list. These personalities, the targets that is, are all repeat offenders.' (He never refers to a person or to people; the word he favours is 'personality'.) He goes on to describe these offenders. 'These personalities are hardcore anti-Hindu. They are activists and communists; even, I am sorry to say, poets and musicians, teachers and professors.'

Sirish Mama says: 'Number 5. Rakshasa Kavi. Devapura University.'

Dr Rajesh echoes, 'Numbers 1-3 in the list are already in progress, being followed up. Number 4 is in hospital undergoing chemotherapy. No point wasting our efforts there. So this mission is Number 5, Code Rakshasa Kavi. Professor P.S. Krishna in the university in Devapura. Please use code from now on.'

Sirish Mama looks at Srikumar critically. 'Confirm training over. Actual, not spiritual.'

Before Srikumar can reply, Dr Rajesh helpfully answers for him. 'Oh yes. That's all done. He's been taught to use the ammunition we have in mind.'

Sirish Mama continues where he left off: 'Funds. Ammunition. SIM, handset, code email. Reconnaissance.'

The children downstairs are done with passing the parcel and are now playing Simon says (or what they call Shankar says). There's no music this time but enough noise to make up for it. A child wails in the background, testing out how much his lungs can do.

Dr Rajesh fills him in on how Professor Krishna has insulted the great saint Kannadeva. 'He claims he has found some poems and done an "analysis". What does he find? That our saint committed suicide. That our saint was the son of a low caste dhobi who came from a family of cattle skinners.'

Sirish Mama interrupts, a suggestion of impatience in his voice. 'Lives in Devapura. Goes to university every day but Sunday. Regular habits. Age 68. Enough for now.'

But Dr Rajesh is not done with showing Srikumar

the rakshasa at close range. 'He is dangerous because he is stubborn; he has not got afraid of the warnings we have given him. And many people in the university, also all the students he has taught and are now spread across the country, take him seriously. They ask him for advice, they respect him, they *love* him. You see how dangerous that makes him?'

By the time Srikumar comes downstairs, the crowd has thinned. The birthday boy, whose wails they could hear upstairs, has been calmed down and is sitting on his grandmother's lap, thumb in mouth. The grandmother looks tired, but she smiles at Srikumar and asks him if he would like to take some cake home for his family.

Srikumar walks to his bike. He's leaving with things better than cake—he has cash for supplies; a mission; a target. He's now part of a well-thought out plan. A plan with a rationale, strategy, lists and information, a network of supporters and organisations. A plan of action.

A week later, Mission Rakshasa Kavi takes the next step. Srikumar is in the shop, checking his email. He scrolls down the new ones in the inbox. There it is, the one he is looking for. It's a message from Sirish Mama, to the point as usual: *Ref Kavi. Children's booklet ready and available. Small, light book, easy to store, dispatch, understand. Four poems. Your child will enjoy.*

Srikumar holds the booklet of poems Sirish Mama told him was available. It's solid though it's small, this 7.65 mm pistol. Srikumar knows how to use stones and cricket bats; then he trained with a gun. That's why he could see, right away, that this one is easy in every way. It's not heavy; it didn't take Srikumar long to understand how to fill it with the kind of poems meant for a rakshasa. There are four bullets, but Srikumar has no doubt he will do the job with one or two. (After all, there are many rakshasas and rakshasis in line. They are in Death Row though they don't know it, writing, speaking, eating, dressing in evil ways, living un-Hindu lives.)

Best of all, the pistol was cheap, and it was easy getting hold of it. So were the cartridges. Sirish Mama knows his job. And so does he, thinks Srikumar. The first stage of the mission has been accomplished, and he's done it alone, or almost.

The message came through one of the other sevaks; Srikumar does not know his name. He came to the shop, actually bought two children's colouring books (*The Prince of Ayodhya* and *The Clever Brahmin and the Stupid Tiger*). Then he gestured at the pen and pad lying on the counter and dictated an address and a date. He nodded at the address Srikumar had written down and said, 'Ten should do. Don't pay more.' Srikumar had looked at him, indignant. As if he would be so stupid! The man added, 'Vijay is the name he uses. He doesn't sell to strangers. He trusts our go-between who's told him to expect a man called Harish.'

Srikumar had decided against taking his bike though he likes nothing better than racing down the highway, past the idiots in cars and buses, weaving his way round the world's slowpokes, flying with the wind like a god. But now that he was not Srikumar but a sevak of Mission Rakshasa Kavi, he had to be careful. He dressed in a pale blue full-sleeved shirt, neither old nor new; he wore ordinary trousers like any clerk in an office; he wiped his forehead clean of the usual orange streak of a tilak; and he carried a quiet backpack like hundreds of young people did. He got into the red and yellow bus and made his way modestly to the back, sat quietly. No one in the bus wasted a second glance on him. He got off the bus once the language on boards and milestones changed script, at the stop just past the border.

He was in a place famous for its monuments. He remembered coming here a long time back on a school picnic. He had enjoyed the trip, even some of the stories the teacher told as they were herded from place to place. Suddenly Srikumar wanted to laugh. Really, he had enjoyed it because he spent all his time staring at a fair girl with pink lips, Shalini. Besides, he didn't realise then how ignorant the teacher was, showing off one building after the other as if she owned them, though they were all built by Muslim kings.

Srikumar looked at the paper on which he had written the address, then tore the paper to bits and threw it away. It was not far, and he wanted a walk after the bus ride. As he turned onto the road mentioned in the address, he could see a red flag fluttering atop a temple. This was auspicious; he could get a quick blessing.

The slim temple, then a building hidden by a façade of Ashoka trees; another building with small shops; then a ruin of a house, with grass and weeds sprouting on its roof, and most of the front wall missing. The bit of wall that was still intact had a sign saying Anand Couriers. This was it. Srikumar had to take the lane between the building with shops and the ruin. It was a narrow lane unwilling to share its secrets.

Srikumar had never seen a gun runner or a dealer or supplier before. This one looked like any of the anonymous men he had sat with on the bus. Srikumar thought, for the first time, that it was good to be faceless. 'Vijay?' he asked the faceless man sitting at a counter watching a TV on silent mode, three cell phones lying by him.

Faceless Vijay stopped picking his nose. He said, without taking his eyes off the TV, 'Who are you?'

'Harish,' replied Srikumar. 'Ravi's Mama told you to expect me?'

Vijay grunted. He had a disconcerting way of never looking at Srikumar as he spoke. 'The cash,' he said to the TV where six women were thrusting their hips at him. The fact that there was no music made their dance even more suggestive.

Srikumar pulled out the brown envelope from his backpack, removed the bundle of rubber-banded notes. Vijay did not bother to remove the rubber band. He counted the notes by folding their tips, or rather his fingers did, because he was still watching the six dancing women.

'Not fifteen?' he asked.

'Ten,' said Srikumar firmly, copying the man's taciturn style. It seemed to work. Vijay's eyes moved from the TV to Srikumar's face, took measure of him. Then he got up, went behind the curtain. Srikumar could hear a steel almirah opening with a low metallic groan, then being closed with one more plaintive groan. Vijay returned with a striped canvas carry bag, the kind a good housewife may use when shopping for vegetables. There was a smaller bag inside.

Once the gun was out on the table, Vijay had become almost sociable. He had forgotten the mute TV. The six women on the screen were now twirling round a man who was mouthing a song that required him to open his mouth very wide.

'See how small it is; you can hide it in your armpit if you need to.' Vijay demonstrated on himself.

Srikumar hid his irritation. Already it was his, and he didn't want it to be in anyone else's hand, leave alone armpit. But Vijay was still admiring the piece though he had already put away the cash and could have sent Srikumar on his way.

'See how the bores have been made to fit in the bullets,' he said. 'And the bullets are easily available. Country-made is best. Your target—it's not like being shot by a regular piece, whether pistol or revolver. This one—the bullet will pierce the target, making a huge hole.'

Vijay looked a little doleful when Srikumar put the gun—his gun now—back in the bag. Then Vijay turned back to the TV. He made a sound of disgust because the women had stopped dancing. He picked up the remote to change channels.

3

How the years have passed by, teaching Chikkiah and Mahadevi to live alone together again. Chandra is under the bauhinia; Kannappa is far away and growing more learned by the day. Rangayya and Parvatamma are bone and dust in the earth. Only the river is still there, both young and old, because it is never one thing at a time.

Sometimes, on waking up, Mahadevi looks at her bare, smooth arm and feels a great sadness. As a child, Kannappa would fall asleep pinching the skin on her forearm. The sleepier he got, the harder he pinched. It used to annoy Mahadevi so much. Now she wants those little love bruises back, an entire bracelet of them that she can wear through the day like a gem-studded bangle. She can visit Chandra easily, she can go every day if she likes to the bauhinia tree that stands full of grace. But Kannappa?

My moon, I used to say.
Now it stares blankly from the sky
or splits its fullness in the water.

My moon is far, O lord.
It is broken, my friend,
My river of a thousand faces.

Kannappa is learning all the time. Sometimes he sends word with Puttanna. Sometimes Puttanna brings them news that Kannappa is busy working hard, and he didn't want to distract him. 'He's the brightest of them all, I hear. Beats the Brahmin fellows hollow,' smirks Puttanna, determined to bring only good news. He is convinced Kannappa will be someone big, grand. He will be of them, of Anandagrama, but not a cobbler or a washerman or a farmer. Puttanna snaps at himself, having waited outside the school without meeting Kannappa for the fourth week in a row: 'He has to be something Chikkiah and I can't be. How can that not happen?'

The old river still flows, though its childish wonders often seem like memories of a lovely tale some grandmother told Chikkiah and Mahadevi a long time ago. Their love is an indestructible bridge between them. But now that Kannappa is not there, the love remains unspoken. Words of love for each other, for Chandra and Kannappa, for the too-faithful river, come readily to their lips only when they are fast asleep and in the place where lost things live. Chikkiah dreams in full, coherent lines:

> How you love green, lord.
> Raw in the fresh sprout,
> emerald on jasmine leaves.
> The rain tree with its distant coolness.
> All the balm of green,
> O river of a thousand faces.
>
> The yellowing coconut fringe
> dangles
> dangerously.
> Is it time, my friend?

There's Anandagrama, steady as ever, though it is thinning a little. Their friends: some have died, some have got old. The wise Prabhu is gone—they miss his serene presence terribly. Elder Brother, clear-voiced as always, looks tired all the time. He speaks less. When he does, he is constant as ever. 'We have dreamt of a better life *and* made it,' he says. 'A life in which we work, pray and live with dignity. We will not let it go. No king or soldier or priest can tear apart the dream we are making real.'

For the rest of the day, they go about their work, a secret strength carrying them through too-sunny days, through the grinding monotony of stitching leather, casting pots, skinning stinking carcasses, weaving cloth too rich for them to wear.

On days when Elder Brother is too weak to speak to them, or even see them, they try hard to wake that bolstering spirit. Those are the days it's hard not to notice: there's expectation hanging in the city. This expectation is still air with invisible particles of poison. *Something is about to go wrong.*

But there are other brothers and sisters who have become Elders, they can keep them all together. These new Elders emerge from Elder Brother's chamber where he lies alone, listening more and saying less. The new Elders give voice to what their old leader is thinking; they also add their own thoughts. On the days when the new Elders argue about how to keep their experiment going and how to make it spread, there is a sense, once again, that they are still doing something. They are not subjects but rulers of their own lives.

Anandagrama is still there, it still hugs the edge of the city. But the city is spreading itself out; its stained mouth is eating up the edge little by little. The rumours begin. The murmurs become audible.

'Why have the rains failed? Here's why: the king's grandmother was a low caste servant. That's why he tolerated this unholy mixing of castes. He didn't see the shadow of Kaliyuga spreading across the sky in the place of rain clouds.'

'No king can rule if we do not give them permission from our gods. Temple before court. That's tradition. That's how it has always been.'

'The old gods know how to punish. That's why there's no rain. That's why the fields are dry and the rivers are sluggish. Farmers are idle, their children are starving.'

'We need a special puja to bring people back to their senses. Get us two hundred kilos of rice, thirty-five jars of milk, ghee, curd, a few kilos of sandalwood. Five hundred Brahmins will have to be fed of course.'

The temples ring with bells, chants; it's a rich and sonorous call to battle.

But still no sign of rain.

Puttanna's nonsensical songs have dried up. He still visits Chikkiah and Mahadevi, they still walk together to Anandagrama, come back as if they have bathed in a fresh spring. But more and more, Chikkiah and Puttanna sit by the river at night, silent. Words, songs, drumbeat—more and more they hear them only in the quiet murmuring of the river, or in their own separate heads. Mahadevi joins them by the river but she is unable to sit still. She walks along the bank. Chikkiah gazes at the small, fine figure, her back to him, receding into the darkness. For a moment he wills her to turn, walk back toward him so he can see her again, see Chandra and Kannappa in her.

Give me just one colour for once.

The tremulous green of leaves,
or the pale blue mouth of sky,
or the hard brown of twig and trunk
that not even you can soften.

Give me just one colour for once.

Don't make my eyes dart here and there,
everywhere.

Give me only one message, my friend.

The rumours in the city have become a disease. An angry rash has covered every inch of the city's skin, afflicted every quarter, rich or poor, pure or impure. This city has always prided itself on being a rich city, a city fit for the gods. But its greatness is in danger. It has a nervous king now, angry nobles and priests, restless soldiers. The markets wear an empty, hungry look. There's food in the temples, but people claiming starvation are stealing food specially cooked to please the gods.

Rumours alone are not enough. They have to come to a boil, that's their point. Soon it's time for action, this side or that. The lines are being drawn. There's the real army, but there's also a temple-funded army that's been growing secretly. Some of the Brahmins who went astray are coming back. Many of them have been frightened into returning where they belong. Others have been convinced by tongues greased with ghee: ananda can be found only in the place that holds honour and prosperity in its brick and gopuram; in the place that houses milk-bathed idols and their priestly guardians.

What eloquent chameleons these priests are, how they turn from guardians of the gods to generals rousing their army of bare-chested soldiers, each with a sacred thread glowing across his chest! They coax and threaten both the faithful and the faithless. 'Who are these people to overturn age-old wisdom, the difference the elders have devised, *sanctified,* over hundreds of years? Anandagrama! An unholy place where weavers, sweepers, merchants, carpenters and Brahmins get together, talk about how to pray and live and love! What god would accept this? A place where men and women eat together, or talk to each other as if they have forgotten all shame. As if ripe breasts and hirsute thighs are the same, as if blood and beating hearts can make man into woman, woman into man!'

There's a young man listening carefully to every word, taking it in, making it his own thought so that it will drive him to action. He used to be called Muthu, his father's peerless pearl, always the first among the boys to pick up a stick, a knife, a spear, and aim it right. His father is in the king's army, but he wanted Muthu to join the temple army—the temple guards. That's what Muthu has just become. He's no longer just his father's Muthu, but Muthuraja. He's going to be as good as a royal pearl, stationed at the most important temple in the land. No one knows him yet. But Muthuraja is sure that his spear will change that. It won't be long before every friend of the temple and the city and the kingdom will know him.

Muthuraja is no cowardly Brahmin; he's always ready to fight. But he's no ordinary soldier either. He's now part of the special band of temple guards in charge of security at the city's Grand Temple. There's a great deal to be kept safe from thieves and the lower castes, what some call the *people.* The lacquer god with eyes, nose and lips painted with gold leaf needs to be protected; the solid little goddess made of pure gold, rubies round her waist, an emerald sparkling on her nose; the god made of stone so heavy that many kilograms of gold can hang around his neck; and the pure ivory child-god, a fixed smile carved onto his face. Then there are the puja vessels, some so large it takes six men to carry one vessel; the deep barrels, mouths open on top for donations from the devout; and, of course, there are the priests and the Brahmins. Without them, it would all go, gold, temple, prayer, the necessary connection to the gods, belief, king and throne, good behaviour, code, tradition and order. The city itself. Civilization itself.

Muthuraja is being trained by the leader of the temple guards. But he is not leaving anything to chance, or the competence or friendliness of his leader. Muthuraja is up every morning, oiling himself, wrestling, running miles to keep fit, drinking litres of milk and eating as many fresh eggs as his mother can send him. He trains himself, not just with spear, but with club, dagger, knife, stone. His bare arms. And he's no brawny idiot. He has friends among the city spies; he keeps in touch with news of alliance, conspiracy, betrayal.

Muthuraja is ready. He waits impatiently for the rumours to ripen, for the priests to finish their long-winded arguments, and for the subversives to finalise their plans, then strike. For Muthuraja, real eloquence comes when the sharp tip of a spear turns bloody. He doesn't know yet whose filthy blood it will be, or how many treacherous louts will blood his spear. But the time for his kind of eloquence, for action and blood, is here. He's at the temple, ready and waiting.

Even in Anandagrama, where shedding blood has never been the way to fight, people are getting ready. They know it's not going to be easy. The grama crowds have thinned even more. But those who remain loyal are meeting, just as the other side is, though the grama meetings are secret, often at night, and in huts, or by the river, or in the forests or fields. There's some fear among several of them, some hesitation, some horrible memory of what they have heard from grandfathers and great grandfathers: 'It's always been like this, that's how the world is. They are up there, we are down here. We are born to obey, born to work, work, work, serve both the deserving and undeserving, then die like dogs.'

But there are brave words too, and they hear this with concentrated attention, because this is what feeds them on days when their bellies are only half full. 'If we go back to how we were, we might as well be dead. They can't make us untouchable again. They can't frighten us with their stony gods or their soldiers or their king.'

Then a young man among them comes up with a startling idea. 'Forget the court and the soldiers,' he says. 'The king is trembling inside his palace anyway. He didn't make all the rules, he only carries them out. He's a mere instrument in royal robes. It's the big temples where we have to go fight.'

They turn over this idea, so new and exciting. So terrifying. Go to the big temples! And do what there? Fight? Pray? But they have given up praying to stone and clay!

'We won't go there to fight,' says a feisty old woman. 'We'll go there and sing.'

The young man speaks again. He is quick to grasp the importance of symbol and gesture in a battle. 'Our mother here is right. We'll choose the biggest, grandest temple, right in the heart of the city. We'll storm the courtyard. We'll sing our songs together. We'll recite our lines of people's prayer.'

Some of the other young men form a semi-circle behind him. Their faces shine. 'We'll sing. But if we need to, we'll fight too. We are not cowards. We can defend ourselves. No pot-bellied priest is going to lay a hand on one of ours.'

Several of the older men are also getting enthusiastic. 'What about the wells,' asks a farmer, thinking angrily of the drying fields. 'We'll storm one of their wells. It's our people who dug them in the first place.'

No one knows what Elder Brother, resting on most days, thinks of the plan to seize upper caste wells. But the new Elders come back with his approval, and theirs, for the plan to occupy the Grand Temple with singing voices.

The city festers. 'We know what this disease is,' say the temple priests, used to diagnosing mysteries through the ages. 'Words that claim to be true but sing heresy—that's the cause. Those songs, those poems, all that illiterate singing and chanting that's filling our pure air with subversive lies. Those words being written down. We need to find those palm leaves they have filled up with trashy words and burn them. If these filthy scum who call themselves poets and singers and writers resist, cut down a few as examples'

Chikkiah is waiting. So is Mahadevi. And Puttanna. All of them—everywhere they go, whatever they do, there is also waiting to be done. They are waiting for a signal, though they don't know when or how or where it will show itself.

Like all signals to battle, it comes too soon though they have been waiting for weeks.

Puttanna comes to them. He does not have to say a thing. Chikkiah is ready. His only condition is that they first arrange for Mahadevi to travel with some of the other women, far away from farm, river, city. To someplace close to where Kannappa's monastic school sits like a haven of peace.

It's midday in the rainless city. Everyone, whether in the palace, the temple or the streets, is being boiled, baked or roasted. The tension that has been building up with the anger, plans and conspiracies, the stockpiling of arms, songs, lines of verse, pujas, a thousand traditions and a thousand challenges to them, come to a head. The pressure has to escape soon. Any minute. Now.

A motley group, but not so motley that they do not have a common purpose or common leaders, makes its way down the streets to the Grand Temple. It's a quiet and orderly procession with everyone walking four abreast, hands linked. Maybe it is this walking, marching image of unity, made up of men and women of all sorts of trades and castes and names and histories, which strikes awe and terror into those who peep out of windows from the biggest houses on the way. By the time the procession has reached the temple courtyard, all the windows and doors in the city houses are shut.

Not far from the huge ornate doors of the Grand Temple, inside its front courtyard where sandalwood is ground for the gods inside, where the big bell is rung to call the gods' attention, where clay and bronze and stone bull and peacock and lion and mouse and other divine vahanas lie like sentries waiting for the commands of god and priest, the crowd—

or the people's army, all infantry—take their position in a semi-circle facing the temple doors. The men in the first line begin to play their drums—flat pan-like drums, long gourd-like drums, every possible kind of drum as long as it has a good beat. Some go at their drums with sticks, others with their hands.

Chikkiah's hands feel empty; he's left his drum with Mahadevi. No matter—let it travel safe, let it remember how it became his. Let it remember, always, the touch of his father who did not meet the word *equal*, or see the flowing river, or keep time to the beat of the Anandagrama songs.

Then one by one, as if on signal, as if they have rehearsed for months, the people around Chikkiah begin to sing. One group sings; another group takes over, then hands over the lead to yet another. It's a never-ending wave, song following song, new voices rising when other voices subside. The refrains are ear-splitting evidence of unity: they sing the refrain together.

When it's his turn to sing, Chikkiah leads his brothers and sisters in singing about the river that brought him here. The Fearsome Four, his most beloved brothers, stand behind him, solid rocks, deep-rooted trees: Puttanna, Siddha, Chenna, Gundanna. How the five of them bring together their distinct voices, how they make their tributaries flow into the same sea. There's one voice missing though. Chikkiah feels it keenly. Where's the woman's voice in his song, what is his song without Mahadevi? But then he hears Puttanna sing,

> This water is holy,
> and this, and this,

Though his pitch is too low and he occasionally hits a false note, what scorn Puttanna can pour into each *this*. When strung on that rough voice, the words come alive as if freshly made.

This water is holy,
and *this*, and *this*,
they mumble in a foreign tongue,
sprinkling a few drops on
stony dolls in the temple,
on the floor of their houses
and outside.

These men
even sprinkle water on themselves
and say they are born again.

Gundanna is enjoying himself. Maybe he has helped himself to a little toddy before getting here. He is practically acting out the words while keeping an eye on the temple, hoping those killjoy bastards are looking.

My river, generous as always,
gurgles as it laughs.

Only those who have sweated day after day
know what it is to be soaked, O friend.

The last two lines rise to a crescendo, soak the air, bring Anandagrama to the temple, turn the temple surroundings into their Anandagrama. The lines say more than just their words. They say: 'Listen to the sweaty wisdom of our work-filled lives.'

They say: 'It's our work that makes us know the land like it is our child. The work makes us know the river like it is our brother. And the carcass and leather and broom and graves and fields are all our mothers. The mothers we break our backs for. The mothers who teach us to love ourselves. The mothers who know that this love and this work make us equal to anybody.' How much those two simple lines can say, how many spaces they fill:

> Only those who have sweated day after day
> know what it is to be soaked, O friend.

The priests and leaders of the Brahmin community are in the temple, watching.

'Kaliyuga is here,' thunders the oldest priest. 'I never thought I'd live to see the day.' He doesn't explain what such a day might bring, he doesn't need to. The day is here. The riffraff of the city, the unbathed, smelly, bare-chested mob is in the temple precincts singing and polluting. Singing!

Muthuraja is getting impatient. What are they waiting for, these priests? What is the leader of the guards waiting for? But Muthuraja inhales deeply, waits. He may be young, but he knows a situation has to build up, the danger to property and temple and palace and law has to be palpable. Then they can unleash a surprise when the crowd thinks they are getting away with it, when the protestors least expect it. Still, one can always help the ripening, bring it to crisis point. All it takes is a stone. No one will remember later whether it flew from courtyard to temple or temple to courtyard.

All it takes is a stone.

There's singing and more singing. Then an evil-edged stone flies swift and hard from somewhere, hits an old woman on the forehead. Her singing stops abruptly; she falls. There's blood spreading on her head. A wave of rage surges, gives way in a seamless movement to a cruel music. The rhythm comes from slapping, beating, kicking. The melody comes out of the fatal sounds: a spear piercing a chest; an axe falling on a neck and chopping it off. The chorus is continuous, it is a combination of screams, curses, moans, grunts, frantic calls to mother and god and heaven. There's a softer music in the background as assorted liquids spurt and fly in arcs, or gush, or drip to the ground.

Chikkiah, Puttanna, Siddha and Gundanna try to stay close together, but it's impossible. 'Siddha, take care of the children—and the Elders and the women,' yells Puttanna. Siddha rushes into the crowd. Elder Brother is on the ground—why did he come—he's hurt. But Siddha can carry him away, save him from being trampled. Gundanna is searching for children in the chaos, rounding them up and leading them away from the temple courtyard.

Where did the guards come from? They must have been hiding all this time, Chikkiah guesses. In the temple maybe, or behind it. No wonder the noble guardians of the temple remained inside as if they were not afraid of a thing. Chikkiah wants to shout to Puttanna, 'Run, they have weapons!' But he can't see Puttanna anywhere. Chikkiah picks up a stick someone has dropped on the ground. He rushes forward.

Meanwhile Muthuraja has fought his way into the melee. He's never seen so much blood before; he's lost his spear; but this is no time to shed manliness or think unprofessional thoughts. The temple's treasures are in danger. The palace's honour, its *security*, is at stake. Ahead he sees a slim dark man, not young, not old, his mouth open as if he is singing aloud. The man is chasing away a guard with a pathetic countryside stick.

Muthuraja steadies himself on his feet, pulls back his body a little, takes aim. He leaps.

Muthuraja lands on Chikkiah, knocks him sideways. Chikkiah is quick; he scrambles to his feet. Muthuraja grabs him by the neck. Chikkiah struggles, frees his neck in one great big effort. He's lost his stick, but he manages a quick kick at Muthuraja's leg. Then he sees Muthuraja pull out a long evil-looking knife. It's come, Chikkiah thinks, and the same instant he is knocked down. A large smelly body has flown at Chikkiah, knocking him flat; it's on top of him now, it's covering him.

'No!' Chikkiah screams, trying to push Puttanna off him roughly. He hardly knows who the enemy is, the guard with the knife or his beloved Puttanna.

'Puttanna, no!' he screams, but Chikkiah can't hear his own words. He can only hear a grunt of satisfaction above him. He can feel the warm blood dripping on him, then the dead weight. Chikkiah pushes the body off, pulls himself to his feet. Screaming like an animal in pain, he throws himself on the guard. Muthuraja is practically waiting for him to do this. It takes less than a moment for a knife to pierce a body. One more body. It takes just one moment for the knife that killed Puttanna to be pushed into Chikkiah's back, pushed deep so it almost reaches his heart, makes it beat slower.

Chikkiah falls.

Chikkiah has fallen. Muthuraja has already moved on to the next target.

Chikkiah lies on his stomach, unable to move. He can't see or hear anything though there must be a crowd around him, still fighting. He thinks he feels a pair of rough and heavy feet run across his back as if Chikkiah is already part of the earth. *I am not yet buried*, he thinks. Then, *I die a better death than my father*. It gives him consolation, this progress from father to son.

He summons the face of Elder Brother. Not as he last saw him, with blood on that smooth face, but the old calm face that could read Chikkiah's mind in just one glance. But wait, this is not Elder Brother, this smiling moonface is Kannappa. The moon slides too soon behind a cloud. No matter. The boy is safe, far away. So is Mahadevi. And also the girl—but what are these colours, so bright they hurt his eyes? The clothes he has dried on the riverbank have got up to dance like demons. It's all right; it's only the old river calling him like his father used to. It must be hard to flow for so long.

'I'm thirsty,' he hears the river say.

'I'm coming,' Chikkiah thinks. He has to plunge deep into the water to nurse the river. It hurts terribly.

Then thought and pain fade, so do those beloved faces. All Chikkiah has is blood, his freely flowing blood, to quench the river's thirst.

My life is my letter

1

It's the first journey of her life. Mahadevi has never been away from the old familiar field and river. The furthest she has travelled is to Anandagrama in the city nearby, the city they are now fleeing. She has heard people talk of travel as enjoyable, with wondrous sights to be seen on the way, people to meet, adventure to thrill, before the pleasure of arriving at the destination. But this journey—she can only hope it is her last. Often she is afraid. Too often, she is hungry, thirsty, too hot or too cold. And the destination—it's unknown, nameless. Can it ever be home? No. For now, her destination cannot be a place; she can only move toward Kannappa's boyish face. That face is the only thing she knows for sure about this journey or its end.

All the time she travels with the brothers and sisters who have escaped their enemies—the marauding stone-throwing, spear-piercing, fire-setting, knife-wielding soldiers, and the fellow citizens who have turned murderers—Mahadevi forces herself not to think of Chikkiah. Chikkiah, living or dead. She forces herself not to think of Chandra, buried under the bauhinia tree, waiting for her mother's visits. Mahadevi makes herself think of Kannappa instead. She must hang on to what matters, a face with a future.

She has not seen Kannappa for several years. But what

she has heard of him off and on, and the childish face she can recall in minute detail, lights up the nights Mahadevi and her friends walk through forests. During the day they hide in dark caves. Mahadevi is terrified of the pockmarked walls of the caves, their inner depths. There may be slimy bats hiding there; rows of bats used to seeing the world upside down. She would not be able to pass the days in these caves without the glow cast by Kannappa's face.

Sometimes, when they cannot find a safe cave, they are forced to travel by day. In the open fields, Kannappa steadies her racing heart when they huddle behind hay ricks as if they are thieves. They do carry treasure, but it is not stolen. Their treasure is only palm leaves wrapped in cloth, leaves weighed down with words. Kannappa would be happy to know that his face has helped protect such a treasure.

Mahadevi tells herself: only when she nears the monastery from where peace can never flee as it has fled an unreliable city, will she think of what she has left, what she has lost, or might lose. What she will do, where and how she will live. How she will wait for Chikkiah. Or not wait. News is best received in a peaceful place, just in case it is bad news. There's supposed to be a little village not too far from the monastery and its school. That's where she and some of her companions are headed. When she sees Kannappa, when she sees his real face, not the face hanging in her mind like a guiding lamp, she will no longer be a fugitive, or a subversive, or an enemy of the city, the palace, the temples, the gods. She will be Mahadevi again, mother of Kannappa. A real mother of a real child. She will be the same as anybody else.

(And Chikkiah? He can go to Chandra, they can be father and daughter, keep each other safe under trees, in the earth or the river. But no—it's too soon to remember them. Mahadevi flicks a hand at the air before her face, chasing away this troublesome thought.)

'Be patient,' the older men and women advise her. 'Every journey has an end. We're almost there.'

'Go to sleep,' says the old woman who smells of fish though she has not been near the river for months. 'The morning will be better.' When it's time to rest, Mahadevi seeks out this odorous memory of the river in a motherly body. Mahadevi sleeps by her. Or if sleep is elusive, Mahadevi lies by her quietly, listening to every bone in her body complain, every muscle whine about a new ache. The bones and muscles fall silent when her foot throbs with pain for three days from the thorn she stepped on in the dark forest trail. Sometimes, on restless nights and days when her patience wears out, Mahadevi feels the old woman's gnarled hand pat her for a while. Her fingers feel like twigs. It's a slow, wordless lullaby, this unexpected loving at the hands of a stranger.

Mahadevi has come to the end of her journey. The village is the smallest and most beautiful place she has ever seen. It's like the last stop to paradise. It prepares those who pass through for what lies beyond, making sure they will not be overwhelmed by too much beauty ahead. The village is more or less new. Not long ago, it used to be just the outskirts of the monastery by the river, just as Mahadevi's field and river were the outlying sanctuaries from Jayapura City. This village will now grow because of people on the run, or people looking for a place to make a fresh start of livelihood. People who need a place to put down roots again, or rest before they move on. Among those who have come with Mahadevi, the jugglers rest themselves, steady their twitching arms and shoulders, then take to the streets. The travelling storytellers collect a few local tales while they recover. They too are used to roaming towns and cities. Many of the farm workers, the artists, singers, instrument players, scribes, fisherfolk, potters and weavers decide to stay.

It's a good place to live. To one side is a gentle swell of hills. Not far away is a quiet river, held in place with the steadying roots of lush trees and shrubs. There's plenty of fish in the river, and it's easy to catch them since the river is so calm and clear. There are also fish-rich streams closer to the village, and happy brooks. The soil is fertile. There's space in and around the village, all the way up to the feet of the hills where the monastery lies quiet and hidden. There's space for fishermen, potters; for looms, dyed and drying rolls of thread; for land in which seeds can be planted, animals grazed. (There may be rats too, but there is no ratcatcher among them. Puttanna is irreplaceable.) There are also quiet, wide open stretches where songs can be made up before they are sung.

Mahadevi has arrived at her destination. The first and last journey of her life is done. Kannappa's face has led her here, forced her to pull herself off the stony ground in caves and the damp leafy floors of forests, take one step forward, then another. But now that she is here, what should she do next? Kannappa cannot leave the monastery or the school or his studies; they cannot live together. But to have him within reach, just a walk of an hour or two, what will that be like?

She packs a bundle of sweet gifts, the most she can afford to make: pancakes of coconut and sugar; sticky balls of peanuts dipped in syrup; a mixture of sesame and jaggery. When she finally meets Kannappa, there's no sign of the face that was her lucky charm on the journey. She knows she has been foolish. Or her memory has been foolish, reverting to sweet-toothed little Kannappa. This Kannappa is too tall, too thin, too sober. His curls are gone, all his hair is gone. He is shaven-headed.

It doesn't matter, there's time to learn this new Kannappa. She begins by kissing his cheeks, his forehead, his hands. It's been a long time since Kannappa was kissed; he is awkward in her embrace. But when she steps back, looks up at him—my god, he's at least a foot taller than she is—she sees how sweet, how serene his smile is.

They look at each other; there's too much to say and no words to say it with.

She breaks the silence. 'Your grandparents would have been so proud to see you grown up like this. A man. A learned man.' Her voice trembles a little. 'And your father,' she adds.

'Have you heard anything?'

'No.' She looks at him steadily. 'But we know what that means. Getting word from the city doesn't matter anymore.'

He nods. They sit for a while in silence, thinking their own thoughts, but they are also mourning together. They have almost become mother and child again.

Back in the village, lying on her mat that night, she thinks wistfully: if only she could have seen the boy become the man, heard his voice break and deepen, seen the hair sprout on lip and chin, witnessed all the rites of passage. Did she and Chikkiah really make a man like this? His face, his gravity, is so unexpected. His face: only the eyebrows are familiar, they are still exaggerated arches like her own. The thick eyelashes are like Chikkiah's. Eyebrows, eyelashes. Is that all a son owes his parents? Her piece-of-moon, her full moon, has gone all the way up to the sky to smile benignly at everyone. That's what he has been taught, not private acts of tenderness for a few, even if one of them is a mother. A lovelorn mother. It would be impossible to stand before Kannappa, lovelorn. A man like that may expect her to be bodiless; to be all mind, or all soul. She should be proud of him, she *is* proud, but she is also a little afraid.

When it was time for her to leave, he had embraced her with affection. How cool and soothing his touch was, but how it felt like it was for her comfort, not his. Her child, comforting her, blessing her. Though he hadn't said the words, she could almost hear them. 'I no longer need you, nor do my father and sister. All that work is done. Go look for your own work. Your own salvation.' What a long sermon in one embrace!

Mahadevi seeks out one of the brothers, a scribe who has remained in the village. She asks him if he will teach her how to read and write. He is surprised, but he agrees. Mahadevi too becomes a student. She works to feed herself, but her real work is learning with her teacher, reading every spare moment of the day, sleeping less at night so she can trace the teacher's letters by the dim and flickering light of a lamp. Though she works hard at it, she is not confident. When she reads, it is letter by letter, and it takes her time to put the letters together and decipher sounds. When she writes, she often makes a hole instead of a letter.

When she meets Kannappa now and then, she does not tell him what her real work is now. Nor does she tell him what this real work, writing from memory, can do. She has to work for one reason alone. She has to insist, through those clumsy, overlarge letters, the words often misspelt, that what she lived and loved did happen.

Slowly, and on many palm leaves, Mahadevi's letters make words; the words make lines; the lines hold meaning, memory. It's enough for her, writing everything she has seen and thought. She only writes about the past. She has few new songs. But she is a faithful chronicler. She writes down every line Chikkiah made, or she made up, or that they made up together. Re-living that life through written words, she learns to live again.

Mahadevi's matter-of-fact air leads Kannappa to assume she is well and content. As for Mahadevi, she does not think of content, or happiness, or love. Like Kannappa, she only thinks of salvation. But for Mahadevi, salvation does not mean prayer or even matters of the spirit. Her prayer is the task which takes up every moment that is her own.

Sometimes though, when Kannappa visits her, he asks her about what is gone. He asks his questions with a hesitant air, as if he is a raw student all over again. His questions come back again and again to Anandagrama, the people who built it or were part of it. He does not talk much about what has happened to it. It's the flowering, the little hopes and dreams, or the big passion of people like Puttanna and Gundanna that he is interested in. Other than the brothers and sisters of Anandagrama, the only person he is curious about is his father's father, the grandfather neither he nor Mahadevi has ever seen.

Mahadevi loves these reminiscences. Like her secret writing, these conversations assure her that what she lived was not some myth or tale, that it will live on as long as she and Kannappa remember it. But Kannappa always looks troubled after they have spoken of Anandagrama. He can't hear enough about it; but there is a look on his face, as if he has been cheated. He was only a little boy when it all happened. He was still a boy when he went away to the monastery. Where was he when his people raised their voices?

And now: there is the path that he has chosen or that has been chosen for him. That's all he has. His memory of Anandagrama, what he is reconstructing with Mahadevi's words, can never be the real thing.

It's not long before Kannappa comes to take leave of Mahadevi. He has been chosen to run a school which is to be attached to a monastery; the monastery is also building a new temple. Mahadevi looks at him with pride. She has heard people in the village talking about him. And they have a new name for him: her Kannappa has grown into a learned man, an almost-saint called Kannadeva. Mahadevi has heard much praise of this Kannadeva, messenger of good tidings such as peace and harmony and the virtue of looking inward. It's this praise that has prepared her for the inevitable parting. Any day, she knows, Kannadeva will be called to set out, walking stick in hand, to take his message to other places. She knows he will travel far with his well-tested map guiding his steps. He is sure to find his way to posterity.

So it has come now, what she has been sure of. She too has heard bits and pieces of the village news. A new temple is to be built in the lap of the open land where a gigantic peepal tree grows. The news has been spreading slowly, with variations. The big peepal has been glowing at night. Ordinary folk may think of ghosts and demons and seductive sorceresses. But the wise know. A temple has to be built there. A temple to go with a monastery and a school nearby. Kannadeva, youngest spiritual guide for miles in the country around the rooted river, will run the school. Who else but he, a man who speaks few words but when he does, the words are measured and weighty?

Kannappa, Kannadeva. Whatever Kannadeva does, whatever praise others sing about him, that piece-of-moon Kannappa is still hers. But once her son has left, Mahadevi's memory often gets confused between her Kannappa and the people's Kannadeva. It's when she writes Chikkiah's words that her memory never fails her.

2

Krishna and Shanta are in the big city for a seminar and are trying to enjoy themselves. They're staying in a simple but comfortable place—not a hotel, but a 'convention centre' located alongside a park with rambling trails. Once they have unpacked the small suitcase they are sharing, Shanta orders a pot of coffee in the room and checks the seminar programme. It sounds ambitious; the session titles and descriptions are peppered with words she finds daunting, such as *intersectionality* or *deterritorialising* or *assemblages*. Some of it is a bit coy: *socially excluded groups*, for example, or *social protection and social inclusion*. Of the titles of papers, she likes Krishna's best. But even his title, 'Fighting to Remember: Kannadeva's Real Voices', sounds distant from the subject of the talk. 'It's a good thing I studied botany,' she announces cheerfully to Krishna, pouring out his coffee.

But later, as he speaks on stage, Shanta is the most attentive member of the audience. She listens carefully to every word, even if she has heard it many times before.

Krishna's paper sums up what he has written on Kannadeva. 'We see multiple processes of forgetting here, all of it choreographed,' he says. 'One involves transforming Kannappa, son of Chikkiah the washerman and grandson of a cattle skinner, into Kannadeva, a figure of indeterminate lineage. His caste is not specifically mentioned; it's almost as if he comes from a casteless society. But this impression can only be created by suppressing all information about who he is, about the people he comes from, or their attempts at resisting a caste-based society. This convenient error of omission makes Kannappa—or Kannadeva as he is generally referred to—more acceptable as a "Hindu saint-poet".'

Krishna pauses, takes off his reading glasses and looks at the audience. 'Listen to the real voice of Kannappa's people. Then ask yourself the question, Can you separate this man from the songs he grew up with? Or from the resistance in Anandagrama?' Krishna then recites, in a strong, challenging voice unlike his own:

In a past life I was untouchable.
In a past life they smelt my shadow and fled.
In a past life the meat I ate was rotten.
In a past life I bathed in a stagnant pond.

That was the past.
Tie me, tether me so I don't stray there again.

Keep me here, in current and whirlpool,
O river of a thousand faces.

There's a disturbance at the back of the room. The door has been pushed open; more people seem to be coming.

Two young men—they look like students—barge in. As if on signal, two others at the back get up. One of them shouts, 'You're insulting a saint! How dare you talk about meat and Kannadeva in the same breath?' The other three begin to shout as well: 'Obsessed with caste … Hinduism is not just caste … polluting our saints …' The organizers, having got used to this sort of disturbance, are efficient. As the audience exchanges indignant shouts with the hecklers, the four young men are led away. Luckily they seem to be armed only with words.

The talk goes on, but the mood has changed. Krishna reads the paper rather than talking to the people in the room. What he reads is a talk by a university professor who is describing, quoting and analyzing, and doing it with reasonable competence. But what he stirred up earlier, for just a few moments, has dissipated into the air. Chikkiah's words no longer come to life through Krishna's voice. Krishna knows this; he hears his voice grow softer as he reads, his tone more tentative than usual.

As he and Shanta leave the seminar hall, a young woman waylays them. She says to Krishna, 'Thank you for your talk, sir. I think your work is really important.'

Krishna smiles.

But the young woman is not finished. 'I don't want to get personal, sir. But you are not Dalit. Isn't this another form of appropriation? You read these poems, explain them to us, deliver them to the world in a sense. I mean, you're talking of a cow skinner. Can you ever understand his life?'

A sadness spreads across Krishna's face, though he can't name this sadness, even to himself. Krishna thinks of saying to this young woman, 'Just as Chikkiah and the others would not leave Kannadeva alone, they do not leave me alone now. They say to me, *Listen to us, speak for us.*' But Krishna doesn't say this aloud. Instead he tells the young woman, with great kindness, 'You're right. I can never directly understand—in the sense of experience—the day-to-day life of a cattle skinner, his suffering, his fears and dreams. But I can listen to his voice. I can read what is written about him. I can translate those words, study them. In fact, I must.'

Krishna turns away so the young woman will not see how moved he is by her question as well his own answer.

That evening, he and Shanta go for a long walk in the park, then find a charming little place that sells ice cream. They have never seen so many flavours before, nor have they heard such exotic names for ice cream. After much discussion, Shanta settles for Seventh Heaven and Krishna for Chocolate Bomb. They eat a spoonful of each other's choices, agree that both are excellent. But secretly, they miss the white-and-green striped ice cream in Hotel Darling, their boring old vanilla and pista. Secretly, they can't wait to get back to Devapura.

It's early morning. Srikumar is already in the shop. He has closed the shutter most of the way, gone into his little area at the back, switched on the light. The man in the picture on the wall continues to look sideways. He's not distracted by what Srikumar has unpacked and is now holding tenderly.

Srikumar admires what he holds in his hands. Who would have thought this black and brown thing of scrap metal, this water pipe made into a barrel, could be the source of such power! He puts it down, picks up a bullet. This hard, pointed thing: it's a perfect shape, a perfect symbol of power; and he has four of them. He will use one or two to silence the rakshasa forever. This Krishna is only the first of the rakshasas Srikumar will dispatch. As everyone knows, rakshasas, like the Muslims and untouchables they love to cohabit with, breed quickly. For a moment Srikumar feels overwhelmed. He can see an army of rakshasas march toward him, growing a fresh head for each one felled by a bullet. Some of the heads wear lacy white caps.

Srikumar places the bullet back on the shelf, takes the gun again. When he holds it, he can feel Guruji and his father and mother and the picture on the wall, and the many people he has met and not met but who must not be linked with him. They are all *in* him, adding to his own strength. He feels this collective strength travel from his hands up his arms, then leap to both sides, filling up his chest. *May he keep this strength in him, may it always defeat his enemies.* Srikumar lines up the gun and the bullets on the shelf before the picture on the wall. He lays a marigold on the gun and one on the bullets. He dabs a touch of kumkum and haldi at the tip of the bullets and on the open mouth of the barrel. *May these blessed weapons be used for auspicious actions.* Ayudha puja has come early this year. Srikumar bends with folded hands, prays. He surrenders.

That evening, he makes his way to Vinay's shop to return the SIM cards and cell phones he has used so far and get another batch. Vinay is waiting for him. He's ordered coffee and jilebis, the kind he knows Srikumar likes, fat and juicy. Srikumar takes just one jilebi. 'Don't want to get out of shape,' he says.

Vinay, who was about to take a second one himself, immediately puts it back on the plate and says, easily, what he's been saying all their lives. 'You're right.'

Their tongues sweetened with syrup, their throats warmed by coffee, the two make plans. They have had their meetings with Sabha members and associates. Srikumar knows he is only one little part of a group, a group that is linked with many others. This does not make him feel small; if anything, it makes him feel the new power of the sevaks, growing in three states, spreading everywhere in the country.

'But now,' Srikumar tells Vinay, 'it's up to us. We have to make it work.' He says 'we', but in the carefully scripted scenarios in his head, Vinay is only a supporting actor. He, Srikumar, is going to fire the bullet that fells the rakshasa.

Both Srikumar and Vinay know Devapura well—it's a couple of hours away if they zip down the new highway. 'I'll go ahead, find a room, start the tracking,' Srikumar tells Vinay. Srikumar wants to start the reconnaissance on his own; he will know everything there is to know about this rakshasa in a few weeks. He tells Vinay, 'You make sure of the phones and the bike.'

'Take my motorcycle,' says Vinay. 'I'll come join you by bus when I get your go-ahead.'

Srikumar feels a twinge, but he sees Vinay's point immediately. Srikumar's new bike is too smart and noticeable. Vinay's motorcycle is a couple of years old but trustworthy. Besides, Vinay can repair anything that rings or rolls.

Srikumar smiles at Vinay. 'Come home one of these evenings,' he tells Vinay, 'come for dinner.' His smile grows. 'My mother is searching for a bride for you.' Srikumar knows what a relief it is for Vinay to have an evening away from home. Going home means tending to an invalid mother, or listening to the perpetually complaining aunt who looks after her.

'How is Susheela Akka?' Vinay asks respectfully. Susheela is Srikumar's pregnant wife. Vinay has barely exchanged ten words with her in the year she has been married to Srikumar.

Srikumar goes back to his taciturn self. A wife is a very private business. He doesn't like talking about Susheela to anyone except his mother. And that's because his mother is supposed to make sure Susheela is the kind of wife and daughter-in-law she should be; and soon, the kind of mother she should be.

Just the day before, Srikumar's mother got Susheela to stand before the gods in the puja room and make a few promises. 'Susheela,' said his mother, 'I have told you why the gods have given a mother such a high position. Will you tell us—tell me, and our men here, your husband and father-in-law, what you have learnt?'

Susheela had spoken modestly but clearly. 'A mother is important because she teaches her son to be strong and patriotic.'

'Yes,' Srikumar's mother had nodded. She took Susheela's hand in her own. 'You're standing before the gods, my girl. This is the time to pray for a son who will fight anyone who disrespects our country and religion. Pray that your son will protect us chaste Hindu women at any cost.' She tightened her grasp on Susheela's hand. 'Swear here, now, before the gods, before your elders and your husband. Swear you will have a son who is not a coward.'

Srikumar slips on his helmet, starts the bike. Tonight he must check with his mother whether his wife is following all the rules of diet, exercise and prayer. He must also tell them at home that he will be away for a couple of weeks. Maybe work or a youth meeting combined with a pilgrimage? Better not mention the sevaks at all? It doesn't matter—he can trust his mother and wife never to ask him any unwanted questions. As for his father—he almost wishes he could tell the old man, he would be so excited that his son is acting on what he has been taught. But best to keep quiet for now. The less people know, even his own people, the better. He didn't need to be told by Sirish Mama and others that though he is not alone, he must act as if he is.

Srikumar is in Devapura. He looks at the three places on the shortlist Sirish Mama has sent him. By late evening, he has decided on the one hugging the outskirts of the town. It's a seedy-looking boarding and lodging house in a side lane, so cluttered with lodges and shops and carts and people that he might as well be invisible. It's called Ishwar Comfort Lodge. It's perfect.

The man at the reception has been cleared by Sirish Mama as a 'friend'. The friend is on his cell phone, his eyes shut, cleaning his teeth with a matchstick. Srikumar waits for him to finish. The friend has a gold chain round his neck and any number of threads round both wrists. The threads are mostly red or yellow, but there's a thick one in black. Srikumar looks at his own bare wrists. He is proud he no longer needs anything on wrist or neck or forehead to remind him of who he is.

The man removes the matchstick from his mouth, opens his eyes to examine his discovery. The phone remains in his left hand. Srikumar quickly says, 'A single room.'

The man barely looks at Srikumar. Even as he speaks into the phone, he takes the cash and pushes a key across the table.

The room is on the second floor and at the back of the building. There is a small window but it faces a brick wall a foot away.

Once he has locked himself in, he has complete privacy. Srikumar opens the single cupboard; it's empty except for a brown blanket like an old sleeping dog, a lone rusted hanger, and a few half-eaten moth balls. But the cupboard can be locked, and there's a hook on its door so he can add, if he wants, a proper lock of his own. He puts away the backpack under the blanket. It's time to go track the rakshasa down to his lair, get to know him better than he knows himself.

The rakshasa is at home in his study, admiring the books he has bought after the seminar in the big city. There's a blissful look on his face. He loves everything about new books, their feel, their smell, and most of all, the sense of expectation they evoke. Once he opens a book and begins to read, who knows what he may find?

Krishna could buy only eight out of the pile of fifteen he had selected in the bookshop in the big city. He told himself not to be greedy; as it is, a chunk of Shanta's savings went into publishing his book. But still—he looked again at the pile he wanted. Shanta had helped him out, saying, 'We can't fit all these in the suitcase, we'll have to pay for excess baggage.' Her sweet but firm voice had worked on Krishna as well as it did on Chitthu. He put back seven of the hardcover books.

Krishna looks at the spoils now, deciding the order in which he will read them. He can hear the electric tanpura begin its drone in the next room. Shanta has begun her hour of music practice with the kriti *Teliyaledu Rama, bhakti margamulu* … Rama, show me the path to bhakti. Bhakti. Devotion; but the word is not enough to hold everything bhakti implies. Krishna turns back to the books waiting for him.

He chooses the fattest of the new books, a hardbound one of course. It has a luscious cover, a painting of a woman wearing all kinds of jewellery: three pieces on each ear, strands of pearls round the neck, and another necklace of red stones. A bejewelled nose-ring hangs over her upper lip. Her wrists are heavy with green and gold bangles. All this, grins Krishna to himself, but the painting is called 'A Lady Holding a Fruit'. She does indeed hold a little globe of fruit in her hand, but Krishna has to look for it; the hand with the fruit has wandered to the spacious spine of the book.

Krishna turns pages, reading snatches here and there. He pauses at a reference to one of the stories about how Hanuman brought a ring from Sita, imprisoned in Lanka, back to Rama.

'In a contemporary South Indian variant of this episode,' Krishna reads, 'the storyteller says that Hanuman dropped Rama's ring into the ocean; then the storyteller asks his listeners, "How can Hanuman retrieve the ring?"Someone in the audience (within the story) jumps up, runs to the ocean, finds the ring, and returns it to the storyteller, who then continues his narration.'

Krishna recalls this story with affection. It sums up everything he believes about the power of the story, how it can become a living thing. How it can become part of the storytellers or poets; part of those who hear the stories or poems or songs so they can't help but pass them on.

Krishna arranges the books in a pile, what he will read first on top, what looks worthy but less pleasurable at the bottom. Before he joins Shanta in the next room, he takes a last look at the bookshelf: there they are, his old friends; and there they are, the new ones waiting for him to fall in love with them.

How he loves his work, the best work of all, taking words

or lines, fragments of knowledge, and stretching them with his mind, his imagination. It's what his young students may call a high. Krishna feels sorry for those who live without experiencing this act, as fulfilling as eating or drinking or sex. The people he feels sorry for take shape in his mind. The likes of that Guru, for example, or those who send him anonymous or signed hate mail, or make threatening phone calls. All he feels for them is pity. Their minds are bound like mummies as if they are dead. The living dead, unable to travel from idea to idea, view to view, one mind to another, one time to another.

3

Satya is looking at the peepal—what he can see of it in the frame his window allows. Over the last couple of months, the tree has shed its leaves. It has undressed itself shamelessly. 'Look,' it seems to say, 'this is my nature, this is who I am. I follow the seasons. When it's time, I turn, slowly, into a gaunt silhouette against the sky.' The bare branches have grown rows of beads. The beads are hard, the branches straight and proud. The tree's arms stretch in all directions and embrace the air. And the tiny coppery leaves—how did Satya miss their birth from the beads? They look wet, shiny in their newness. A few of them are still in the midst of unfurling themselves, sticky with their afterbirth. But not everything is new and fresh. Satya can see an untidy twiggy nest now that the tree has rained its old leaves. How vulnerable the nest looks now that it is exposed! Or does it look old and sad because it is empty?

These days, small things startle him, or move him. He sees everything as if the living world is magnified. The world is growing bigger, louder, even as his place in it is shrinking.

The peepal speaks to him though it's in a place where everyone speaks *at* him. It's his tree of a thousand faces, like Chikkiah's river of a thousand faces. Chikkiah's poetry, Satya's peepal tree: how many messages he gets that despite all, something new, something beautiful, can grow even in this rotten, divided world! But can the likes of Chikkiah and Satya ever make something of these hopeful messages? Can their lives be lived as they should, can their humble words become everyone's poetry?

Like the peepal tree, like Chikkiah's poems or his river, the week that unfolds shows Satya almost a thousand faces. But far too many of them speak of despair.

His mother's friend, their neighbour Suja, calls. She's in a hurry to tell him what she has to say; maybe she has promised to return the borrowed cell phone soon. 'That bastard Ganesh is bothering your mother for money. He's been haunting her place with that account book of his, talking of interest.' She lowers her voice, a difficult thing for Suja. 'Your mother doesn't want to tell you. Please don't tell her I called, she'll be angry with me. But I thought you and Prasad better send her something soon. Keep the greedy sonofabitch quiet for a few weeks.'

'Please don't call Prasad,' begs Satya. He hesitates. 'I'll get my scholarship money soon. It … it got delayed this time.'

Satya is in the finance office, waiting for Mr Murthy to give him time. He has been waiting for almost an hour. He has already missed the first class, but it can't be helped. He has to find out what's happened to that money, get it released, and send it all to his mother. As for himself, he can manage on practically nothing.

It's close to noon by the time Mr Murthy waves him over to his desk.

'My scholarship money,' begins Satya, but Mr Murthy holds up his hand to stop him.

'It's easy to come here asking for this money and that money,' Mr Murthy says. 'You people are very good at making demands.'

'But Mr Murthy, I have earned that scholarship.'

'Earned? What work have you done? Let me see—you've not even bothered to go to class.' He pulls out an attendance sheet.

Satya leans over, shocked. Murthy pulls himself back to keep the distance between them. He does not let go of the sheet, only holds it up for a moment. 'Here, take a look and stop acting so innocent.'

Satya's been marked absent for at least two classes a week in Dr Sharma's anatomy class. The big red X's stand in a row, ready to take on Satya.

'But I wasn't absent all those days,' says Satya. 'You can ask the other students.'

'Are you accusing your professor of tampering with your attendance? Or are you accusing me? That's right, blame someone, anyone, because you can't cope with your studies. When will you people learn?'

Murthy slips the sheet into a file, pushes his chair back and gets up. 'You can put in a formal complaint if you want. It will be processed'—and Murthy now looks and sounds like an official who lives and breathes procedure—'in due course as per the rules. But I can't release the scholarship money till all the requirements are met.' Murthy sheds the official look. He shrugs casually, as if he is offering avuncular advice, but his eyes look anything but casual. 'You better do that soon if you want to sit for the exams.'

Satya rushes to the dissection hall, worrying that he is late, worrying that he will not recall what he watched and heard and did in the last session, worrying about the complete silence that has greeted his letter of complaint, worrying about his scholarship, worrying about money. He already owes Ravi and, as always, his brother Prasad. Even worse, he owes a little to Rahul, whom he hardly knows though they have been roommates for months. How can he ask either Prasad or Ravi again? And nothing would make him ask Asha. He might be worse off than Ravi and Asha. But they too bear the weight of borrowed money to be returned in driblets; the guilt, possibly, of depriving brothers and sisters; the knowledge of parents struggling every day, every week and month.

In the dissection hall, everyone's already around the four cadavers, one for each batch of twenty-five students. As always, the pungent smell of formalin hangs in the air; it seeps into every pore of his skin. Satya blinks to clear his eyes. He can't possibly remain at the back with the students who just watch. He pushes his way forward, ignoring the usual barbed remarks.

In his room at night, the cadaver's face comes back to him. How peaceful it looked, embalmed in sleep. On his own face—and he doesn't need a mirror to look at it—he can see a thousand miseries. No, he can see only one, with a small single-syllable name but as big as a monster, many-headed like some mythical beast, too many heads to be killed by Satya in just this one life. The creature is taking up every inch of space in his life, gobbling up all his air. Yes, Satya has his armour, his weapons. His yearning, his hard work, his mother's love, his brother Prasad, Asha, Ravi. Chikkiah's words like distant memories. And his own words—but they are still so simple and raw, how much can they do?

He picks up the blue notebook, opens it to a new page, and writes.

This is a cobbler's child.

Don't sit next to him.

This is a washerman's child.

Don't speak to him.

This child's mother lifts buckets of shit.

Run away from him.

My tears for these children have dried up.

Must my voice too grow silent?

There are several pages in the notebook still, inviting him to fill them up. But they too will have to learn that not all dreams are allowed to live.

It's night again.

But this is not a night for studying, for memorising long words, lists of points, entire paragraphs. He has piled up his notes and diagrams neatly. Rahul can use them, just as Ravi and Asha used to do earlier.

It's not a night to read poetry, even words by Chikkiah and his friends, brave words of comfort. Besides, he no longer needs the book Ravi lent him. In the short time he has had it, Satya has learnt the poems well enough to recall almost every word.

It's not a night to write in his blue notebook, Asha's gift that has patiently heard the thoughts no one else wanted to hear. For a moment he misses it terribly.

But really, all he needs is his pocket—or what is in his pocket. That, and the night, and his readiness to move.

He walks into the night.

He walks in the darkness. The roads are empty. The roads

have emptied themselves to let him know that this is what night is. In the end, you have to walk alone, completely alone, in the dark. But wait—now that he is looking, he can see a huddle here, and a few huddles there across the road. Bodies in sleep. There's one that's completely covered with a sheet. Should he go lift that sheet, uncover the body, see if it's still alive? No, he's done with that; he's done with cadavers; or with bodies struggling to breathe. He hears a dog bark and a muted growl of a response. Satya walks on.

How long it's taking. He has always cycled to the pond, he didn't realise how long it would take to get there on foot. It's like preparing for the entrance test again. Will the exam never come so he can be done with it?

He's left the road now; he's walking past fields, trees. His damp shirt sticks to his back. He misses his textbooks. Where will everything he has learnt from them go? Satya mumbles to himself, 'The brain. A hundred billion neurons that make us who we are. A complex, highly organised living structure.' A breeze stirs; the leaves rustle in response. Satya says to them, 'The cerebrum. Frontal lobe, temporal lobe, parietal lobe, occipital lobe, limbic lobe.' What's that he can see on the sky in between the branches, like the knobbly skin of a nut? The cerebrum's surface, convoluted into hundreds of folds. He greets the neocortex where all the higher brain functions take place. 'The frontal lobe,' he mumbles. He touches his forehead. 'The centre of reasoning; planning; problem solving—' but he's here. Or the pond is here. He can sit now, fall silent. The lessons are over.

It's almost dawn. The world will wake up just as he goes to sleep. But he has prepared well for this long sleep. He has already sold the cycle Prasad bought him. Gone to the post office and sent a money order and two parcels by registered post, though not acknowledgement due. The parcels were, of course, books. One was the book Ravi gave him. The other was the blue diary. He bought himself his last meal at a chemist. Then he set out on his solitary picnic.

He pulls the packet out of his pocket, tears it open, looks at the colourless granules. For a moment his mind is empty. What is this, who is it for? And why? Then Dr Sharma arrives, except this Dr Sharma is eager to help. He shows Satya how he and many others have, over years, with either deliberate or careless intention, turned Satya's head, his knobbly-surfaced brain, into a place difficult to live in. Sharma opens Satya's mouth. 'See, it doesn't even need to be diluted in water.' Sharma places the granules lovingly on Satya's tongue. It tastes of nothing. Sharma shows Satya how to swallow this nothing. Having done his part, Dr Sharma disappears.

Satya lies on his back, looking at nothing, seeing everything. But why has the whole picture around him turned so black and white? It's neither night nor day; is that why the world knows only two colours? Ah—now the black is lightening, the white is deepening, and everything is a palette of greys. He likes that; his watery, stinging eyes and his pinpointed pupils prefer this blurry grey.

There's a body lying not far from the pond.

It's still not a body; he's twitching, trembling, drooling. How wet he is—is it sweat, saliva? Tears? What does it matter? And why is he alone? No, he is not. Here's Prasad, and behind him, holding hands, Ravi and Asha. Satya wants to say something to them but he has forgotten what it was.

It's so hard to breathe, it's such an effort, worse than the worst of exams. Only Amma can help. And here she is, as always, her love following him wherever he goes, faithful as ever. She doesn't want him to lie there like an orphan, there's water nearby, water that can flow if it is allowed to, give life to what she has planted in the fields. He gets up—how hard—he stumbles then crawls. The sky and trees and pond swim around him and he retches. But Asha and Ravi are here, one on either side of him. How gently they guide him into the water.

He sinks almost at once. No, this water does not flow. It lies there, still, stupid, and without an idea for the future. But the sky is lightening, there's a streak of pink waking it up. What will it do? Will it bring the day sooner, move the water so it finally flows, then shout aloud, 'Look! Here's my child, what have you done to him?'

Keep me here, in current and
whirlpool

1

Morning is already here, touching Asha gently, showing her what a nurse's fingers should feel like. Asha resists opening her eyes—surely she's been asleep for just an hour or two? She turns over onto her stomach and burrows her head into the cave of her pillow. But sleep is gone; morning has won. Still, before she can open her eyes, acknowledge that she is awake, Asha has to make sense of last night's dream. There was nothing to see in this dream; nothing to hear. There was no information, no detail. It was nothing but the haze of a mood, and even that was not good or bad; it didn't have a name. But how powerfully that haze comes back to flood her mind now. A sense of waiting, that's what the mood or dream was. Waiting for someone? For something to happen? She must call home today. She dreads hearing that her sister is sick, or that her father has lost his job, or—Asha's eyes fly open. She meets the day; it's dull, ordinary, a day like any other. She yawns, looks enviously at Priya who is still fast asleep. She gets out of bed.

In the second class, she finds she has forgotten her notebook. She races back to her room. On her way out of the building, she sees the day's post lying unsorted on the long table. There's a slim flat rectangular parcel right on top with her name on it. Asha picks it up. There are many

Ashas in the hostel but yes, it is for her, this brown envelope that says Registered Post. Who sends anything by registered post anymore? Universities and colleges. The courts. The government. The police. She turns it over, sees the two words with a colon in between. From: Satya. There is no address below.

Asha tears the brown cover open but she knows what it is even before she sees it. It's the notebook she gave Satya months back, though it seems like years now. The blue cover and the label she had decorated with flowers and his name look fresh. He's taken good care of it, the way he always takes care of books, notes, people. And himself? Is he taking care of himself?

What is she thinking, admiring the cover and the label, when she knows, when she doesn't need to open the book to learn why it has come back to her? She has to sit. Her legs are hollow—no, they are filled with gravel, cement, stone. She limps back to her room carrying herself like an old woman. She carries the slim book as if it is heavy, as heavy as a limp body.

She sits on her bed, stroking the book with a finger. Is this paper or skin? The book looks at her, daring her to open it if she wants answers.

Asha takes a deep breath, opens the first page. But she's only able to read a phrase here, a sentence there. It's never been so hard to make sense of letters, words, even if only some of them are in English. *Medical student... hard to believe... have to be worthy of it... Ravi and Asha... would be less alone if...* She turns to the last page—the last page in which there is writing—and this, every word of it registers, every word is cruelly legible though it is written in a scrawl unlike the neat handwriting in Satya's notebooks in school. *Asha and Ravi: I can't write a letter to the two of you. My life is my letter. You know it better than anyone else.*

Asha is in a bus, on her way to Ravi's college.

In between the phone calls to and from Ravi, her ears fill with Satya's voice. What's the point of hearing him if she can't make out a word? She's not sure what language this voice speaks. What words, what poetry, can rise to the challenge of giving language to a broken dream?

She shuts her eyes and the voice goes away. But now she can feel him sitting next to her. She can see him. Not the Satya who has written in the book and sent it to her, but the Satya to whom she had given the empty notebook. She remembers his deep pleasure at receiving a gift, however small and unimaginative. He looks at her now as he did then, as if he wanted to hug her. He didn't, he doesn't, but made up for it—makes up for it—with a smile. That smile. It contains—contained—every promise in the world.

There's someone tapping her shoulder. It's the woman who's sitting next to her, asking if she is all right. Asha nods grimly. How can that Satya no longer be here, there, anywhere? Can you love someone even if there is no body? And how will she remain Asha, Ravi remain Ravi, if a part of them is missing?

Already they have changed. Asha, who has never been to Ravi's college before, is taking a bus there alone. She has not waited to see if the letter she left with Priya has got her permission to leave college and hostel because of 'a personal emergency'. Asha, who cries when she sees a sad film on TV, has not yet shed a tear. And Ravi—when the bus finally comes to a stop and she sees him waiting for her—looks nothing like the Ravi she knows. This is a childlike face, bewildered, frightened. All the old humour and newfound activism have deserted him, left his face naked. They walk in silence till they reach his room. Luckily his roommates are not there. It's only then, when they have sat down on his bed, face to face in the cluttered room that smells of food, sweat and cigarettes that words come to them; words and, finally, tears.

Ravi brings Asha the book on Chikkiah and Kannadeva, the book Satya has sent him back in the post. He places it on Asha's lap as if it is a baby. Asha pulls out the blue notebook from her bag, places it on the bed between them.

'Is there a—a letter?' Ravi picks up the notebook gingerly. He doesn't know why he is whispering.

Asha's eyes leak; her nose runs. She can feel a thin stream making its way down her face. There's a stream clogging her throat too, drowning words. When she finally speaks, she sounds hoarse with the effort. 'Look at the last page,' she says. She gestures at the book in Ravi's hands. Ravi opens the diary at the last written page with trembling fingers.

Later, as night comes to mark one more day without Satya in the world, Asha stands with a small group, all of them strangers except for Ravi. Ravi's Bhim Shakti comrades hold candles; Professor Senthil speaks. Asha listens, surprised by what she hears. Senthil didn't know Satya, but he describes what happened to Satya exactly as if he knew him. How does that happen? Do the familiar details, the words *discrimination* and *no support* and *institutional murder* make Satya only one more name in a long list?

There's no wind in this place. It's on strike; or it's

expressing solidarity by its absence, letting the candles burn straight as needles. The needle of flame she holds looks Asha in the eye. It's asking her hard questions. Is there any point in picking up a needle and thread, in one pair of hands, or a few hundred hands, seeking to repair a torn life? But the life is not just torn, it's lost; and it's left behind other torn lives that may, like Satya's, fall entirely to pieces. How is she to live, how is anyone to live, if that frayed rag of a life is beyond repair?

Ravi's tears have dried up; it's anger that fills Ravi now, a cold anger. He doesn't want to talk any more, he doesn't want candles or speeches or poetry, he wants to be *doing*. But what can he do? Ravi sends messages to WhatsApp groups; he writes on Facebook.

As always, the story hides behind the old smokescreen. A Dalit student's suicide: it's a case of academic weakness. Inadequate merit. In Satya's case too, the College Principal and the police have agreed on that. The College Principal has issued a statement: 'The unfortunate suicide of first year MBBS student Satya was because of his inability to cope with academic pressure. We try to help all our students, especially those from a weak or humble background, but some students give up because they can't keep up with academics or because of personal reasons.'

Ravi responds, punishing the keyboard furiously.

> Weak. Humble. We are neither weak nor humble. Why don't they name us, why do they hide behind these lies? And merit. Satya not have merit? What merit does his college have if it drove him to death?

Ravi struggles not to feel alone. Senthil Anna has told him how important it is to be part of the group, to feel connected to the community, to the idea of Dalit, to Bahujan. But Satya is not Satya for the rest of them. How is Ravi to explain this one man, his beloved friend, to anyone else? For now, his only friend is anger. If he lets that go, what will remain but sadness and despair? Somehow, in some way, he, Ravi, must punish that medical college; get it to admit that the college, the entire system, not just a single professor or student or official, murdered Satya.

But a few days later, a news story breaks its way out of the ground and swallows up everything else. It's like a firecracker that goes on and on because it's eye-catching, ear-splitting, brain-addling. A movie actress has managed to get a visa to Pakistan to immerse her grandfather's ashes in a river. The river is near the place where his family lived before partition. She made her grandfather a promise on his deathbed.

Everyone in the country has something to say, it seems; on the grandfather's wish, on the granddaughter taking him seriously, on the Pakistani embassy's evil designs in granting a visa to grab an Indian body even if it has been burnt to ash. Little boxes on television explode with screaming that is supposed to be debate. The story spreads across the maps of Facebook, Twitter, WhatsApp, real news, fake news, print, digital. It's a crowded conversation, though many do not converse but deliver serial monologues. The trolls march out in orderly formation. Shankar@hindupatriot and his brothers, sisters and cousins threaten the actress and her family for anti-national behaviour. The trolls' granduncles perform pujas to assuage their hurt feelings—how can the rivers and soil of Mother India be insulted like this? When a young woman trapped in one of those speaking boxes on TV points out that this is a good sign, a woman immersing ashes, the granduncles leave their pujas and issue a call to rape both the young woman who was on TV as well as the actress. A long-time member of several India-Pakistan friendship committees speaks up, says human attachment is superior to any nation state. Intellectuals and legal experts strain to see the 'larger picture' or examine multiple layers, whether of history or philosophy or law. For less exalted readers and viewers, there are discussions, accompanied by photographs of the actress carrying the urn to the plane in Mumbai airport. Should she have worn a green kurta to Pakistan? Should she have displayed bare arms on such a solemn journey?

The Bhim Shakti campaign, whether on social media or in real life, fades to its proper place, outside public space, to a place that must be right because it's almost invisible.

Asha has returned to her college with both books, two hard bundles of sorrow.

It's Sunday again. From now on, Sunday, or any other day, is never going to be the same, because it is a day Satya will not see. She doesn't like what she can see either. She doesn't want to see the fragmented film in her head: here's Satya walking alone, looking for his final home; there's Satya, walking past fields to a stretch of water. A stretch of water—there was no river nearby to call Satya into its flowing embrace. No sea either, no lake. Her pain would have been the same whatever it was; but her heart breaks every time she imagines a small, mean pond. She tries hard not to think of the poison that came before the pond.

Asha opens the blue notebook, looking for refuge; the only refuge she has for now is Satya's own words:

Books, newspapers, TV.
Movies. Court and classroom.
The streets.
I am looking for missing persons.

I am looking for them everywhere.
My mother, back bent, humming to herself.
My invisible father.
My lost sister.
My open-hearted brother.

There's no word about them.
No tears, no anger.

If they never lived,
If they do not live still,
where is my story, my own history?

Asha turns the page. She blinks furiously so the tears will flow and she can read.

Me, a doctor? Me, write poems and songs?
I can hear laughter.
Their laughter.

Medicine, they call it.
If this is healing,
I do not know it.

Poetry, they call it.
If this is poetry,
I do not know it.

They don't want to know me either,
the stuck-up bastards.
This medicine, that poetry,
has no place for me.

Poem. Song. Word. Like the word *human*, they map far too much, tease you with despair or hope. But is there anything else? Asha can't bear to be in her room, or even her college, for a minute longer. She puts away Satya's diary in her cupboard, looks around for her slippers. She heads for the door.

'Going out?' Priya's voice startles Asha. She's actually forgotten Priya is in the room.

'Just going for a walk.'

'Shall I come with you?'

Asha shakes her head and Priya looks relieved. Priya has heard the story, she felt bad hearing it. But since Asha's friend died—since he killed himself—it's been hard to say anything comforting to her. Besides, every time Priya hears the word *caste*, she feels tired. It seems a fixture in the life of everyone Asha knows, and Priya wonders sometimes if it is an unhealthy obsession. Why should people not just be people, instead of remembering their caste and their problems all the time and complaining?

Asha has not noticed either Priya's watery sympathy or her uncomfortable silence. She goes for a walk, returns, takes the blue notebook and the other book out of her cupboard.

Asha studies Satya's notebook and Professor Krishna's book on Chikkiah. She has never studied two books as hard, as closely, for any exam. Unlike Ravi, she does not have a Senthil or a Bhim Shakti group to listen to, and take heart from. But how can she keep quiet? How can she put away the two books as if the words in there, those lives chock-full of dreams and sufferings, are relics of another time or species?

Asha too begins to share WhatsApp messages and the

Bhim Shakti Facebook posts. Finding the right words: it's hard to do that. But she discovers other people's words; they can be used as crutches till she learns to walk on her own. If she learns Satya's words, or Chikkiah's or Mahadevi's or Kannappa's, she too can write her sorrow someday. She can write or speak her plea that Satya should live on, in her own heart and in the hearts of others.

Chikkiah says to us, she posts. *Where is my land where water flows free?*

And Satya says to us, she posts. *Where is my story, my own history?*

From the washerman poet Chikkiah to the medical student Satya, born an outcaste, dying an outcaste, she adds. Has anything changed in all the years in between?

There's someone who is anxious to answer Asha's question, someone who is very sure of his answers. *You're born where you are because of the sins you committed in your past life. Stop blaming everyone else now. Bharat Mata ki Jai*. That's from Shankar@hindupatriot, the same troll who took on Senthil the Dalit professor of physics.

Shankar has just discovered Asha. It's a delicious discovery, because there's so much more he can say, there's all the body to be stripped and ravaged when he is trolling a young woman. Shankar@hindupatriot has plenty of serious trolling tasks, each one a step toward a glorious new nation. But can he neglect even this small task? Especially when it gives him so much pleasure?

He tracks Asha's posts several times a day. Asha's Messenger inbox fills. Several times a day, Shankar assures her that he will never let her go.

2

This is the first time Srikumar has seen, up close, a rakshasa and his life—what he does every hour of the day. It's all a little disappointing. *This* is his fearful enemy? To begin with, the man looks quite old. All right, he isn't bald. The rakshasa has quite a bush of hair, but it's completely grey, white, in fact, and he hunches even while he is walking. It must be all those hours he spends slumped at his desk, bent over papers, pen in hand, or at the computer, reading and writing rubbish. Srikumar has never seen a person spend so much time just reading. And for this they pay him a salary?

Srikumar checks the notes he has made—not on paper, he is proud to say, but in his head.

5:00 am: the lights in the ground floor go on. 5:30: Krishna sets out, walking stick in hand. He gets to the lake by 5:45, and walks till 6:15, 6:30, with three others. They sit at the same green bench every morning and talk for a while before they go their separate ways. (One of these is an old man, even older than Krishna. Of the other two, one is called Hasan. Krishna walks every morning with a Muslim; that's the kind of puja he does at the sacred hour of dawn.) Krishna is home anytime between 6:45 and 7 am. He sits either in the living room or outside in the garden, drinking coffee. The son and daughter-in-law leave for work together in their car at 8, and a while later, 8:30ish, Krishna's wife walks with the grandson a few streets away where she leaves him for the rest of the day. Krishna leaves for the university in his car and gets there between 9 and 9:30. Krishna has a little room of his own in the university. The department seems busy on weekdays, with all kinds of people coming and going all the time. Krishna eats the lunch he brings from home in the department. He leaves exactly at 5:30. He always parks his car in the same place, in the same parking lot at a distance from the building. The car is a green Maruti 800. (Srikumar feels both indignant and scornful. This old man who has written books, who dares to write his rakshasa-lies about Hindu gods and saints and scripture, drives a beaten up old Maruti. Pathetic.) The husband and wife often go out in the evenings, but there is no pattern here. Sundays they have many people coming home for lunch; and Sunday evening husband and wife go to Darling Ice Cream Parlour by themselves. Srikumar, standing by his motorcycle pretending to be on his cell phone, sees them coming out of the parlour, hand in hand. He feels ashamed for them; they have grandchildren and they hold hands in public! Sirish Mama is right; it's not just the Muslims. All Hindu-haters are lustful, even their women. Srikumar spits on the road in disgust.

All the same, Srikumar would prefer not to involve the wife or the other members of the family. It's not because he is soft that he wants to get hold of Krishna when he is alone. It's not even because of the instructions he has been given. Srikumar wants it to be a fight like old times in Hindu history, man to man, or sevak to rakshasa. The rakshasa has his words; he, Srikumar, has the silencer of words in his backpack, biding its time.

So maybe when Krishna walks to the lake, or the time he is alone at home in the morning—about fifteen or twenty minutes? Srikumar frowns. He doesn't like the idea of catching him at home. This street is full of houses close together. There are enough trees and parked cars and scooters; he can easily hang around as if he belongs there. But there are too many ifs, too many risks. The university when he is setting out in the evening? He will need to consult Sirish Mama anyway.

Srikumar follows the Maruti at a discreet distance as the old lovers make their way home from the ice cream parlour. At home, they sit outside in the garden, playing with the grandson. Across the street where he is, Srikumar can hear the child's shrieks of delight.

Srikumar heads back to the Lodge; Vinay should be arriving soon. Once Sirish Mama has given them the go-ahead, it has to be finished quickly. If it's the morning, on Krishna's way to the lake, then it has to be the day after, Friday. Saturdays and Sundays there are too many people heading to the lake, even that early in the morning. If it's the university in the evening, it has to be Saturday, when there are fewer people around.

Back in the room, Srikumar lies in bed, waiting for Vinay to find his way to the lodge from the bus station. There's a smell coming in from the open window. It's something rotten, like a dead animal. All of a sudden, he feels tired. He can't make the effort to get up from the hard bed, close the window, switch on the Good Knight to counteract the smell that may linger in the room.

The smell of death. It's terrible. It's impure. It pollutes every particle of the air, it goes into you through your nostrils and spreads like a stain. Srikumar breaks into a light sweat.

Srikumar jumps up, shuts the window, switches on the fan full blast, checks that the Good Knight container is not empty of liquid. He goes back to the bed but does not lie down. He sits cross-legged as if he is about to do yoga. He picks up his cell phone, goes to the Gallery and looks at the photo he has taken of the picture on the wall of his shop. He looks at it, waiting for it to take its usual effect. But strangely, it's not the picture that fills his mind but an image of his father.

He sees his father, much younger and still straight-backed, walking briskly to the shakha, little Srikumar and even smaller Vinay almost running to keep up with him.

Once in the open maidan, Srikumar and Vinay would be impatient to begin their games, but they knew they would have to wait. First the saffron flag had to be raised; they would have to salute the Bhagwa Dhwaj. Then the warm-up exercises and the Surya Namaskar. Srikumar would feel his father's watchful eyes on his back. Srikumar didn't like the yoga—it was too slow and boring. (He knows better now. Guruji and his senior disciples have taught Srikumar so much about control, control and surrender.) Srikumar's father insisted that before the boys went to play, they had to go through the practice of fighting with sticks.

On the way back, his father would not walk so fast. He was also quite talkative then, especially on the days Vinay was not with them. 'Never forget who we are. We don't get the respect our ancestors were used to. My grandfather and great grandfather could remember a time when our world was not destroyed by Muslims and missionaries and untouchables and modern fellows who worship anyone with a white skin. But you—you must remember, like I do.' His father held Srikumar's ear with his fingers to emphasise his point, then let it go before it started to hurt too much. 'Never forget who we are, do you hear?'

But there was that one day his father was especially pleased with Srikumar's performance during the stick-fighting practice. That's the day his father told him, 'When you were born, I had your horoscope made.' His father's face shone at the memory. 'You have a special horoscope. The positions of several planets compared to the constellations and nakshatras were auspicious. The sun was in Aries, Saturn in Libra. Cancer was rising in the east. Only the moon was not as perfect as it should have been.' His father frowned, looked at him searchingly, as if Srikumar's face would reveal whether he had the strength, with the sun in Aries, to overcome the moon's shortcoming.

Srikumar feels a mixture of tenderness and pity now, remembering his father's pride. He will show his father that he can go beyond exercising or fighting with sticks. Or throwing stones or lashing out with a cricket bat. It's best and fastest to pick up a gun. By the time his own son is born, Srikumar will bring them all that much closer to a country that will respect the family for who they are. He will take his family to Hindu Rashtra. A rashtra which will really be home, at last, not just for them, but for Hindus from everywhere in the world.

It's Friday evening. Krishna leaves the university at 5:30. But this evening, he does not dawdle as he usually does, admiring the trees and shrubs in the campus, or trying to match them with the resonant botanical names (*Allamanda cathartica, Begonia rex*) he has learnt from Shanta. Krishna is in a hurry to get to the car and get home. He's promised Shanta an evening of music. The concert is by a young musician both he and Shanta admire.

Krishna finds he has forgotten to lock his car. This has been happening a little too often, he tells himself sternly. He really should be more careful. By the time he's dumped his bag on the front passenger seat, reversed the car out of the lot and changed to first gear, he's forgotten all about his resolution. He does not notice the grey coloured motorcycle or the two young men getting on to it. He does not hear the motorcycle take off once he has got into the car.

Shanta has brought Chitthu back from his grandmother's and he's in manic mode, running around the living room, or climbing the sofa and jumping off it. His smile when he sees Krishna: it makes life worth living, coming home to a smile that holds so much friendship in a perfect round face. Chitthu wants to welcome Krishna home properly. He runs to the kitchen, picks up two small steel plates drying in a plastic basin, runs back to the living room. He's past the spoon-hitting-the-plate phase. He has discovered the Chitthu version of cymbals, two plates being hit against each other.

Shanta looks harassed. 'I don't know why he's so excited today,' she says. 'He must have had an afternoon nap, and now he's going to drive poor Ram and Leela crazy with all this energy after they have had a long day at work. Go get ready, Krishna, we'll take turns.'

By the time Krishna and Shanta have got dressed for the concert, Chitthu's parents are home. But Chitthu has decided he doesn't want to go upstairs with them. He holds on to Krishna's leg as if it is a tree trunk that he is never going to let go of; he's conducting a small chipko movement of his own. 'Car,' he shouts. His father promises him a ride in his car. Chitthu looks at him scornfully. 'Geen car,' he says decidedly, tightening his hold on Krishna's leg.

'We'll take him with us,' says Krishna.

Chitthu's mother looks doubtful. 'But if he doesn't sit still—I don't want the concert spoilt for you. You've been looking forward to this so much.'

'He'll listen to the music. Don't worry,' says Krishna. Chitthu must have someone on his side, since both parents and Shanta look doubtful about his love for Carnatic music.

At the auditorium, Chitthu insists on standing on Krishna's thighs so he can see everything and everyone. It's not his fault that the people in the row before them are so grown up, blocking his view.

The singer is a maverick but he's an intelligent, sensitive one. Most Carnatic music concerts follow a set pattern; and while this means a certain understanding between the musician and the audience, it also makes it all rather predictable. The weighty precedes the 'lighter pieces' of devotion. But this evening's recital is unpredictable. The singer clearly loves the music he is making. He loves it enough, and knows it enough, to play with it, tease out its technical possibilities and its emotional content. Krishna and Shanta are riveted. It's impossible not to be infected by the man on the stage, enjoying himself thoroughly as he sings.

Chitthu settles down on Krishna's lap, puts his thumb in his mouth. There's a glazed look in his wide open eyes.

Then, like a gift to Krishna, the singer begins a languorous alapana in Sahana ragam. Krishna shuts his eyes. The world—or the mundane world—recedes. A line he read somewhere floats into his mind: I am not this. I am not that. Or that. All the rest is your knowledge … But wait. All the games Krishna's mind knows how to play, the seizing of a text, the unravelling of its ambiguities, are irrelevant now. Here, they've slipped out of his mind. Only the music remains. This singing voice does not need words. It's reaching out as high as it can, it has gone beyond words. Sometimes music, or even poetry, does not need a language.

When the voice dissolves, there's silence for a moment; the air is holding its breath. Then the silence breaks into applause.

Krishna opens his moist eyes, turns to Shanta. How beautiful to open his eyes on that face, framed by greying hair twisted into a bun and encircled with jasmine, the body on which he knows every city and country wrapped in soft yellow silk! Shanta's eyes meet his. They could be alone in the world, so intimate is the look that passes between them. Then Krishna looks down at his lap where Chitthu is fast asleep. The music, life itself, shared with Shanta and Chitthu. How lucky he has been, how lucky he is still!

They are silent on the drive home; Chitthu is still fast asleep, but now he's on Shanta's lap. Leela is waiting for them downstairs. She senses their reluctance to chat, so she quietly takes the sleeping child and makes her way upstairs.

Like the best part of the music, entirely wordless, Krishna and Shanta undress and get into bed, switch off the bedside lamps. They lie close to each other. The four arms and legs go exactly where they are most comfortable. They have curved themselves into a tight C, his back attached to hers, his arm holding her close, a hand on her right breast. Krishna suspects Shanta is smiling. Maybe it's the mischievous smile he saw on her face the first time he saw her. His fingers seek her face in the darkness, trace her lips. Yes, she is smiling.

3

Years have passed, fathers and mothers, sisters and brothers have come and gone. Only temple and palace remain, and the city that carries them on its shoulders. The palace used to look a little battered for a while, but then a new king came along, as kings tend to do. The palace has been repaired, parts of it painted; all bloodstains and unpleasant memories have been washed and scrubbed clean. A few new wings have been added. Extra guards have been stationed before the locked doors of the treasury that is filling up again, now that the army has brought in fresh loot. The poor and miserable, the lowly in the city and the countryside, are back on duty, the duty they are born with, like an extra finger or toe.

The palace looks fresh, impressively ornamented; the king looks promising. It is time to start a new dynasty. The temples approve of developments, at least the temples that matter, not the ones so neglected that grass and weeds grow on their stony heads. The temples that matter assure the king, and so everyone else, that this dynasty, though born only yesterday, has had royal blood all along. If anyone wants proof, they have only to listen to the ballads and chronicles sung by the most favoured court poets, or the humble vassals of neighbouring regions, always in fear of conquest.

There is a king again in the old city now, the one where Anandagrama used to be. The new king has been blessed by the gods via the temple. King, court, gods, temple—all are secure as they should be for a city to run, grow great once more. Order is back. Those who were mad enough to think they could live without order, without the necessary highs and lows of caste, are gone. Those drunk out of their senses with a heady brew called equality are gone. If they are still there, they are sensibly quiet, or biding their time. Just in case, the city and temple have devised foolproof security plans. A new Security-in-Charge has been appointed. He's a quick, decisive man called Muthuraja who has risen through the ranks, having proved his valour as a temple guard.

And that piece-of-moon, Mahadevi's sliver that grew full with her love, Chikkiah's ray of sunshine in the river, Puttanna's pet, Chandra's stunted soul, the favourite child of not one but two rivers: where is he?

Kannappa lives, though no one knows him by that name any more. He has been Kannadeva for many years. The name grew like a halo around him with his years in the old then the new monastery, studying then studying more, teaching and testing and chanting and reciting, meditating on the unseen mysteries of the world, contemplating the uncharted land and river and sea inside himself.

It has not turned him into a king or a priest, all this hard work. It has not turned him into a leader either, or not quite. But still, what a triumph. Kannadeva, son of Chikkiah, carcass skinner turned washerman, and Mahadevi, daughter of fisherman and field labourer, initiates young minds into the mysteries of salvation. How the old friends of Anandagrama would have enjoyed it, Elder Brother and Puttanna and the rest of the gang, Siddha, Chenna, Gundanna! And, of course, the proud parents, Chikkiah and Mahadevi.

Do people know? In the temples, for example, or even in the monasteries, not exactly ignorant of caste? Maybe there are some deaf grandmothers or senile grandfathers in the old city who recall Kannadeva's lineage. But who cares to ask them, or listen to the stories they get mixed up or tell too often? Kannappa, Kannadeva. How does the name matter? It's his life that is the best example of what he teaches. He is distressed by injustice, inequality, exploitation. He is selfless, kind, honest, charitable, a spiritual guide to all those who come his way, whether rich or poor.

Kannappa himself has never kept where he came from a secret. But who can he share the secrets of childhood with? And when does he ever talk about himself, at least the self that is not part of some universal consciousness or soul or spirit? The abstract is more real to him than flesh and blood. Absence of passion; the spiritual aspect of every single thing. The rest of it may all be true, it may be just, it may be important. But it's just too disruptive. At least it disrupts progress on his path, or the path chosen for him.

That path. The path to learning. First the boat, then the bullock cart, then the long long walk. The first week Kannappa was at the monastery school, everything was too hard. Being away from Mahadevi, Chikkiah. The river. Anandagrama. In between study and recitation, or drawing water from the well for the teachers, he sneaked away into the far end of the grounds where some monks were working on large patches of vegetables or trees with fruit ready for picking. For many days he felt less ignorant and stupid as he helped plant field beans, water them, pull out weeds. The soil he had turned looked fresh, a rich black-brown. The bean rows were straight. He washed the mud off his hands and feet every day with a sense of achievement. One of the monks must have told Kannappa's teacher what a good farmer the boy would make. The next day, the great teacher summoned Kannappa and took him to the river.

This river was a quiet, peaceful one, bound by trees. At a distance, the skinny legs of the trees were not visible. To Kannappa it looked like the endless clumps of trees had no trunks, they floated just above the water. The trees in this river could levitate.

The river was still as glass. (How different from that unruly river he had left behind!) Kannappa could look into this river and see all the way to the bottom, the smooth pebbles laying restfully on the bed. Above the bed, the fish, milky white and grey, swam in orderly patterns. They swam so quietly they barely stirred the water. 'This tranquil river has something to teach you,' the teacher told him. 'This is what you can learn from the river—absence of passion; mental discipline; self-control.'

It wasn't the river alone that taught Kannappa these qualities. There was his special teacher, kind but rock-firm. There were the monks; the scholar-teachers; the manuscripts of handwritten wisdom which could never age; the memorising night after night so the morning chants and recitation were perfect. He learnt to follow a hundred rules, live with his teachers keeping a close eye on him. If he remembered his earlier life, what his parents did, the secret bit of him called Chandra, everything he had heard in Anandagrama, it would all grow limp, faint, drown a little more every day in his memory.

By the time he met Mahadevi again, he, Kannappa, had already become Kannadeva.

But still, somewhere in those watery depths, there must be evidence left, bits of wreckage; pieces of where he came from and who he was. It's only now, when there is no one left to call him Kannappa, that the name, and everything that the name is tied to, floats now and then to the surface, insisting on his attention.

Then a monk from the old monastery school comes to visit Kannadeva's school near the peepal tree that had asked for a temple to be built. The monk brings with him a large box from the monastery storage room used to heap firewood, and also the possessions from the past lives of scholars and monks. 'I was told this is yours,' he tells Kannadeva respectfully. 'It's apparently been lying there for years. I was told to deliver it to you.'

It's his mother's box. When Mahadevi died, her friends must have taken it to the monastery, left it there for Kannadeva. He had made a quick journey to say goodbye to his mother and all family ties. Could he have been told about the box then? Did he forget about it all this time?

Kannadeva opens the box that night when he is sure of being alone. He examines Mahadevi's legacy, the heirlooms that have been saved for him in this box. It's almost comic, this sight of a monk-scholar dipping his hands—which he washes at least five times a day—into a dusty box of childish treasures. Right on top, there's a very long green cloth bleached by the sun so it looks ghostly; it is full of holes. It's tied to a dirty-looking dhoti which must have been white once. Under these intertwined corpses of lovers from another time, a time Kannadeva does not know, he sees a stack of palm leaves.

They are like bones; they may soon grow brittle and crumble. He picks one gently. He sees the too-large scrawl, the letters often tripping one another. He reads:

In a past life I was untouchable.
In a past life they smelt my shadow and fled.
In a past life the meat I ate was rotten.
In a past life I bathed in a stagnant pond.

That was the past.
Tie me, tether me so I don't stray there again.
Keep me here, in current and whirlpool,
O river of a thousand faces.

The letters no longer trip each other one at a time. Rows of them rush ahead; there's a stampede as known and unknown pasts push their way forward. Kannadeva—no, Kannappa—can hear Chikkiah loud and clear, Chikkiah and his old drum. How quickly these words have taken him back to being Kannappa, son of Chikkiah, carcass skinner turned washerman, and Mahadevi, daughter of fisherman and field labourer!

Kannadeva shakes his head free of the noisy drum, reads another one. This he does not recall; Mahadevi must have made it up after he left.

Crossing.
Life can be left behind
without dying.

Death too is a crossing.

Did we cross each other,
Coming and going?

Tell me, friend.
Which one died, which one lived,
O river of a thousand faces?

Kannadeva picks another. He can remember this one, word for word.

How light this boat is
        how light
how it holds us safe
        lightly
in its long-eyed belly,
O river of a thousand faces.

How light, how light—the phrase bobs up and down, rocks gently to left then right. How lightly it floats, takes him so far from himself; how swiftly it takes him far back into himself.

Kannadeva bends to pick up one more. But on this dry leaf he sees a bracelet, a black thread with rough and uneven blue and black beads. Chikkiah bought this for Chandra in the city. She had never seen anything like it and she treated it like it was a queen's jewels, wrapping it in a fresh leaf every few days, changing its hiding place every few weeks. But Kannappa found it. He didn't want to wear it, but he couldn't bear it that she loved something so much, a silly girlish thing he couldn't see the point of. He hid it; she found it and hid it; he found it. It went on like this for a while, till it disappeared altogether and was forgotten. No one remembers beads and bracelets when there are bigger things to be forgotten, like a little girl's dying, or a little boy's grief.

Kannadeva does not touch the beads now. He has seen something else. A hard and weather-worn drum. He finds he has to sit down. He feels breathless, as if he has been running hard.

He sits awake all night, considering the box that has come to tell him that learning is not at an end. He can see the boy Kannappa: he's crossing the river; he's sitting in the bullock cart; he's walking; he's homesick in the monastery. Quickly, too quickly, the scenes dissolve. The boy Kannappa is now clay in his ambitious teacher's hands. Maybe that's too simple. Maybe the boy was seduced by the power of being better than the other students? And later, more learned than the people he came from, a pillar of the monastery, almost as powerful as the temple?

But the price he has paid, how terrible this price looks now. He lost Anandagrama; by the time he wanted to find it again, it had dissipated; it was gone. He had missed being part of something—something, what was it? Was it the people's voice?

Kannadeva, son of the people's poets, now makes up a poem of his own. He recites it to himself.

> He dives into himself,
> practises his alchemy.
>
> Bodies melt into words,
> Word turns spirit.
>   Friends, foes,
>   all buried
>   one by one,
>   ash in his earth.
>
> There's only one man left.
>
> Is he the one?
> Who's left to tell him?

Who's left to tell everyone else, those who will come after him, the generations to come, about the brave people he, Kannadeva, comes from? They lost him; he lost them. He didn't fight palace and temple like they did, harnessing their work and words to sing equality, live it or die for it. But he can record them for all time. He can make sure no one forgets what they began, because remembering is the first step to taking up the fight again.

Kannadeva gets up, approaches the open box, dips his hands into it. He sets aside the green cloth and the bracelet tenderly. Let their stories end with him. But the drum, Chikkiah's drum. The drum Chikkiah told them belonged to *his* father. Chikkiah never told them his name. Kannadeva knows him only as the unseen grandfather who skinned carcasses, drank and sang songs, one song in particular, to his faithful drum. Let this drum be the witness: Kannadeva will make sure those voices, the words and lines that rang so simple, hard and true, are never forgotten.

It's time to go to work. Kannadeva goes looking for a fresh roll of reddish leaves, soft and malleable.

By the light of the lamp, late at night, every night for the next several weeks, he works hard, copying one poem after another. At the bottom of each, he meticulously records the name of the author. Chikkiah. Mahadevi. Puttanna. Wise Prabhu. Grandfather. He also adds the name of the copier: Kannappa-Kannadeva. He inserts one or two of his own poems. It feels wonderful to belong to his parents again, to Chandra, and to Anandagrama.

He looks at the originals once more. There's Mahadevi's large wandering miracle of a collection. The leaves are a faint yellow, and just eight inches long; the cheap brittle kind given to students for copy work. How childish his mother's script, how many holes and splotches and falls in between, and how prodigious her memory, how tenacious her intent! These leaves of love must be there too. He intersperses the originals with his copies; he collates. Then he makes holes in the margin of each leaf. He passes silken thread through the holes and ties the leaves carefully. Now her short yellowish pages and his longer reddish pages are bound together forever. On the top but one leaf he inscribes: Kannadeva. In this name, the key to his manuscript, leaves and words make up three lives; more than three lives.

He entrusts the wooden box of leaves, all those lives rustling inside lightly, to the librarian in his monastery. He has to go back to his life. But the old lives do not let go of him. They remain with him. They grow inside him, turning into niggling questions. These questions are no longer about the past. It's the questions about the present that make him restless.

The school, the monastery, the temple. Kannadeva was never caned in his old school. He followed rules; if he had any questions, he kept quiet about them, figured out the answers for himself. But the others? Were they caned or punished or thrown out if they asked uncomfortable questions, or thought for themselves? He does not recall. But here, in the present, in the school he is supposed to supervise, the cane remains a teaching tool though Kannadeva frowns on it. There's too much rote learning; the students are being turned into sheep.

Kannadeva has let it go on too long. Then the memories in his mother's box, and the old words lying there like messages waiting to be rediscovered, woke him up. Or maybe they have got him ready to be woken up. All it takes now is one boy's questions, his acts of dissent, for Kannadeva's eyes to fly wide open.

The boy is smaller than the others of his age and often sick. But there is a sharp look about him; he doesn't miss a thing, if the thing can be seen or heard, felt or thought. And he asks questions about everything. Kannadeva doesn't have favourites among the pupils, but he can't help warming to the boy every time he sees the intent face trying to understand why this is this and that is that.

A questioner among sheep: of course the boy is going to get into trouble.

He asks one of the teachers: 'Are we parrots?'

The teacher looks at him, amazed. What on earth does the boy mean?

'We repeat what's in the manuscript or the lines you recite. It's the same day after day. They're just words that put us to sleep. We think we have found peace because we are fast asleep.'

The teacher has never heard such a thing before from anyone, leave alone a runt of a pupil. He can't think of a thing to say. The boy, he has heard, is Kannadeva's pet. But he can send the boy to the head of the monastery, bypassing Kannadeva. He can add another complaint to give weight to his own. The boy has not been going to the daily common prayer at the temple; he will pray but he doesn't need an idol or a temple to do that, he is supposed to have said.

It's not a question of one pupil or one teacher any longer. It's bigger than that. The monastery and temple decide to make an example of this boy and throw him out. How can they allow every student and teacher to challenge the authority of the school, or the sanctity of worship practices in the temple?

Kannadeva, wide-awake after his nights of copying out the words of Anandagrama, objects when he finds out what is going on. 'It's good to encourage independent thinking,' he says in defence of the boy. Kannadeva is overruled. The boy is sent away.

It's just the one boy, but Kannadeva feels the entire student body has been disbanded. It's as if there's no one left in the school. It's terrible, this emptiness of a place of learning without anyone to ask questions. More and more Kannadeva sees that the students, and many of the teachers, wear faces devoid of expression. Their voices grate on him. They drone their lesson, their throats working hard while their minds are fast asleep. If only they would all wake up, come back to life. If only they would all go away.

It's he who needs to do that.

It's he who needs to keep learning, but without the comforting accomplices of text and manuscript, the orderly room of pupils, and the river that preaches and practises tranquillity. The river that has made him believe that sattva is the highest quality of qualities, and that truth and wisdom can be sought only in stillness. This river has made him a monk. It's time for the monk to take leave of stillness, go back to the flowing, ever-moving world.

Kannadeva packs a small bundle, picks up his walking stick and sets out. He knows it will be a long journey, and not just in days and hours, or in miles to be covered.

I have become the tide

1

Kannadeva is back at the beginning. He has made his way back, not to the place where Anandagrama used to be, or the city that has swallowed it. He is back in the place with a river that helped Chikka become Chikkiah, the fields where Mahadevi and her mother laboured, and where Chandra and he, Kannadeva—no, Kannappa—were born.

Kannadeva goes to the field first, the shack on the edge of the farm, not far from the old row of fishermen's huts. On the way, he looks for his sister's bauhinia tree. He can't find it though he knows exactly where it should be. It's gone. Which devil would take an axe to such an innocent tree? Which thoughtless storm would knock it down? Chandra is not under the tree, or in the tree, any longer. He walks on to the shack.

Chandra and he used to think this field was theirs, because it was always filled with the voices or bodies of their own people. Then they learnt that not one blade of grass, not one sprout or bush or tree, not even the shack, belonged to them. (The river then became theirs. 'Everyone has something that belongs to them,' said Chandra. 'It's only fair.')

The shack is empty. It's almost not there, it's just a ruin. Can a mere shack be ruined? Silence lives here now, fills it to the brim in the place of all those full-throated voices. The shack Chandra died in: Kannadeva sees a host of silent invaders there, ants, cockroaches, lizards. The mice are not to be seen but they have left trails of droppings.

Kannadeva walks to the small farmhouse. On his way across the field, he does not meet anyone he knows. Everyone he sees is a stranger. It's as if his childhood never happened. Those nights Chandra and he slept so close to Mahadevi and Chikkiah that they became one body with four heads, eight arms and legs, is a fantastic animal from a dream.

When Kannadeva meets the farmer and his family, they treat him with great respect. They stand at a distance and dispatch a naked child to carry an unpolluted bundle of raw rice and fruit. There's firewood too at a safe distance, they assure him. They know how it is done, they know how to be hospitable and do their duty by the upper castes. Kannadeva does not disillusion them. He does not see the point of it, telling them he used to live here. What good will it serve?

But it slows him down, this past that he wants to embrace but which does not fit well in the present. When he makes his way to the river, he treads cautiously as he goes down the slope they used to take at a run. He sees, first, the two trees Chikkiah used to hang clothes between. The rope is gone but the trees are flourishing. Their lush foliage has merged to make a bright green canopy between them. A tunnel. Kannadeva goes through the tunnel, brushing off a large cobweb that clings to his face.

Then Kannadeva is at the river. The old river.

So this is home—the place he left behind, and that he has taken so very long to come back to. Unlike the missing bauhinia, the ruined shack and the farmhouse that told him he is someone else, this river is exactly the same as it was. He knows it immediately. And the river: does it know who he is, does it know him better than he knows himself?

Kannadeva sits by the river as Chikkiah used to.

It is a dry, unhappy summer. Nearer the city, the parched, sore air and the sun's kindling rays must be stoking fire like arsonists in the clusters of untouchable hovels. But here, by the river, it is possible to believe, for a moment, that the rains are not far away.

Kannappa hears the frantic cheep of a bird. His eyes fly from the river to the tree by the bank. He locates the nest. The little bird is out of the nest. It is trying to fly, its mouth open, its terror obvious. The mother bird is nowhere in sight. The little bird flutters its wings too hard, flaps them too fast. It loses control, drops like a pebble through the air. Then, despite its panic, its wings learn how to beat the air. The bird manages to fly up to its nest. It sits there, surveying the world it is setting out to conquer. The air fills with its shrill cheep.

Life goes on, birds learn to fly or die. Anandagrama too died because it was cut down, its people had to be cut down before they became people, citizens, like the priests and soldiers and merchants and royals. Kannadeva sighs. All that's done and gone. But he, has he done everything he could? He has disciplined himself, he has meditated and prayed. He has not neglected the people around him, or ignored the quarrels that periodically break out between rich and poor, the overfed and the starving. He has taught his students that harmony, in the individual, or in school or monastery or temple or palace or field or village or city—harmony in and among all these—is what matters the most. Still—he has not felt as alive as he has since he copied out the words of those who put passion before harmony. Those words from Anandagrama he has stitched together for posterity, the people's voices: will those words survive, will those lives be remembered?

Kannadeva turns back to the river without a name, or so many names that it's best to just call it the River. It stirs. It's reminding him that his father sent him away so the son would not have to go through what his father did.

How strange, it's also reminding him of words spoken by another river. He hears that old teacher as they stood waist deep in a quieter river, purifying themselves at sunrise, then sunset: 'Order is the path to the ultimate blessed silence, the best of worlds. See how gently the river moves so you can barely see movement. This river knows that it's not movement we seek; we move only to get to stillness.'

The river before him has always scorned stillness. Even now its watery heart swells, promising high tide.

The river rises as if it is about to ask questions it has no business asking him. It was always challenging, this river. How do you find out what it was really like, the place, the people you come from? Who would have thought the past would be so hard to read?

He moves closer to the water. There must be a reason the voices he inscribed on palm leaves called him here.

The old disorderly river before him has heard the songs, laments and loving whispers of Chikkiah and Mahadevi. It has absorbed the desperate hope, the brave action, then the defeat and the lingering memories of Anandagrama. What choice does he have but to go into its dangerous arms?

When he is waist deep in the water, he finally hears his father Chikkiah.

This bee with its insistent hum:
what is it doing here, droning mantra?

There is no temple here,
no chanting.

Only the prayer in
the net the fisherman casts wide,
the potter's wheel spinning in a trance.

His father's voice grows soft so he can barely hear: *Only my own friend. Only the hide that falls, the drum that speaks—.* His father falls silent. Kannadeva is treading water now, looking into the river, waiting.

The river looks back at him. It can outstare him, never blinking for a moment. This river. Why does it make everything so difficult? He could get out of it, head to the temple he sees in the distance, rest awhile before he returns. But wait, he can hear something.

The river has begun a slow, deep rumble. The sound has a human quality to it, as if many people, too many people, are talking.

No, they are shouting. A lot of voices, many people's voices.

How can he listen to all of them? He doesn't even know many of them.

Then he sees a wave. It's not an innocent wave, the one coming toward him. It's not just a piece of Chikkiah's sunshine, a little sliver of Mahadevi's moon. It's more, too much more. There's one wave, then another behind it, even bigger. Wave after wave after wave. He sees the waves; he hears the tide. The river is bringing them all back for him, giving him a last lesson in the roar of people's voices.

It sounds almost holy, he thinks.

Then he can't think any more because the river is roaring so loudly. It's deafening. It's grand, this voice. The roar comes at him, hits hard. It hits him so hard that *he* becomes the roar, going down through the ages.

2

Is something missing? Krishna opens his eyes to find that Shanta has already left the bed. But her side of the bed is still warm. Her soft pillow dips in the middle, remembering the weight of her head. He lies in bed awhile, scratching his stomach then stretching luxuriously. Last night comes back to him; its memory fills him. He feels alive, and being alive means either those brief moments of joy, or these enduring memories. Either way, it feels like a perfect morning. He stretches one last time, gets out of bed.

The air at the lake is cool. He listens only now and then to Natraj's chatter and an occasional mumble from Hasan. 'What's the hurry, where are you rushing off to,' says Subbiah, catching up with him. Only then Krishna realises how briskly he has been walking, and that he has gone a little ahead of the others. He slows down, falls in step with Subbiah. Natraj and Hasan lag behind. Natraj has gone back to his WhatsApp videos with a vengeance now that Krishna's book is published and their Plan of Action has been carried out.

Subbiah and Krishna reach the green bench and sit down, waiting for Natraj and Hasan. It's impossible not to look at the new cement island rising from the lake. It's a hideous round platform and it's shaped like a giant rook from a monstrous chess board. Krishna is not sure he wants to continue his morning walk at the lake if he has to see a poet, his friend Kannadeva, marooned on this cement rook. But he forgets about this as he walks home. There's no point being sad about what you have no control over.

Krishna picks up the newspaper lying near the gate, goes into the living room. A lovely complex smell floats in the room, freshly ground coffee and mustard seeds popping in oil. The radio is on, the volume soft; Subbulakshmi is singing Suprabhatam. Shanta emerges from the kitchen, trying to carry too many things. She gives him a sharp look. He groans, puts down his paper, and relieves her of the coffee and the dish of chutney.

They're eating their slices of papaya when Ram and Leela bustle in with Chitthu. 'You two look cosy,' says Ram, 'I wish I taught in a university. Then I wouldn't have to rush like this.'

Leela is busy with last-minute instructions to Chitthu on good behaviour during the day. He's obviously heard it all before. He looks bored. He wriggles out of her arms, comes over to inspect the one uneaten slice of papaya on Krishna's plate. 'Boat,' he shouts, delighted.

'You eat this half of the boat, I'll eat this half,' says Krishna.

Chitthu ignores his parents as they wave goodbye and leave. Krishna spoons papaya into Chitthu's mouth, while Shanta gets his bag ready for his day at the other grandmother's.

The papaya is all gone. Chitthu bursts into tears. Krishna feels guilty about having eaten his half of the slice. 'There's more in the kitchen,' he says to Chitthu, carrying him in there. 'See, there's a whole papaya.'

Chitthu cries even louder. 'Boat,' he yells.

Krishna carries him back to the living room, makes a series of little boats out of the newspaper. Shanta, ready now, seats Chitthu on her hip.

'Boats,' Krishna says to Chitthu. 'See? Lots of boats.' Chitthu looks at them solemnly.

'Boats are better than a boat,' Krishna tells him, equally serious. 'And no one will eat up these boats.' He hands them over to Chitthu.

Chitthu doesn't say a thing. He stuffs all but one of the newspaper boats into the day-bag on Shanta's shoulder, then looks at Krishna. There are leftover tears on his lashes, making them shiny. But he gives Krishna a radiant smile.

Krishna is still at home when Shanta gets back. 'What's the matter?' she asks, seeing him in the garden, the bag with his papers and lunch box sitting by him.

'Nothing,' he says. 'I'm so comfortable, it's making me lazy. Shall I take the day off today?'

They smile at each other like co-conspirators. But she says, 'No, no, the music teacher is coming later in the morning. I'm going to learn a new kriti to surprise you.'

'In Sahana?' he asks, still smiling. He gets up.

'Anything you order, my lord. Go now, your Shiva must be waiting for you.' She gives him a quick hug and a gentle push.

At the university, Krishna parks some distance away from the building. He always parks here because of the grand old tree nearby. It's a lush peepal; its roots make visible bumps on the ground, its leaves make a roof shielding everyone from sun and rain. Krishna pauses outside the car, listening. He likes to wait for a minute or two to identify the birdcalls.

For the last couple of weeks, he has heard a barbet mark his arrival with its call. Once it starts, it can go on for a long time, as if its poems have far too many verses. But the tree is silent this morning. He gives up, walks to the department building.

Shiva is waiting for him, his face shining. He is about to give his beloved Prof a present. Even before Krishna can sit down, he says, 'The history department wants you to join their syllabus revision meeting, Prof. As Special Invitee.'

The barbet may have been silent, but it was watching Krishna's arrival from its leafy hideout. So were Srikumar and Vinay. They had been walking, hanging around the grounds for more than an hour. 'You said he's always here by 9:30 in the morning?' Vinay asks Srikumar. Srikumar doesn't reply. For two weeks, the rakshasa has been so predictable, and today of all days, he is forty minutes late! But he's here now; there's no point getting infected by Vinay's nervousness.

'He's in the department now,' he tells Vinay. 'He won't be out till 5:30 in the evening.'

'Though it's Saturday?' asks Vinay.

'Yes, I told you, he's here 9:30 to 5:30 every day except Sunday.' Srikumar speaks patiently, as if they are children again, and Vinay needs to be given courage to take part in some mischief. 'Let's go get some coffee and something to eat.'

Vinay looks relieved. He's been hungry for ages. As soon as they got up, Srikumar got busy with his morning exercises and prayer. They were at the university by 9, parked the motorcycle, walked about, sat on the ground under the trees. Vinay had pulled out his cell phone, plugged his ears, and listened to music. But Srikumar had sat still, on the alert, waiting, looking and looking at the parking lot as if he could will the rakshasa into appearing there.

Now, back at the lodge, after a good breakfast, Vinay finds the excitement trickling back into him. He no longer feels nervous, or the need to chat, or go over the plan again. He too can be as silent as Srikumar. He goes out to check the motorcycle one last time. Srikumar joins him in a while, carrying his backpack. They set out to top up the petrol. Srikumar has chosen the petrol pump as well. It's on the way back to the university, and it's also near a small temple. He's already prayed once today, but no one can pray enough on a day like this. He especially wants to ring the temple bell hard, once, twice, thrice, to make sure the gods are listening.

The motorcycle runs like a dream; the petrol tank is full. They have been to the temple, rung the bell three times, circled the structure three times.

They're at the university. It's only 3:45. They stop at a stall outside the university gates, where Vinay buys a plate of vadais and two oversweet coffees. Srikumar refuses a vadai. He wants to keep his stomach light, almost empty. Being hungry will keep him quick and alert. He drinks the coffee though. The sugar will make him feel energetic, ready for anything.

They go into the university grounds, come to a stop on the road that leads out of the parking lot. The lot is deserted. There are just two cars, Krishna's and another that's covered with a torn old sheet of tarpaulin. It's 4:05. Srikumar takes the backpack, goes behind the tree. He comes back; it's 4:15.

'All done?' Vinay asks him.

Srikumar nods. He doesn't want to waste a word or a particle of his concentration.

Vinay goes behind the tree, pees, dawdles a bit, returns. It's 4:30. That leaves them an hour if the rakshasa sticks to routine.

The rakshasa is reading a story. Saturday afternoon is when Krishna likes to read the submissions from research scholars—everyone leaves by lunch or soon after lunch, and there's no danger of being interrupted. Even Shiva has left but not before asking him three times if it's all right. 'I would stay,' he had said, hunching over so he could look modest. 'But I have to . . .' Krishna hadn't let him finish. 'Go run your errand, I am fine, Shiva. And thank you.' Krishna had smiled at Shiva. Shiva looked as if Krishna had just done him a big favour, letting him leave early, though both of them know Shiva always left after lunch on Saturdays.

Krishna looks through the research papers he has to read and react to. There's one on the role of the drum in different folk performances. He reads the first paragraph, puts it aside. There are three on Sita. He feels a twinge. Why always Sita? Why not more papers on Draupadi? Or someone no one usually notices?

The first of the three is on songs woven around Sita. Krishna reads through it, stops at a lovely example on how to recognise Sita. It's called *Sitadevi anavahi*: Identifying Sita.

> O Hanuman, I will tell you how to identify Sita, listen.
> Her dark tresses are undressed; they are matted and very long.
> She looks as if she has taken an oil bath, though she has not.
> She looks as if she has applied collyrium, though she has not,

She looks as if she has applied a beauty spot, though she has not,
She looks as if she has put on ornaments, though she has not,
She looks as if she is chewing betel leaf, though she is not,
She looks as if she is decorated, though she is not,
She looks like a gem tied in a worn-out black cloth
She looks like the water in cold winter
She looks like the Veda studied on Padyami day,
Shorn of all her glory and brilliance.

Krishna's gaze wanders from Sita to Shanta. Shanta does not need jewellery or lipstick or eyeliner, or even combed hair, to be beautiful. He shakes his head. What's happened to him, he's acting like a boy mooning about the first girl he's fallen in love with! He's done with the paper; he puts it aside, picks up the next one.

The second is an analysis of a contemporary Hindi novel called, simply, *Sita*. Sita here is a Dalit woman. Krishna has not read the novel. He keeps this paper too on the pile for more work he has to do before he can offer any comments. The third Sita paper is on her culinary skills, and how that was the real reason for her being abducted by Ravana. Who can resist a really good cook? Krishna reads this one carefully, makes comments with his pencil.

He looks at the time. He can definitely read one more. This one too is on the Ramayana—a national obsession, Krishna thinks wryly—and begins to read. He's hooked by the first few paragraphs about a Telugu folk song, *Lakshmanadevara navvu*—Lakshmana's laughter.

The paper sets up the story beautifully; it helps that the

song is profound though 'only a simple folk song'. After the great war in Lanka, everyone who is anyone in the Ramayana is gathered in the court for Rama's coronation. Suddenly, in the midst of this solemn scene of pomp and splendour, the ideal brother, the king's brother Lakshmana, begins to laugh. He laughs and laughs; he can't stop. His laughter is so uproarious that everyone in the royal assembly begins to feel he or she has something to do with this unstoppable laughter. The king feels humiliated; kings, of course, are notorious for their thin skin. He thinks he is being laughed at for taking back Sita, who was a captive of another man for so long. The god Shiva, who is present, thinks that Lakshmana is laughing at Ganga, the fisher-girl on his head. Sita wonders if the laugh is directed at her. All of them search their pasts, their words and actions: what did they say or do that is making this man laugh at them? There is a simple explanation, of course. Lakshmana is sleepy. He's laughing because he had kept the Goddess of Slumber at bay for so long, but now, on this important occasion, she refuses to be sent away. At the king's coronation, the happy ending of an epic story, the Goddess of Slumber dances on Lakshmana's eyelids.

Krishna chuckles. What a song! Maybe Chitthu would like it? No, he's being silly, Chitthu is too young to find it amusing. Krishna looks at his watch, sees it is close to 5:30. Time to go home, his attention is wandering. Tomorrow is Sunday and he will have all day with Chitthu and Shanta. He will come back on Monday and work better.

Krishna slips a few papers into his bag, looks around to see if he has forgotten anything. He switches off the light.

He locks his room, slips the key into his pocket. He goes down the stairs and walks to the parking lot.

Srikumar is relieved. The rakshasa is behaving himself. He's leaving the department at his usual time in the evening, though it's Saturday and most people have already begun their weekend. It's silent as he walks to the car door, opens it, dumps the bag on the back seat.

Krishna hears the insistent call from the thick foliage. The barbet! This tree hides so many mysteries. He's never seen the barbet though he hears it so often. He leaves the car door open, walks to the tree, looks up. Where is it?

What is the rakshasa doing under the tree? What is he looking for? Srikumar has his helmet on. The sweat trickles down the back of his neck.

A motorcycle whizzes past somewhere; the noise drowns out the bird. Krishna feels annoyed. But here it is again, the call. The barbet is singing again. Krishna narrows his eyes, looks. Is that the bird? No, it's only a leaf curled up over another, green and brown.

Srikumar makes a swift decision. He walks to the car, waits by the open door.

The bird has fallen silent. Krishna turns back toward the car. He sees a young man wearing a helmet waiting at the car. Krishna smiles. The man does not return Krishna's smile, or if he does, Krishna cannot see it. The man has a gun in his hand. A gun? What's he doing with a gun on the campus? But Krishna doesn't have to worry about any more questions. The bullet is already flying the short distance from gun to Krishna. From Srikumar's hand to Krishna's forehead. It's a perfect shot.

Krishna looks astonished. There's only a moment when he sways, a stingy moment in which it must all be packed, Shanta and Chitthu and Sahana ragam and the river that roars because it has too many voices. The moment passes; Krishna slumps to the ground.

Srikumar thinks, *How easy, just one shot and he has crumpled.* But still—he fires one more shot at the fallen head. Then he races to the man waiting on the motorcycle behind the bushes. The motorcycle revs, then it's gone. The place is silent. It will take a few minutes for the barbet to begin its requiem.

3

Asha was not always a regular reader of the newspaper. But since Satya's death, she has begun looking out for the paper first thing in the morning. She's not sure what she expects to see when she unfolds the paper and runs her eyes down the page. But without this new ritual framing the day, beginning with the newspaper and ending with Facebook, she feels irritable, restless.

This morning she has woken up with a dull ache behind her eyes; she decides to skip the newspaper. But when she goes down to the mess for breakfast, she can't resist; she might as well have a quick look. Besides, she's waiting all the time these days for news. She's waiting though she doesn't know for what. To see if Satya is paid reparation in some way, or at least remembered? To see if something has happened to another Satya, a boy she doesn't know but can recognise immediately? She opens the newspaper.

Her eye goes to the item at the bottom of the front page. The headline says *Devapura Professor Shot Dead on Campus*. She scans the first paragraph. Professor P.S. Krishna. He wrote a book called *Kannadeva's Family: The Poets of Anandagrama*. Asha gasps. That's the book she has been reading diligently, side by side with Satya's notebook.

She reads the rest of the piece. The professor was shot in

a university parking lot by an unknown assailant or assailants. There were two bullet wounds, one on his forehead, the other to the side of the head. His body lay near his car; the door was open. The assailants probably fled on a motorcycle. The police have begun their investigation. Though it was Saturday evening and the campus was on holiday, there may have been a witness.

Asha cannot take in more details. All she can think about is the book that sits safely in her cupboard. That's the last book Professor Krishna wrote, that Senthil lent Ravi, that Ravi lent Satya, that Satya read to find the brave poetry of his ancestors, that gave courage to Satya for a brief interval but finally let him go, that Satya returned to Ravi, and that Ravi has now given Asha. A slim book that holds so many, far too many people. A bit of Satya, a bit of Krishna, a bit of Chikkiah and Kannadeva and all their family and friends, a bit of Ravi. A bit of Asha too. A long line of words and people, a chain hoping to be a chain of courage.

Asha runs upstairs to her room, takes out the book. She doesn't open it, but she wants to hold it.

The book is waiting for her to *do* something. She picks up the phone, calls Ravi.

The news of Krishna's murder has spurred warriors from many camps to arm themselves and make their way to the battlefield. Shankar@hindupatriot has forgotten Asha for the time being. He has to take his place in an army, the one that's going to make him feel as big as an epic hero but also let him play victim. That comes in handy when the enemies insist on everyone's *freedom* or their *right to think or speak*, or when they tearfully point to fresh wounds and old scars, or to fallen bodies that ask too many questions despite their bloody stillness. Shankar the loyal soldier joins his army online. Maybe this time he will also go public on the streets. But for now, online, this is how Shankar and his army ride to battle, or psych the enemy by mocking and gloating.

Mock Hinduism and die a dog's death. This dog deserved to die. Guess who's next?

This is what happens when you write against Hindu dharma. Commie bastard.

Can't take being a Hindu for granted. Good lesson to all Hindu-haters and Hindu libtards. #ProudtobeaHindu

Teachers must teach the greatness of Hindu thought and philosophy. If they insult our saints, we will send them to Pakistan Or kill them. #Killallrakshasas

Talking about caste all the time, insulting Hindu philosophy. Bad karma caught up with casteist Krishna.

Leftie liberal pseudo-secular anti-national Krishna shot for writing lies about Hindu saints. Salute the killer. Good start to cleaning up our country. #CleanIndia

Is it a crime to worship our Hindu saints? No place for atheist commies or Allah lovers in my Hindustan.

Slip on a banana peel somewhere and these anti-Hindu forces will start shouting Hindus did it, or caste did it. Is being a good Hindu a crime?

Luckily, Asha can also hear and read the words of other soldiers. She wants to learn more about this Professor Krishna. She has learnt a little about Chikkiah and his small family, and his bigger Anandagrama family, first from Satya's notebook, then from Krishna's book. But Krishna—how does he fit into it all? What made him say and write and teach what he did?

Asha sits in the back row in Mrs Kumari's class so she can sneak a quick tap on her phone, silently ask Google her questions. She finds a post by Ravi's Professor Senthil on the Bhim Shakti page:

> There are some truths we need to remember as we recall Professor Krishna and the subject of his recent controversial work. Many scholars and poetry lovers have studied and written about those who broke away from the ways of the religious establishment. In different parts of the country, at different points of time in the past and the present, the common people have found ways to experience a spiritual life outside the temple or mosque, or customs and rituals, and without the medium of priest or mulla. Sometimes it was just the one man or woman; sometimes many people came together and found new ways to think, pray and live. They found god close to them, in places and things and people and experiences that were part of their daily lives. This god was a friend. Sometimes this friend was close enough to complain to, scold, or make love to.

Asha tries to imagine such a thing and gives up. Maybe Chikkiah and Mahadevi and the rest did something like this. Who can tell what really happened all that many years ago? But today, and for real people—does it make sense for people like herself or Ravi or Senthil—or Satya? The next paragraph also seems to be about gods. Asha races through it.

> Sometimes this god and that came together, the gods of different castes, or even of different religions. What mattered was whether the new god was still a friend, not someone locked up in a building because he or she was made of gold, or was owned by someone, or had to be guarded by watchdogs.

Asha frowns. Why is he going on and on about gods? Senthil spoke about Satya in such a way at that candle-lit meeting. She could understand every word he said; she could even fill in what he didn't say. But this piece—why can't he just get to Professor Krishna or the murderer?

> Every time the lowly and powerless raise their voice, or make their own choices, they challenge the existing hierarchies, especially that of caste. This is also what Professor Krishna's book shows us. This is why the book made so many people angry.

Ah, he's getting there finally. Asha can let go of her frown.

> The small outbreaks in the past that we can only guess at, and even the bigger ones recorded by historians, did not necessarily bring about lasting change. Caste and other inequalities remained. But the experience of dissent, individual or collective, small and unrecorded or otherwise, remained in bits and pieces to give ordinary people comfort and hope. Hope that their lives could change for the better.

Asha looks up and just about escapes meeting Mrs Kumari's eyes. She puts away her phone. But she's still not listening to Mrs Kumari or writing down anything. Bent over her class notes, pen in hand, she puzzles over Krishna's friendship for a history, for people, who were not really his. He was not Dalit or ST, or even OBC. What made him interested in their words and lives, what sustained his interest? Is it just the poetry or the story, is it part of the university job? Asha would like to know what this Krishna was really like. He must have been more than this one little book. After class, Asha sits alone in the cafeteria, phone in hand, the cup of tea on the table growing wrinkled skin on its surface as she reads.

> Professor P.S. Krishna studied oral and written poetry in several languages, but mainly in Kannada and Marathi. He was no ordinary scholar. For him, those texts, those people in the past, were real. They lived and suffered, they sang and wrote.
>
> The university was his second home. He loved the library, the university grounds, and most of all, the students and research scholars. Some of his students were practically his disciples, such was the devotion and respect he inspired. His standards, as a teacher, a critic and a translator, were high, but he was always patient and generous to his students. I was lucky enough to be his student for two years. I will always remember his starting every critique with a gentle 'Good', or 'Very good', before he went on to make suggestions to improve my work.

There are other tributes that reveal tiny parts of the man Professor Krishna may have been. Asha puts away the phone, takes the teacup to her lips. Senthil's lines come back to her mind. She's surprised that she recalls every word. She wants to keep these words near her; if they stay put in her head, maybe they will become real, become something more than words. *The experience of dissent, individual or collective, remained in bits and pieces to give ordinary people comfort and hope.* How Asha wants comfort, how she wants hope, enough for herself and all those living, and all those for whom it is too late.

Resistance. Dissenters. The people. People's words, people's voices. These are the words Asha is getting to know through what she is reading. Maybe they are only words. But these words can be voiced, can't they? They can be written, spoken, shouted out; and they can be heard. These words, and the lines they make up, come out of living mouths, or living pens. These words, these truths: can they ever die, even if mouths are forced shut, pens broken?

Satya is gone; his pen—his soul—broken. But can his words die while she, Asha, is alive?

Ravi sends her messages and email in a steady stream. 'There's to be a rally,' he says. 'A big one. You must come. All of us are going.'

The most recent message adds, in a tone new for Ravi, 'Please, I really want you to be there. With me. With us.'

Once again, Asha leaves the hostel alone, gets on a bus.

The crowd has gathered though there's still time for the rally to start. Banners are unfurled; placards distributed. Only some of the placards have thin ropes attached to them so they can be hung round the protesters' necks. The others will have to be held up.

The police have stationed themselves; Asha sees a stout policeman looking at her. She looks away. Young men and women roam with cameras and microphones as if they are their eyes and ears. Asha sees one of the TV people thrust a mike at the girl standing next to her. He asks her, 'Why are you here, why are you protesting?' What a question! Asha stares at the TV man, wondering if he is pretending not to know. A poetry teacher has been killed because he tried to find the truth about a poet. Because he showed that one of their saints is actually Dalit. And all the TV man has to do, anyway, is read the big banners people are holding at both ends, in more than one language, saying *Condemn the political murder of P.S. Krishna!*

Asha walks away. Where's Ravi? Or his friends, and Professor Senthil? Suddenly she feels alone; she doesn't know anyone here. It's the first time she's come alone to a protest, not long after she first read a book on poetry from hundreds of years ago, not long after the first time she ever went to a candle-lit public meeting. Not long after a friend, a friend who may have become more than a friend, killed himself. So many firsts.

But there he is, Ravi has arrived, ready with his old drum and his new friends. Ravi's friends distribute placards and unfurl a banner. Senthil is there too, with a young woman carrying a child. Ravi sees Asha, smiles, waves vigorously for her to join them. She goes up to him, admires his drum. It's made of the hide of cattle. It can be beaten hard enough to shake walls and smash prisons; it can send its stout-hearted messages far and wide. Asha takes a placard from Ravi, hangs it round her neck.

She looks at the swelling crowd; she remembers, once more, that Satya's death did not make headlines. But Krishna's has. Maybe she can use Senthil's words to conjure up a long link of words, dreams, suffering and thwarted hope. Chikkiah is at one end, Satya at the other; Krishna is a narrow bridge in between. Can she really make believe that when she marches today to protest against Krishna's murder, she is also marching for Satya? For the Satya she knew and all the Satyas she doesn't know?

The people ahead are moving. The rally has begun. The banners have been stretched out; the placards go up, high enough to be seen and read. And the slogans—how many there are, how they mingle words and languages! Then a long one-voiced call fills the air; the reply is many-voiced.

It's like a song Satya's mother and her friends may have once sung in the fields.

The rally is moving slowly, but it's moving; people are crying themselves hoarse. They fill up the road. The march has so many groups with their own banners; they look like the segments of a very long insect with a hundred legs. Then the insect is gone, or it has metamorphosed; it's melted into a sea of arms, legs, voices. From where Asha walks, she can hear one wave shouting *Lal salaam!* The wave that meets this one roars, *Jai Bhim!* Asha walks between the waves as if her thin dark body, her voice, can make a bridge. Every time she responds to a slogan, Asha feels her chest tighten. She means what she says; she means it so much she has to shout it out.

The people's voice, Senthil called it. Senthil's voice; Ravi's voice; Ravi's drum that beats like a powerful heart. The voice Asha hears coming out of her mouth. Together, they may make up a song with many verses, with or without rhyme. And the refrain: it must boom its way into the air, into Ravi's airless home and Satya's mother's lost field and Asha's father's government office. It must roll like a tsunami, find its way into the classroom and court and parliament and Satya's grave. The refrain is the one part of the song that must be sung together.

It's going to be hard work, this song that demands words and voices, knowing and speaking. It's going to be hard work, Asha making Satya live by remembering his life and speaking of him; Ravi having to be both Ravi and Satya from now on, combining his slogans with Satya's love for his mother and work and poetry. It's going to be hard work, learning from the words and ideas of people Asha will never meet, Professor Krishna, Kannadeva, Kannappa, Mahadevi,

Chikkiah. And Asha's new shadow, Shankar@hindupatriot? Does she really have to get to know him?

The sun shines so hard, it could be the most powerful slogan shouter in the crowd. The road ahead of them is as lustrous as water. The sweat pours down Asha's back; her kurta is stuck to her skin. Ravi's face is wet but he's hammering his drum, stopping only to wipe the sweat off his hands. Then an unexpected breeze arrives, turns into wind. It amplifies the people's slogans. The wind blows, teaching everything, every scrap of junk, every person there, what it is to move. To refuse to stay in the same old tight-fitting place. The slogans get louder and the drums beat harder. In this blur of faces, words and voices, Asha can almost believe that this crowd is not alone. There are other crowds in places across the country, their strong currents flowing down roads and fields, through villages and towns and cities.

The crowd mills around Ravi and Asha. Ravi's drum has finally gone silent. She takes Ravi's hand. The red and blue flags; the words; the voices; the people: is it only today, or has this river of living bodies been flowing for a thousand years? The river rises; it fills Asha with anger and grief, but also a strange joy. She can hear Satya tell her, or maybe it's she who's telling Satya and Ravi, even Professor Krishna and Chikkiah: *I have become the tide.*

Acknowledgements

The lines quoted from J.V. Pawar's poem 'I Have Become the Tide' are from the English translation by Jayant Karve and Eleanor Zelliot. The full poem, translated from Marathi to English, can be found in *An Anthology of Dalit Literature, Poems*, edited by Mulk Raj Anand and Eleanor Zelliot (Gyan Publishing House, New Delhi, 1992). The lines are reproduced here with permission from the translator, Jayant Karve, and the poet, J.V. Pawar. I am grateful not only for this powerful poem, but also for its title line that I have used as the title of my novel.

The lines by L.S. Rokade that Satya quotes are from his poem 'To be or Not to be Born', translated from Marathi by Shanta Gokhale. The full translation can be found in *Poisoned Bread, Translations from Modern Marathi Dalit Literature*, edited by Arjun Dangle, (Orient Longman, Bombay, 1992, pp. 1-2). Reproduced with permission of Orient Blackswan Pvt Ltd. © Orient Blackswan Pvt Ltd 2009.

The English translation of 'Sitadevi anavahi' (Identifying Sita) is quoted from D. Rama Raju, 'Versions of Ramayana Stories in Telugu Folk Literature' in K.S. Singh and Birendranath Datta (eds), *Rama-Katha in Tribal and Folk Traditions of India: Proceedings of a Seminar* (Seagull Books and Anthropological Survey of India, 1993). Reproduced courtesy of Seagull Books, Kolkata.

The quotation Professor Krishna reads from the story of Hanuman's taking a ring from Sita to Rama is from Wendy Doniger's *The Ring of Truth, Myths of Sex and Jewelry* (Speaking Tiger, 2017, p. 66). The lines are reproduced here with permission from Speaking Tiger, New Delhi.

The quotation from Dr B.R. Ambedkar, 'Turn in any direction you like, caste is the monster that crosses your path...' is from the section 'Why social reform is necessary for economic reform' in *Annihilation of Caste*.

I would like to thank those who have supported the writing and re-writing of this novel in some way or the other: Ritu Menon, Shanta Gokhale, Himanjali Sankar, Gargeya Telakapalli, Samar Vanaik, Prava Rai, Valerie Borchardt and Rajesh Kalithody. I must add that they are innocent of the results, and I remain the sole guilty party. Closer home, I thank Prabir for conversation and argument. And as always, for better or worse, Rishab and Nishad.

Finally, an acknowledgement of another sort. No privileged person in terms of caste or class can, despite choices made as an adult, really 'know' the lived experience of those who have been historically oppressed. *I Have Become the Tide* has been written with this awareness. But it was also born out of the conviction that no writer can engage with life in India today without taking a stand, in some modest way, on the terrible inequalities that continue to ravage the lives of so many of our fellow citizens.